HERE WE STAND

BROOKE RILEY

HOW WE RISE TRILOGY

How We Rise (Book One)

United We Fall (Book Two)

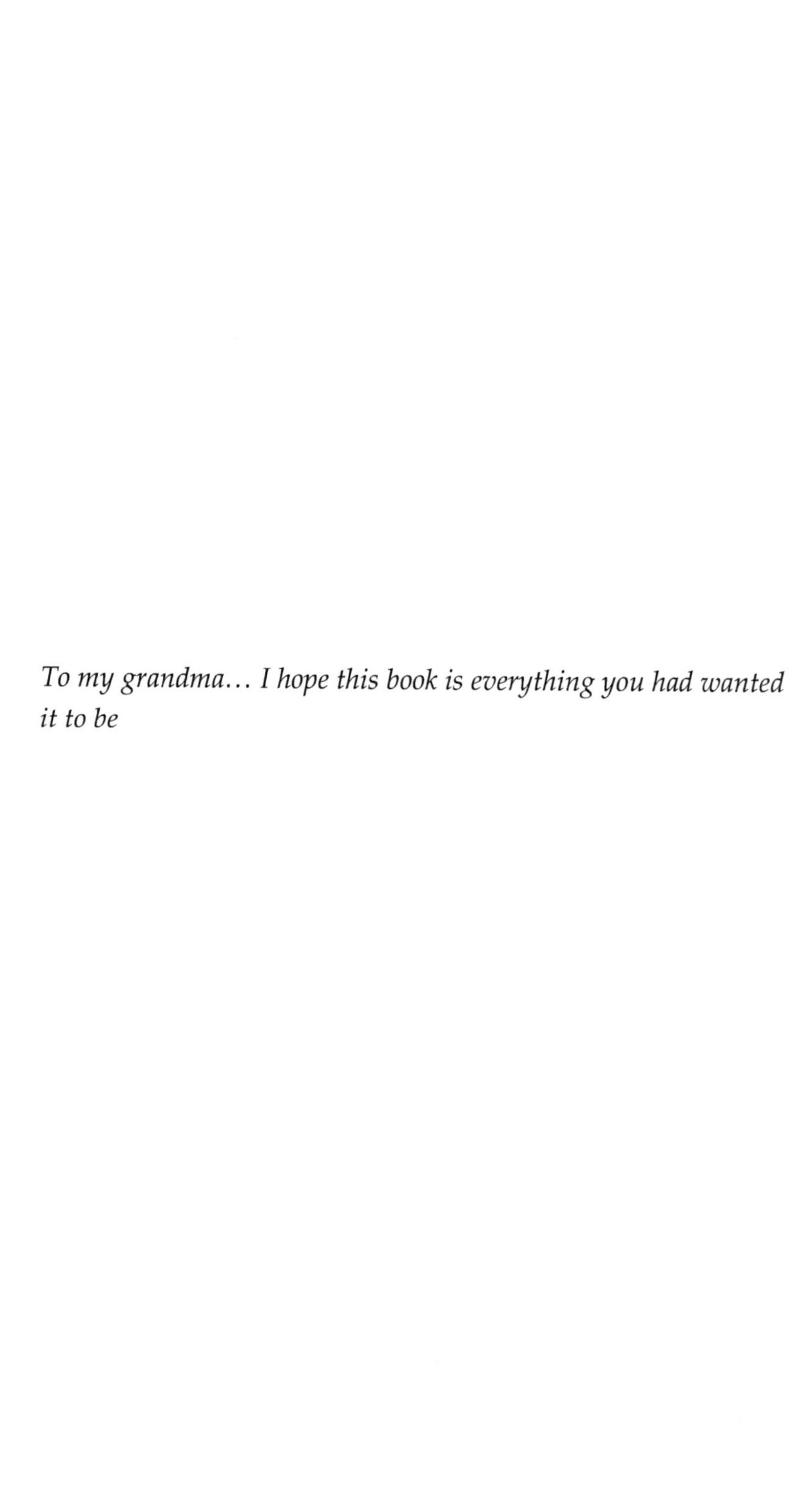

To my grandma… I hope this book is everything you had wanted it to be

PROLOGUE

WHEN THE WORLD IS QUIET, MY MIND IS LOUD.

Sometimes, I hear the gunshot, feel the bullet piercing my shoulder. Phantom pains creep up my shoulder, despite the fact it's healing nicely. Usually, I feel nothing. Numbness from the medicine or maybe from the nerve endings that were broken when the bullet went through me.

Other times, I hear the front door bursting open, the sound of boots marching up the stairs. The way it felt when Peter's hand was roughly yanked from mine.

The noise is loud in my head. But there's nothing hiding in the darkness of the night.

No gun being fired.

No soldiers rushing through my house.

All is silent.

But Peter is still gone. And my shoulder is still numb.

Tears soak my face, falling to the pillow beneath my

head. I don't bother wiping at my eyes or trying to stop the onslaught of emotion from flowing from me. It's no use. My heart is too heavy. And I am too weak to stop it.

Sitting up, I take a few deep breaths. Sleep never comes easy. Although, I don't remember the last time it really did. But the lack of it doesn't help my healing. Dr. Ho told me so yesterday when she came to see me and check my progress.

I don't know what progress I'm supposed to make when my whole world is falling apart. The only solace I have in any of this is that Mr. Williams determined it's safe for me to stay home. I don't have to be locked away in some bunker, hidden from the world. Even though I can't be seen by any neighbors, either. I have to be careful.

Dr. Ho advised against putting me back underground. And after everything that's happened, it's not likely that Evan will be returning for me. Especially when the world thinks I'm dead. Although I don't entirely understand why he cared much to hurt me in the first place.

As long as I'm careful to not answer the door if a neighbor comes knocking, then all is well. The town thinks I died in a car accident. If I show up alive again, there will be too many questions. Questions Mr. Williams says are too complicated to answer right now. And bringing attention to myself may not be in my best interest, anyway.

I nearly ruined the ruse when I ran outside after Peter as he was taken away. But no neighbors saw me, by some miracle. And my dad got me back inside just in time.

I don't really care that I can't go anywhere. What's out there for me? Everything in this town makes me think of Peter. The only place I really desire to go is the tree—our tree. But even that feels too heavy to think about.

I rise from my bed, my bare feet hitting the cold wood floor. My room feels warm and the wind outside invites me to let it in, to inhale its fresh autumn scent. Carefully, I walk to my window, avoiding the floorboards that creak in my room. I don't want to alert my parents that I'm up. Patrols come by every hour. I have at least a good twenty minutes or so to open my window and let in the cold night air.

I unlatch the lock on the window, then slide it up slowly. The wind howls as it dances around my room, blowing back my curtains. My thin shirt and shorts don't do much to keep the gooseflesh from crawling up my arms and legs. I embrace the feeling, hugging my arms to my chest and closing my eyes.

The air smells of fallen leaves, and there are dewdrops clinging to the window pane from the humidity. Maybe the rain will come soon. The leaves of the big oak tree outside my window rustle. I imagine them falling in waves of brown, orange, and red. It's late in the season, but autumn is usually late around here.

The rumbling of a truck breaks my calm. They're early. I dive towards my window, pulling it shut ungracefully. Then I duck to the floor, waiting as the headlights pour into my room. Soldiers' voices carry on the wind, but I can't hear what they say. They pass just as quickly as they come, taking the light with them. The rumble of the truck grows fainter and fainter. All that's left is the wind.

I crawl over towards my bed. My head pounds as all the sudden movement brings a wave of nausea over me.

I'm still so weak.

My room has taken on the cold of the night, something I welcome compared to the normal stuffiness. My heart is made of ice and the bitterly cold air is a welcome touch.

My body doesn't agree with the sentiment, though, and I begin shivering violently. Defying my urge to stay here and freeze over, I climb back under the covers. Somehow, I drift back to sleep.

When I wake again, sunlight floods my room. It would be helpful if the dust that's been settling in our air for the past year could choke out the sun. All the light does is remind me of Peter. He loved bright, sunny days like this one.

I ease out of my bed, careful not to aggravate the

mild headache that still throbs against my temples. I'm tired of feeling so weak. I want to be normal, not ill all the time.

I enter my bathroom, seeing myself in the mirror for the first time since Peter's been gone. I haven't showered since they took him away. And every time I've used the restroom, I've kept the light off. I have no desire to take pity on myself, to see my own downfall.

I'm a porcelain doll. One small touch and I might break apart.

My hair is matted to my head, tangled and knotted. My clothes hang off my body. My eyes have dulled, seeming to sink further into my head. That's probably the dark circles, though.

I stare at the gauze that encases my right arm from my elbow to my shoulder. I've never cleaned or dressed my own wound, too afraid to see the damage that's been done. But I'm tired of my mom having to do everything for me.

I take a deep breath as I start to pull off the wrappings. They come off easily enough, though trying to work with my left hand is awkward.

When I see how bad the wound looks, I almost throw up. I turn away from the mirror, taking deep breaths.

The gunshot echoes—

Boom.

I shake my head. "It's not there," I mumble to myself. "He's not there."

There's no gun aimed at me. No bullet to pierce my skin. How I sat there, defiant and strong, is beyond me. All I am now is weak.

Not daring to look in the mirror again, I start the shower before my mind can slip further into its downward spiral.

When the water's warm enough, I strip free of my nightclothes and step in. I clean the wound first, letting the warm water rinse it. I try not to look at it. The feel of the hot water rushing over my skin keeps the anxious thoughts at bay, at least. After my right shoulder is clean, I wash my hair, hoping the shampoo and conditioner can save me from these horrid knots.

I finish washing and rinsing myself, cleaning the wound one more time. The hot water washes over me, relaxing the tense muscles in my shoulders and back.

When I can't take it anymore, I stop the water and get out, pulling my towel around me. The bathroom mirror is fogged up, a small victory. I don't have to see my weakness as I dry off and pull on some clothes. I apply the ointment recommended by Dr. Ho to the wound, then I try my best to wrap my arm. But no matter what I do, I can't get the gauze to tighten properly around my shoulder.

"You're not overdoing it are you, Raegan?"

I startle at the sound of my mom's voice. I find her standing in the doorway to my bathroom. "No." I shake my head. But a wave of dizziness rushes over me.

My mom senses this and guides me over to my bed. She takes the gauze from my hand and carefully dresses my arm. When she's done with that, she goes back to my bathroom and grabs the comb from my vanity. I don't have to ask. She already knows what I need.

She climbs onto the bed behind me and begins combing my hair. "Did the shower help you feel better?"

"A little."

For a moment, I'm a little girl again. I can't take care of myself. I can't wrap my own arm or comb my own hair. So my mom does it for me. She gets through the knots in my hair easily, as moms always do. When she's done, she braids my hair down my back to prevent any more tangles.

"Are you hungry?"

Not really. "I guess."

"Raegan."

I finally look up, meeting her eyes. "Yes?"

She sighs. "I know… I know I should…" Another sigh. "No one trains you on what to say to your daughter when her best friend is taken away like this. What do I say? I want you to heal. I want you to get healthy. And not eating or taking care of yourself isn't going to bring him back."

She's right. Even if I won't admit that out loud.

"I know," I say. "I don't want to stay like this. I want to get better so I can fight. So I can…"

So I can have a chance to bring him back.

My mom offers a sad smile. "Would you like to come down to eat? Dr. Ho says your lack of nutrients isn't helpful."

I nod once, letting my mom help me rise from my bed as I fight dizziness and nausea all at once. I let her help me down the stairs, even though I want to take them myself. One slow step at a time, we make our way down.

I will eat.

I will take the vitamins Dr. Ho recommended.

I will do whatever it takes to get better. I will not keep being a victim of this horrible world. I will get Peter back.

I have to

CHAPTER ONE

Evan

MONDAY, NOVEMBER 6TH, 2023

"EVAN? ARE YOU IN HERE?"

Light floods into my dark office from the hallway. I realize I'm slumped in my chair, head on my desk. Another night of working too late gave way to a morning of waking up in my office. I should really have a cot put in here.

"Unfortunately," I say, my voice still hoarse from sleep.

Sam approaches my desk, only the light from the hallway guiding her. "What happened to you?"

I sit up, stretching my arms above my head. Something in my shoulder pops. My neck cracks. And I'm not sure even a chiropractor can fix what I've done to my spine from the countless nights of falling asleep at my desk.

"I guess I fell asleep in my paperwork," I finally answer, suppressing a yawn. "What time is it?"

"Just before dawn. They're expecting you to address the new soldiers in training on their first official day.

Remember? We talked about this."

Shit.

I rise too fast, my head spinning as my vision grays out. Sam reaches out her hand, touching my arm to stabilize me. A shot of electricity races through my arm at her touch, making my heart race.

She pulls her hand away, taking the spark with her. "You really shouldn't stay up late like that for paperwork."

"I know," I sigh. "But there's so much the emperor wants from me. I have to get it done somehow."

Sam bites her lip, holding back whatever it is she wants to say. I glance down at myself. "I need to change," I say. "For the event."

She brings her focus to my rumpled, slept-in clothes and nods once. "Agreed. Come on, then."

She takes my hand in hers, making my mind go blank. But I know what she's doing. We have to leave my office together, appearing like the loving couple the world thinks we are.

We make our way through the halls, making sure every agent and worker within the White House sees us. No one else is in on our ruse. Even though Emperor Morgan chose this for us, we're playing him and everyone else.

At least… that's what we're supposed to do.

I'm not entirely playing a role or a game. Even

though allowing myself to get caught up in my feelings for Samantha is dangerous. But it's hard to ignore the way my heart beats wildly in my chest or the way my breath catches in my throat whenever she walks into the room.

Sam escorts me to my room. Once I unlock it, she follows me inside. As she seems to float over to the lounge chair, I close the door behind me and say, "What are you doing?"

"Waiting for you to change?"

My face burns with heat. "Are you going to watch?"

She rolls her eyes, leaning back in the chair. "You have a bathroom, genius. We have to be seen everywhere together to make this work. I know it's exhausting to keep this up, but we want to be believable. And the only way to make them believe anything is if we commit to it."

My heart deflates slowly. I grab a button-up shirt from my closet and some dress pants. Before I can stop myself, I say, "It's not exhausting."

I slide into the bathroom, shutting the door. I lean my back against the bathroom door, taking a moment to myself. I shouldn't fool myself into thinking any of this might be real to her, too.

Not long ago, she confessed that it might not all be an act on her part, but since then it's like this is a business transaction. She's acted like she always does, ready to put on a show when we're in public. Yet… so cold when we're alone.

I wonder if I imagined her telling me she's falling for me. But I know her confession was real. I want it to be real.

I *need* it to be real.

I dress quickly, tucking my shirt and making some effort to look like I tried. I run my hands through my hair, but nothing I do helps with the mess it's become. I'm going to have to deal with it like this.

I step out of the bathroom, slipping on my dress shoes. Sam looks up from the book she's reading. "What's wrong with your hair?"

"I'm trying something new."

"It looks like you just escaped a wind tunnel."

I shrug. "Maybe I have."

Sighing, she rises from the chair, leaving the book on the armrest. She grabs my wrist and pulls me back into the bathroom.

"Careful," I say. "You seem to have bad intentions."

She shakes her head, turning on the faucet. But I catch the mild tint of pink on her cheeks as she lets the water run over her hands.

"Do you have gel?" she asks, ignoring my comments.

"No," I say. "I'm not Jackson."

She turns off the faucet, running her wet hands through my hair. My mind goes entirely blank at our proximity. She's standing on her toes to reach my hair. I don't quite know what she's doing; my eyes are trained on her face, her lips, her eyes. The scent of something soft, like mint and citrus, floats around me.

When she steps back, I look in the mirror, regaining some of my senses. My hair is slicked back but doesn't look entirely like I struggled with it. Better than anything I could've done to it. She's not standing close now, but I wonder what could've happened if she was. If I had let my hands go to her waist like I wanted to. If I had leaned in ever so slightly...

"We should get going," Sam says, interrupting my thoughts. "They were expecting us ten minutes ago."

"Right," I say. I follow her out of the bathroom.

I can't let my mind feed me these delusions. There is nothing between us. There never will be anything between us. The sooner I accept that the better off I'll be.

I follow Samantha down the hall. Through she holds on to my arm, she leads us with her confidence.

We're escorted to the car, my guard sliding in the front seat with the driver. The ten-minute drive is silent. Sam makes no attempt to speak to me, even though we're in the presence of two people. Maybe the act doesn't matter as much with my guard and my driver. Perhaps neither of them holds any consequence for our ruse.

We arrive at the base; General Kahn and some other generals wait for us. Though we're now about twenty minutes late to this event, General Kahn smiles widely. A disturbing sight.

"Welcome, Your Highness," he says. "We're so glad you could make it."

His fake niceties grate on my nerves. He'll say whatever he thinks he needs to say to stay on my good side. Not very trustworthy in a general, but I ignore it for now.

"Good to see you, General Kahn. I apologize for being so late. Time slipped away from me this morning."

General Kahn's smile never wavers. "It's no worry at all. Don't apologize. We've waited for you to arrive before we begin. They've all been gathered in the open field, ready for your speech."

Speech? *Shit.*

We follow Kahn and I nudge Samantha softly. "I'm supposed to give a speech?"

"Yes," she says as if I should already know this.

"I don't have a speech planned."

"I noticed."

This is not going to go well. I can BS my way through a conversation, but a speech? With hundreds of new soldiers who hate me watching my every move? Highly unlikely.

I have no time to figure this out as I'm rushed to the platform and plunked in front of a microphone.

General Kahn and a few other generals stand off to my left. Sam stays near my right.

I look out into the crowd; the sun is shining down now. The air is far from hot, though. I find Peter in the crowd and I'm suddenly inspired. I know what I want to say.

"Thank you all for being here today. I know for *some* of you, that wasn't a choice. But I also know that being here means you will learn to trust us more. I understand you'll have concerns and hesitations. But we've chosen only the best of you to fight for us."

A simple lie. I know I'm not convincing to a crowd made up almost entirely of rebels who've been drafted as part of the emperor's new initiative. But the point isn't to convince them. It's to send a message to every rebellion and every rebel. It's about taking apart all the different resistance networks, one person at a time. And welcoming their demise.

"I want to personally take a moment to welcome every one of you who's here today." My eyes find Peter's in the crowd. His burn straight through me, almost as if he believes glaring hard enough will cause me to combust into flames.

"We value you and want you to feel like you're taken care of." Another lie. They're cared for enough. But they are our machines. Nothing else.

"I look forward to hearing updates on your progress and on returning in six months when it's time for you to be assigned to your new bases across the country. Until then, good luck with your training and blessings to our wonderful emperor."

I want to spit on those last words, but if I want to play the role of grateful heir, I have to act like it. According to every headline from the last couple of months, I owe my life to the emperor, for pulling some random nobody like me and making me his heir.

If only they knew the truth of what he's done to me and my family.

I dismount the stage, my security escorting me and Sam back to the front of the base where our car waits. General Kahn walks alongside us and when we arrive at the car, he thanks me for such a wonderful speech, shaking my hand as if his life depends on it.

Then I'm in my car and on the road back to the White House. My exhaustion slowly returns now that the rush is over.

I'm surprised when Sam's hand comes to rest on my thigh. I glance over at her, finding that she's looking at me. "What's wrong?" I ask.

She leans in. "That speech was impressive."

"It was?"

"Yes," she says, coming closer. When her lips are near my ear, she says, "Your guard and driver have been glancing at us in the rearview mirror. I'm giving them something to look at."

Maybe it's the exhaustion, but I play along. I let my hands skim her waist as she's whispering in my ear. I risk a glance to the rearview mirror, finding the driver sending curious glances back at us as we come to a stoplight.

"I have an idea," I whisper. "Kiss me."

I expect some sort of delay, but Sam's lips are on mine in an instant. My hand reaches for the button on my door that brings up the divider between the front and back seats in the car. Once it's up, Sam slowly pulls away, her face flushed.

"Good job," I say, feeling like I'm finally the one in power. "Now they'll have something to report back to the emperor."

"Right," she says.

It feels good to have these small victories. In six months, we'll see how these soldiers shape up.

And we'll see where Sam and I stand

CHAPTER TWO

Peter

MONDAY, NOVEMBER 6TH, 2023

"MORE EFFORT! KEEP UP THOSE PUSHUPS, MAGGOTS! ARE YOU SOLDIERS OR ARE YOU WIMPS?"

The commanding officer screams as he walks past each and every one of us. It's the first official day of training, but I'm doing my best to tune it out. Pushups aren't my strong suit, but I like them more than the pull-ups, the sprints, but less than running around the base with the heavy pack. I've enjoyed that one, despite it being hard.

My training in the resistance has made me fit enough to endure a lot of these training methods. But I'm by no means the fastest at any of this. The intensity of soldier training—and the way we're belittled as we do it—is not something the resistance had. I'm both grateful and weakened by its lack.

I complete my fiftieth pushup, nearly collapsing on my stomach in the grass. But Officer Dunlap pauses in front of me and barks, "Oh, you finished? FIFTY MORE!"

I stop myself from groaning out in pain as I begin another round of fifty pushups. I don't know how many rounds they've made me do at this point. Sweat trickles down my neck and back, my shirt long since tossed aside.

My arms begin to shake as my stomach rolls in on itself. I close my eyes, trying to distract my mind.

We value you and want you to feel like you're taken care of.

I don't know what kind of crap Evan thinks he can spew to win us over, but he's going to have to do better than that. It didn't take long on the drive here from Texas to learn that a lot of the men and women drafted were from other, smaller resistances. We were targeted for a reason.

It also didn't take long to learn we all have one united hatred for Evan Williams. But mine... mine is more personal than anyone else's here. They might be here against their will—something that shouldn't be taken lightly—but Evan didn't personally threaten their girlfriends. Evan didn't shoot their girlfriends and leave them so fragile.

I finish this second set of pushups, finally collapsing on my stomach. So do quite a few others. Officer Dunlap laughs.

"You lot will do just fine," he tells us. "You held up longer than I thought you would. But don't worry, it gets worse from here. Time for dinner, maggots."

I'm slow to get up, comforted more by the feeling of the grass than the idea of food. But I'm pretty sure they won't tolerate me falling asleep out in the field. I jump to my feet, regretting it as a wave of nausea courses through me. I swallow it down, grabbing my army green shirt from the ground and shaking it out. I pull it over my head, getting in line with the other soldiers as we file out of the training field.

We march to the mess hall, single file, like we've been shown. Mess hall is a generous term for the large tent that sits near the hub of the base. I glance around; the entire base is surrounded by concrete walls topped with barbed wire.

Scattered throughout the base are watch towers. In them, guards stand alert, watching out for oncoming enemies.

Or maybe just for soldiers trying to escape by climbing the walls.

I wonder if anyone's tried to climb the walls in the middle of the night. How soon before someone would get caught… or shot at?

I'm at the mess hall sooner than I realize. I shake my head, grabbing a blue tray at the entrance.

Blessings to our wonderful emperor.

Seeing Evan up on that stage this morning left me with a burning hatred that leaves fire in my veins. His eyes, full of pride for what he's done.

"Yo, Daniels," Jose says, nudging me from behind. "Some of us would like to move forward."

I realize there's a rather large gap between me and the guy ahead of me. I set my tray on the rails in front of the serving counter, releasing it from my death grip. "Sorry," I say, turning to Jose. "I got lost in thought."

Jose and I bonded on the journey to DC. He came from another resistance, somewhere in Virginia. A few years older than some of us, he tries to protect us as much as possible. But he's also an extreme goofball.

I push my tray forward. The girl behind the counter hands me a plate of chicken and vegetables. She smiles too kindly at me, leaning forward as she hands me a small portion of mashed potatoes. "Are you new?" she asks, looking me up and down.

I grip my tray, the anger rising up in me again. I think of Raegan, of her heart beating and her small frame fitting in my arms perfectly. "I have a girlfriend," is all I say, turning away and marching off towards a table.

The other guys jeer at me from the line, but I ignore them. I don't care what they think. I'm not here because I want to be. I find a table near the back, hoping to be left alone. But Jose and a few others join me shortly after getting their food.

Tyrone, who came from Texas as well, smirks at me as he sits down. "Popular with the ladies already, Daniels? You should pace yourself."

I roll my eyes. "I don't care. I have someone waiting for me back home."

Jose squirts ketchup into his mashed potatoes, much to the horror of Tyrone. Jose sets the ketchup down, sighing. "You realize we've been brought here to die, right? Might as well have a little fun before then. We're not going home. Especially not you. Care to explain why Evan Williams, heir to this very nation, found it in his best interest to look at you like he wanted to kill you?"

I shovel a spoonful of mashed potatoes in my mouth, chewing slowly. I'm not answering their questions. I've bonded with them; we've been thrown in this miserable hell together because we fight for the opposite side of the government. But... I can't trust them to keep my secrets. I know how people in rebellions operate. It's everyone for themselves. They could be willing to betray me to save themselves.

It's unfortunate, but necessary.

Jose doesn't repeat his question. Instead, the talk of the table changes. I don't contribute much to conversation. I focus on eating, then on getting out of the crowded mess hall. I head out to my barracks, hoping for a quiet moment in the bunks. The light of the day has started to dip beneath the horizon, the air growing colder.

Unfortunately, there's already a line of new

recruits and seasoned soldiers trying to get into the barracks for the night. A couple of officers I don't know of check off names on their clipboards as we enter.

So much for a quiet moment.

They even have to make sure we're all here before we can relax or sleep. A check and balance to make sure no one's missing. Or trying to escape.

If escape could even be possible.

I've heard rumors of a few people making it out, but anything that could resemble hope is shut down quickly. No one's supposed to talk about the people who made it out. To freedom and beyond.

Once we're all inside, Officer Conrad enters. A rather burly man with a red, bushy beard, he doesn't walk gracefully around the barracks. His boots clomp up and down the aisle as he checks the bunks. When he gets back to the door, he turns to all of us and says, "Aye, this is a clean one. Cleanest I've seen."

His accent is strong, but I can't quite place it. He sounds like he could be a pirate. He could look like one, if not for the military uniform.

Conrad writes a few things on his clipboard, then nods at us once. "Aye, off to bed with you lot."

When the door is shut, we climb into our respective bunks. I never hear a lock click, and I wonder if it would be difficult to slip out of the room undetected. I almost consider trying, but the ache in my body overcomes my desire to find out. I close my eyes, trying not to feel every shake of the bed as Jose tries to get comfortable in the bottom bunk. My body, sore and tired, relaxes against the firm mattress. Everything begins to fade away.

Then I hear it.

Heavy boots on the ground.

The door bursting off its hinges.

I shoot up, nearly hitting my head on the low ceiling. All is dark. Some snoring fills the quiet spaces, but nothing is going on. The door is still shut tight.

No one's come in for an attack.

"Daniels?" Jose whispers from the bunk below me. "You good?"

"Yeah," I mumble, unsure if he can hear me. "I'm fine."

I roll to my side, feeling for the keychain under my pillow and wishing for an escape. I want to be home again. I want to be with her. The others may think we're here to die. But I won't die within these concrete walls. I'll survive. I'll go home, and I *will* see her again.

CHAPTER THREE

Jackson

DATE UNKNOWN

VOICES.

I follow them.

All around me are voices.

Dancing around me, like faded music coming through speakers at a party, but I'm tucked away in a different room.

I don't know who the voices belong to. I don't know if they're male or female. I don't know who they are.

I don't know anything.

But I swim towards them, wanting to find something tangible in this empty, dark void.

My body is numb and cold. Everything is dark. I don't know where I am. All around me is a void. If this is death, I must be in limbo. There's no angel choir or bright gates to welcome me. Assuming I'd even make it to heaven. But this doesn't feel like hell, either.

It's nothingness.

Empty.

The voices fade in, muffled. Muted.

I search for whoever it might be. Suddenly, I sense something—or someone—near me. And someone's talking. It sounds like Spencer, but I can't be certain. But as quickly as I hear muted words, they're gone again.

A soft, delicate hand wraps around mine.

Something to hold on to.

I realize I'm not swimming in a void. My eyes are closed.

My fingers wrap tightly around the hand in mine. I hear a soft gasp coming from my left… or maybe it's my right?

"He squeezed my hand," someone says.

Carissa.

My Carissa.

"What?" another person says. Spencer.

"He squeezed my hand. I felt it. He's still in there."

I start to drift away again, but I fight it. I squeeze her hand again, trying to find her in this emptiness. I try to speak, but I find my mouth doesn't move when I try. I want to call out to her, but that won't be possible. I need to see her, need to know I can escape this place.

If this is limbo, I have to fight death.

"He did it again," she says excitedly. I love

hearing her excited.

"Okay," Spencer says. "I'll go get the nurse."

Did he say nurse? Where the hell am I?

"Jackson," Carissa says softly near my ear. "Everything is going to be okay. You're so strong. I know you're going to make it. Please, please hold on. I need you."

She needs me? I don't know what happened or why I'm here in this state between life and death. But I know Carissa hates me… at least as far as I know.

But I follow her voice. Light begins to leak through the darkness. My eyes, heavy and shut, start to flicker open. The light's too much. Blinding, searing pain rips through my head. But I push through. I need to see Carissa. I need to know where I am.

I need to live.

Carissa releases my hand as I hear the door swish open. Another person enters the room. "You're saying he's showing signs of brain activity?"

"He squeezed my hand," Carissa says. "He has to be in there."

The nurse doesn't say anything. Cold fingers wrap around my wrist, checking my pulse. I force my eyes to open, but the bright lights above burn. I groan. The nurse's cold hands instantly fall from me.

"I'll get the doctor. If he's coming to, he may need assistance. We don't know what the blood loss will have done to his brain."

Blood loss? What happened to me?

Clearly, I'm in a hospital. But I don't remember coming here, or why I'm here to begin with. But as my body regains sensation, my abdomen burns with pain. A headache pulses at my temples. But pain feels better than numbness.

The door opens again and a new voice speaks. "We need to run some tests before we can get too excited."

This must be the doctor.

I force my eyes open, blinking rapidly as tears form. I don't know who decided bright lights in a hospital room was smart, but I will hate them forever.

The nurse gasps. "He's awake."

The doctor looks at me, shocked. She brings those same cold fingers to my neck, feeling for a pulse. But the *beep-beep-beep* of the monitor tells me I'm breathing and alive.

"Wha—" I cough, not able to fully form words.

"Take it easy, Mr. Maverick," the doctor says. "You've been through a lot."

A sharp pain rips through my gut and I groan. The doctor turns to the nurse. "The dose of pain medicine isn't enough now that he's awake. We need to give him something stronger."

The nurse nods, rushing from the room again. Carissa hugs herself, a pensive expression on her face.

But for a moment, all I can see is her beauty. She's a sight for literal sore eyes. She shifts her weight and says, "Won't more medicine knock him out again?"

"Yes, it might make him drowsy, but if he's waking up, the bullet entry wound is going to sting a heck of a lot worse."

"Bullet entry wound?" I realize the words do actually fall out of my mouth. Raspy and broken, but everyone in the room is shocked.

Tears fall down Carissa's face. The doctor looks even more shocked. "Mr. Maverick, I regret to inform you that you're in the hospital."

I groan, my hand instinctively going to my stomach. "Yeah, I got that. How did I get here?"

"You were shot in the abdomen. You lost a lot of blood and have been in a coma. But you're awake now, which is a good sign. We're going to give you medicine to help with the pain. You may fall back asleep, but don't fight it. You won't be back in the coma. It will be normal sleep."

I don't know if I trust that, but I don't know that I have much choice either way. The pain sears through me. The nurse returns with a cart and they change out the bags hooked up to the IVs in my arm.

After they finish, the doctor and nurse leave again, promising to return in half an hour to see how the new dosage progresses. I'm left with Carissa and Spencer. Carissa looks faint, taking a seat in the chair next to my bed.

Spencer leans against the wall.

The room is quiet for a long while, save the soft hum of machine noises.

Then Carissa stands, approaching my bed. "Jackson?" she says, hoarse.

"Yes?" I ask weakly, looking up into her beautiful brown eyes.

Tears fill her eyes again. I want nothing more than to reach up and wipe them away, caress her face and comfort her.

Spencer approaches the other side of my bed. "You just had to go and take a long nap, didn't you?"

"Always. But I'm not sure what happened."

Spencer glances over at Carissa, then back at me. "You don't remember what happened?"

I shake my head slightly. "No. I remember following Carissa over to the warehouse where we knew Linley would be. I know Evan was there. But after that, it's all blurry."

Flashes of a gunshot and blood fill my head, but I shove them away. Carissa clutches my hand again, her hands warm and shaky. Spencer takes a few steps back.

"I should probably head home. I'll fill in Uncle Andre and bring him up here in the morning."

Carissa nods. "Okay. Drive safe."

Spencer leaves, closing the door behind him. I

realize it's night. A clock ticking on the wall catches my attention. It's almost nine p.m., to be exact. But Carissa makes no move to leave.

"Won't you get in trouble?" I ask. "For staying."

"I've fought them the first few days of being here. They gave up after a while."

"How long have I been out?" The question scares me. The idea that I've been in a coma for any length of time is terrifying.

"Today marks fourteen days, if you count the day it all happened."

I shift a little in my bed. "What exactly happened? How did I get shot?"

Carissa turns away from me, hugging herself as she stares out the window into the night. At first, I think she might not answer the question. But then she says, "We were tracking down Linley. We found out she was back at the warehouse. Evan and Samantha were there, too. I don't know why. I don't know what they were looking for. I assume it has to do with Raegan. But we went inside. To find Linley and to get her out. But… there was a fight. I got out with Linley because you were fighting with Evan. And…" She pauses, turning to me.

Pain is clear in her eyes. This isn't an easy part to get through. Whatever happened, I think I can fit the pieces together.

"Evan shot me, didn't he?"

She nods, not saying a word. Maybe neither of us believed Evan to be capable of this. Not with Raegan alive. Not with his own admission to being unable to kill anyone.

Yet he tried to kill me.

The doctor comes in, interrupting us. If she senses this, she doesn't show it. She does a few checks on the medicine. Asks me a few questions about my level of pain now and how I feel. Then she leaves and the lights in my room go out.

The only light left comes from the crack beneath the door.

"You must be tired," I say to Carissa. "Have you gone home at all?"

"A couple of times. And only because my father made me. Spencer stayed here while I'd take his truck back home, to shower and change into new clothes. My mom made me eat. Then I'd come back and Spencer would go home until the next day. He's been with me a lot."

"Thank you. For staying by my side."

The room is silent. I clear my throat. "That hospital chair can't be comfortable."

"It's not." There's a heaviness to her voice, like this is something she didn't want to admit. I scoot over in my bed as much as I can and pat the spot next to me.

She huffs. "You can't be serious. That won't be

comfortable for you."

"I don't care. I want you close." I'm surprised by my own forwardness. I'm even more surprised when she comes over, climbs in and lies down next to me. Her small frame fits easily, her head resting on my chest. The heart rate monitor beeps furiously.

"Am I hurting you?"

"No," I say. "No, that's called 'the girl I used to date is tucked into a hospital bed with me.'"

I expect some kind of witty comeback, but instead she snuggles closer to me.

"Well, if I knew it just took almost dying to get your attention again, I might've done it a long time ago."

"You don't remember what you said to me before you passed out, do you?" she asks, ignoring my flirtations.

She's tense, and I realize this is serious. I clear my throat. "No. I'm sorry. What did I say?"

"I should probably finish telling you what happened to you."

Whatever I said, I can tell Carissa is upset that I don't remember. She shifts, turning away from me. I want to wrap my arms around her, but I can't when she lies that way.

She sighs. "Linley and I got out of there, but then there was a gunshot. When I found you… you were lying on your stomach in the alley, bleeding onto the concrete. Linley helped me get you into the car. We brought you to the hospital and you passed out before we could get you out of the car."

"What did I say to you?"

Silence.

"Carissa, whatever it is, it's important. What did I say?"

"You said you loved me."

BEEP-BEEP-BEEP-BEEP

The heart rate monitor does nothing to help me disguise my thoughts. I lift my hand up, stroking her hair. The only movement I can do. "I do still love you. I never stopped loving you, Carissa. I made a stupid decision. But I was trying to protect you. I should've done more for you. Honestly, you deserve someone way better than me."

"I still love you," she murmurs, rolling back over to face me. She buries her face in my chest again.

"You...do?"

"Yes."

"You don't..." I swallow, feeling the nerves rise up in my throat. "You don't have to say it back. I know I almost died and everything, but that doesn't mean you have to give me pity like that."

"Jackson," she whispers. "I'm the last person to look to for pity. I love you. I never stopped. I'm not saying this because you almost died. I'm saying it because I realize that we're fighting for our lives. Any moment could be our last."

Wrapping my free arm around her now, I hold her close. "Don't leave me again," she says softly.

"I won't."

We're both silent for a while. But I'm unable to sleep. Even with the pain medicine coursing through my veins and a lingering drowsiness, I'm more alive than before. My mind flits to different things that I can recall. I helped save Raegan. I was locked up in the resistance base. Carissa and I went to find Linley.

"Rissa?"

"Yeah?"

"How's Raegan?"

Carissa tenses beside me. "Things aren't great. Peter… was drafted. He was taken to DC about ten days ago. I haven't left your side, but Spencer's gone to see her. She's not doing well. And according to Peter, a lot of the men and women drafted came from rebel backgrounds. It's part of the initiative Emperor Morgan has taken to break down resistance."

"But Peter's name should've been removed."

"Spencer did remove his name, as well as any other eligible person in our resistance. But Evan must've done something for his own personal idea of revenge. I don't really know. And my father has decided to focus on some secret project. Something he says will help us all."

"And how's Linley?" I ask. Linley, a girl full of teenage

angst and family trauma.

"She's staying with Peter's mom. She refuses to return to her mom. Apparently, her birthday was the other day, but she didn't tell anyone. She decided she wants to train, so my father is letting her for now. Something to burn off the energy, he claims."

So much has changed while I slept. I hate that I've missed so much. "I'm sorry I've left you alone for so long."

"Don't leave me again."

"I won't. I won't leave you."

Soon, Carissa's breathing evens out and I know she's finally asleep. My eyelids grow heavy, the quiet whirring of the machines lulling me to sleep.

I don't know where I'll go after all of this. Maybe Andre will let me stay with him, but I don't know if I should ask that. I want to help the resistance and fight against what's going on. For too long, I've fought for the wrong things.

I won't be a prisoner to Evan's games anymore. It almost cost me my life.

I look to the woman at my side. I'm living for her. To provide for and protect her. Evan may have tried to kill me. But I'm coming back stronger.

CHAPTER FOUR

Raegan
WEDNESDAY, NOVEMBER 15TH, 2023

THERE'S SOMETHING ABOUT MY NEW ROUTINE OF waking up in the middle of the night and opening my window that I find calming. Tonight, the air isn't as cold as it was a week or so ago. That's the thing with Texas… the cold doesn't linger in the night like the bitter wind that helped me freeze my already ice-covered heart.

Sometimes, it warms up in between the cold spells. Tonight, it's only a mild chill. But the humidity signals rain. Even the air smells of it. I like the rainy days. They cover the sun, reflecting my mood. I don't want to exist in a world with sunshine when the light inside me has been snuffed out.

But life doesn't care if I want sunlight or not.

Thankfully, in the dead of night, I can imagine that I'm always in the dark.

Dr. Ho says I'm making progress. My mom says color has returned to my face.

But that's about all the progress I've made. Maybe I'm a little stronger. I can live outside my room longer than I used to. I'm not as skinny. I'm still small, but my clothes seem to fit better. Dr. Ho thinks I need to get more sun. Something that's difficult to do when I'm not allowed to be spotted by any neighbors.

Peter's mom brings Gunner, their dog, over sometimes. She's thrown herself into work a lot. Sometimes, Linley comes over with Gunner. He's comforting to hold onto. And he reminds me so much of Peter. Dr. Ho thinks interacting with Gunner is good for my healing, since my contact with nature and the outside world is limited.

Nicole visits me when she can. Sawyer does, too. But never at the same time. Never like it used to be.

I inhale, closing my eyes. The humid wind shifts, changing. But before I can analyze it to see if perhaps another change in weather is coming, the rumble of the patrol truck draws closer. I shut my window, placing the curtains back, and go back to bed. Tonight, my body feels tired.

I haven't had night terrors the past few nights. But I still wake up around two or three in the morning. I think I'm making some sort of penance out of it. A vigil of standing by the window and watching silently as the night shifts. An act of rebellion since no one is supposed to see into the night. But I do it despite the rules, throwing caution to the wind.

For Peter.

For the other souls torn from their homes for the stupid draft.

Peter communicates with Mr. Williams every so often. A lot of the other men and women pulled for the draft were from other rebellions. It seems as though this was part of Evan's plan. Despite rebel leaders removing the names of their members, Evan knew how to put them back in.

I've begged Mr. Williams to let me talk to Peter. But every time they've communicated, it's been late in the night. Past curfew.

Past my parent-enforced bedtime.

Spencer gives me the notes he takes from every call, visiting often to do so. I've noticed he writes down almost every word Peter says so I see them. So I can *hear* the words echo in my head.

I roll over onto my side, closing my eyes. All is quiet. Sleep should be simple. But it never is.

When I wake again, birds chirp outside my window, but rain beats against the glass panes. There's a comfort in that simple sound. The skies crying out in agony, just like my soul.

I rise from bed and shower. My routine for the past couple of weeks. I don't take too long in the shower, though. It warms me up enough to feel like perhaps I am still human. Then I get out so I don't have to thaw completely. My body runs so cold lately. I'm sure I've grown anemic; among other issues, my body has developed. Or maybe it's the result of all the nights I've been letting the cold air chill me to the bone. My body must be developing some sort of tendency to stay cold.

I pull on a t-shirt and jean shorts. It's probably going to be cold out again by the end of this storm, but that's exactly what I'm counting on. I grab Peter's forest-green hoodie, the one that brought out his eyes. The one I stole from his closet a few days ago when I snuck over to his house to see his mom.

I exit the bathroom and slip on some socks. My room is cast in a faded gray light from the skies. I throw my curtains open; the rain pounds heavily against the window.

I wonder if it could be raining where Peter is now. I doubt DC has the same crazy weather pattern that Texas has. It's probably cold. Maybe it's even snowing. Do they make him train in snow? So many questions I want to ask him. So many words I may never get to say.

I close my eyes, feeling his arms come around me again. His even breathing on my neck. The way his lips pressed softly to my shoulder just before he faded into a quiet, peaceful sleep.

And when the soldiers marched in, his first

instinct was to protect me. His arm was tight around me, and he was ready to jump up if he had to.

I wish I had been strong enough to fight for him. It wouldn't have mattered. But watching him get dragged away was gut-wrenching. My mom hurried me back into the house before neighbors got a good look at me, comforting me when all I could do was collapse against her and sob. I wanted to lie in the street screaming. I wanted the world to know my grief.

Instead, I grieve alone and in silence.

Because of Linley's similarities to me—same dark hair and smaller frame—my parents were able to convince the neighbors that it was Linley they had seen out in the street, sobbing on her hands and knees.

Not their dead daughter who was taken so soon by a car accident.

Part of me hates the lying and the cover stories. But I'm also anxious, wondering what Evan would do if people found out I'm alive.

My phone chimes from my bedside table, shaking me from my thoughts. I turn away from the window and the soothing rain, taking a seat on the edge of my bed. A text from Nicole sits on my home screen. I click it open because Nicole is one of the few people besides my family who know I exist.

Nicole: good morning, boo! how are you feeling?

Me: I think we both know the answer to that. but I'm enjoying the rain.

Nicole: up again all night?

Me: kinda. it's okay. I'm okay. I'm making progress.

Nicole: good. I want to stop by after school. should be okay, right?

Me: yeah. not like I have anywhere to go.

Nicole: so not what I meant. but okay. I'll see you later! try to have a good day.

Me: I shall attempt.

Nicole has been so wonderful to me through all of this. She brings me candy—not approved by my doctor, but we eat it anyway. She distracts me with things going on at school. At first, she didn't even want to talk about her life happenings, but I begged her to. I need something normal to hold on to.

Now I look forward to Wednesdays, when she stops by to give me snacks I shouldn't eat, and tell me gossip I care too much about.

I pocket my phone and head downstairs. When I see Gunner sitting in the center of the living room, I realize Peter's mom, Michelle, must be here. Entering the kitchen, I see her sitting with my mom at the table. She's sobbing into my mother's shoulder, her body shaking. My heart cracks further.

"What's going on?"

My mom gives me a soft, sad frown. "Just a hard moment."

I walk up to Michelle, giving her a hug. She leans away from my mom, latching onto me. "You smell like him," she says softly, her voice hoarse.

"I'm wearing the hoodie you let me steal," I say sheepishly.

Despite the emotion in the room, Michelle leans back and wipes her eyes. "Thank you. It helps to remember he exits. It's not like anything bad is happening right now. He's in training for six months. Andre says everything is going well right now. I just… miss him. But I'm happy to have Linley and Gunner. They make me feel safe. I don't know if Linley's mother is happy with this arrangement, though."

I nod, taking a seat. "Linley comes by sometimes when you're working. I think she likes hanging out at your house instead of being with her mom right now."

My mom rises and says, "I'm going to get us some tea.

I just brewed a pitcher."

"Thank you," Michelle says to her. She returns her attention to me. "Greg didn't mean to hurt anyone by keeping the secret," she says, referring to her ex and Peter's father. "I think he worried how Peter would feel. He's never been good with words. And I think Linley's mom worried about the same thing."

"Not really the right way to go about it," I sigh. "But I think Linley will warm up to her mom again soon enough. She misses her. She'll tell me about her sometimes."

Michelle gratefully takes the cup of sweet tea from my mom. "She talks to me about it, too. Greg found a good one, I think. Hopefully someone who can make him focus on family a bit more than work."

I don't know what to say to that. Peter's parents divorcing was a hard thing for both him and me. They had been my second set of parents when they lived here. And for them to go through that when Peter was in California was so hard. But from what I can tell, Michelle and Greg are pretty friendly; at least they seem to be. They aren't bitter exes fighting at every turn. Peter told me they were always really amicable, especially for him and his sister, Emilee.

But knowing that another woman might make Greg Daniels slow down is frustrating. It's all Peter ever wanted, being handed to a new woman and a kid that's not his own.

"How is Em?" I ask, needing a change of topic.

Michelle sighs. "She doesn't talk to me much anymore. She's a lot like her father. Work hard and keep working. I hear from her once a week. When I told her Peter was drafted, I don't know if she knew what to think. She knew of the resistance, but she wasn't interested. I think she blames the rebellion for her brother being taken away."

Emilee was always a bit more driven towards isolating herself from everyone. It doesn't surprise me that she doesn't give much reaction. Peter's dad was always that way, too. Peter hated that about his dad and sister. He wanted emotional connection and they were all business.

My mom brushes a hand on my shoulder. "Are you hungry? You need to take your vitamins."

"Yeah, I guess."

Michelle stands up and says, "I should get going. It's my day off and I promised myself I would clean my house and take Gunner for a walk."

My mom meets Michelle at the kitchen door and wraps her in a hug. "Everything will be okay."

I take in my mom's words, wishing I could believe them. I wonder if Peter's mom believes them. I don't dare ask. Because if those four words give her some sort of hope, I don't want to be the one that breaks it.

But I can't stop the vicious cycle of thoughts that live in my brain. Every scenario, playing on repeat. Peter dying at the hands of the enemy, tortured and with no one to fight for him. Evan coming back to take me away from all that I love, to finish what he started at the warehouse.

I know these are all worst-case scenarios, but life is a worst-case scenario right now. Everything is falling apart. I can't find hope or light or peace in anything going on.

I do know one thing. And that is I will fight for Peter. As long as it takes.

CHAPTER FIVE

Carissa

WEDNESDAY, NOVEMBER 15TH, 2023

I STUDY JACKSON AS HE LIES ASLEEP ON THE GUEST bed. His eyes are closed, one hand resting on his stomach, near the wound. The doctor said the pain medicine would probably keep him pretty tired. Most days, he sleeps between meals. It's the best thing he can do for healing.

I miss talking to him, though. We haven't been able to talk much in the past few days. But I'm grateful he's here.

"Are you stalking?" I jump at the sound of Spencer's voice behind me.

I close the door quietly, turning to my cousin. "No. But they said to make sure he doesn't roll onto his stomach."

Spencer brushes past me and goes down the stairs. I follow suit, still feeling that invisible string tug between me and Jackson. But he's asleep. And he's safe.

Spencer says, "I don't think hovering over him is doing you any good. You should relax. The worst part is over. He's awake… mostly. And he's healing."

Shaking my head, I cross my arms and lean against the wall behind me. "The hard part isn't over. It's barely begun. We've lost Peter. Raegan's health is dancing on a single thread. My dad is obsessing over the information Peter is collecting while he's in the military. And knowing my father, he's using this information to plot things for the demise of the government regime. But it's not enough. We're falling apart, though he's not going to admit it. And he keeps going on about war. Some of the other rebel leaders of even contacted us, suggesting we take the fight to them."

Spencer sighs, running a hand through his chestnut-brown hair. "We can't go to war. We don't have the numbers."

"Apparently… a lot of the other men and women who were drafted were rebels. Not for my father. But for other rebellions. Smaller ones. Established ones. It's a theme. They're slowly chipping away at our forces using Evan's knowledge of who's a rebel and who's not."

Eyes wide, Spencer says, "What the—what are we supposed to do with that? That means numbers are even lower."

"I know… and so does Evan. He's forcing our hand. He wants to lure us into making a move."

"Rissa?" Jackson's voice calls out weakly. I hardly

hear it. Part of me wonders if I imagined it. But then Spencer glances up the stairs.

I run up, the wood creaking beneath my feet. I'm usually more careful not to make noise, but I throw caution and stealth to the wind in my own home.

I open the door to the guest room. Jackson's awake, but he's entirely loopy.

"I missed youuuu," he says, his voice almost sing-songy as he sleepily drags out his words.

"You were sleeping," I reply.

"I thought you left foreverrrr."

I sigh. I cross the room to the bedside table, pour him a glass of water and help him to sit up a bit. Hopefully it will help him wake faster than the last time.

"Nooooo… I'mnotthirsty."

I roll my eyes at his slurred declaration, but I can't stop the smirk creeping onto my face. "Too bad. Drink it."

He takes a few sips, blinking the sleep from his eyes. We stay in silence for a little while as he slowly drinks the water. I take a seat in the lounge chair near the bed.

"Ugh," Jackson says, finally waking from the fog-like state between dream and reality.

"Welcome back, sleeping beauty."

"Yeah, yeah. Whatever. I have a splitting headache and I feel like I've been repeatedly punched in the gut."

I frown. "You still have an hour before you can take another dose of medicine. Are you hungry?"

"No. Not even a little bit."

I nod slowly. "Well, you have some time before you need to eat. Can I get you anything?"

"Nah. I'm okay. How long was I out?"

He doesn't say it, but I see it in his eyes. Jackson's scared of slipping under again. Of falling into a coma and waking up weeks or months or even years later. Despite constant reassurance from the doctors and from me, there's fear.

"Only a few of hours. You took your dose with breakfast, slept through lunchtime, but it's only the afternoon."

He sighs, leaning his head back on the headboard. "Okay. Any updates?"

I look away, unable to meet his eyes. "Not really."

I hate lying to Jackson with every fiber of my being. But after everything he's been through, the last thing I want is for him to be stressed or worried about not recovering fast enough. My father agreed that as soon as he's made a full recovery, he can stay in the resistance if he chooses to.

I want to tell him everything I know about what's happened so far. But it will only cause him unnecessary stress.

"Carissa May Williams."

My eyes meet his instantly at the use of my full name. Jackson's eyes hold an intensity I've never seen before.

And a bit of hurt.

"I know you're lying to me, Rissa. I'm not a child. Tell me what's happening."

"But your healing—"

"Being updated doesn't stop my healing," Jackson says, cutting me off. "I asked for what's happening. I wouldn't ask if I couldn't handle it."

He's right. I know he's right. I inhale slowly before telling him everything I told Spencer at the bottom of the stairs. When I finish, he's contemplative.

"We should join forces with the other resistances."

I laugh dryly. "You think my father would be willing to link our resistance with other ones? Have you met him?"

Jackson's jaw hardens. "Yes. Many times. And if he's wanting to go to war, we'll need numbers. The other resistances have been damaged, just as we have. It's Peter now, but the draft could happen again at any moment. They could take anyone else. Evan is willing to stop at nothing to bring us down. So how do you think we'll build an army strong enough to defeat the government?"

"My dad isn't one to share leadership. And you know how all resistance leaders are. They think they know best. There's no way we'd get through anything, let alone plan out an actual battle tactic."

"Maybe," Jackson relents. "But maybe this is the key we're waiting for. At least suggest it to him. I don't know if he'd listen to me. But if it comes from you, he'd listen."

I shake my head. "He doesn't trust me all that much yet."

"Don't make this difficult."

I rise from the chair, standing near the table and filling his cup with more water. "I'm not being difficult. I know my father. He's not going to be willing to hear any ideas from me."

"But if we don't join with other resistances, we'll never have the strength to win. It would be suicide."

"You're right," my dad says from the doorway.

I turn on my heel, nearly spilling the water in Jackson's cup. "Dad?"

He lingers, not quite entering the room. "I heard voices so I thought I'd check up on you, Jackson. I see my daughter is taking good care of you."

"Yes, sir. Always."

Dad nods. "You're both right. I am stubborn and I don't like to take suggestions. But Jackson has the right idea. I've been in communication with the other resistances. We're working on a deal to unite as one front. Some are a bit more… uncertain. But I think we can all agree that time is of the essence. But as you were saying, resistance leaders are stubborn."

I glance at my father sideways. He waves his hand at me. "Yes, yes. I know. But there is talk. And there is hope that maybe we can gather enough of us under one resistance that our numbers will matter."

"I… I'm shocked," is all I can manage to say.

My dad smirks. "Well, maybe I've got a few tricks up my sleeve. I'll let you two get back to it. I'm heading to a virtual meeting."

With that, he's gone in an instant. I look at Jackson. "I guess I was wrong."

Jackson shakes his head. "I've never known you to be wrong. He's incredibly stubborn, and it's going to be a difficult process. But I think there's strength in numbers."

I hand him his glass of water, a small half-smile creeping onto my face. "Maybe you're right."

Jackson sips his water. "I've never known myself to be wrong."

"CARISSA, YOU'RE NEVER GOING to believe this!"

I land another blow to the punching dummy before turning to give my cousin my attention. Sweat drips down my neck, and I'm breathing heavily. I grab the water bottle near my sweat towel, flipping the cap open. "What?"

"The other resistances are talking to Uncle Andre right now and they're considering an alliance. *An alliance*! They want to join together into one."

I don't have it in me to pretend to be shocked. "I know."

"He never compromises on anything."

"I know."

"This is either going to be the best thing ever, or the biggest disaster in American history."

I smirk. "Probably both."

When Spencer goes quiet, I take another gulp of water before closing the lid and setting my water bottle aside. Motioning to the punch dummy, I ask, "Here to train?"

He shakes his head. "No time. I'm working on a major project."

"What kind of project?"

"The classified kind."

"Does it involve figuring out how to talk to Raegan's redhead friend?"

Spencer's face goes beet red as he stutters, "I— what? No. It's the type of classified project that those of weaker minds could never comprehend."

Glaring at him, I say, "Go check on Jackson for me, Mr. Classified Secret. I have another round of boxing before I can call it a night."

Spencer nods. "All right. Don't stay up too late, okay?"

I don't agree, but everyone knows my lack of answer means I'm going to do whatever I see fit. They've learned to accept it.

I start again with my sparring, imagining that this

training dummy is my own brother, Evan. I don't know that I'd be able to attack him in real life. That's what scares me. I can let all my anger loose on this fake person.

But if my brother, armed with a gun, were to be in front of me right now… could I defend myself? Or the people I love?

Some part of me hurts knowing I still care for him. He's a psychopath. But he's my brother.

The last of the workout has me breathing heavily. I lie on my back on the training mat, trying to catch my breath.

Memories of my childhood flood back to me. Moments where Evan was all I had. He's four years older than me, so we were never in the same grades at school. Sometimes we weren't at the same school at all. But regardless of whether we were in the same building or not, he protected me from the mean girls by marching up the front steps with me every morning.

He helped me balance on my bike when I first learned to ride without training wheels. My parents were always busy with their jobs, and then when my father inherited my grandfather's money and things started going bad with our world, he used the inheritance and began building a resistance.

And my mom was always helping my dad. But Evan was always there. He never complained about helping me when I asked. Even when he was in the middle of homework or something he wanted to do, he would stop everything to help me.

Could this psychopath, the one trying to help destroy everything we've ever known, really be my brother?

Tears well in my eyes and spill onto the mat as I let the grief finally hit me.

I miss my brother.

"Rissa?"

I sit up, quickly wiping my face with my hand. "Jackson? What are you doing down here? Who let you down the stairs?"

"I asked Spencer to help me."

The doctor said the best thing would be for Jackson to walk around the house a little, maybe even outside. We weren't supposed to overdo it. And if he wasn't up to it some days, that was okay.

But he's most definitely not supposed to go down two flights of stairs, never mind having to go back up again.

I rise from the floor, turning and taking a step away from him. I don't want him to see me like this.

Weak.

Broken.

"Baby, why were you crying?"

I shake my head. "I wasn't."

"I saw you. You don't have to hide from me."

I don't realize he's right behind me until I turn to

face him. His hands take hold of my face gently, his brown eyes searching mine. Our faces are mere inches apart, the tip of my nose touching his.

"You can tell me anything," he says softly, his breath brushing across my lips.

"I know," I reply. "I just… miss my brother. I know it's stupid."

He shakes his head. "It's not stupid. He's still your brother. You grew up with him and you were close as kids. This is only natural. You haven't processed any of this since leaving him."

My head comes to rest against Jackson's shoulder. "I've let it build up and I'm realizing…"

The words are lost as I begin to sob. Jackson wraps his arms around me, gently. I'm careful not to press up to close to him, cautious of the wound to his gut. Still, hearing his heart beat against my ear is a strange form of comfort.

I let it all out. The anguish of thinking I helped murder Raegan. My time on the run from Evan. The heartbreak I felt because of Jackson choosing my brother. Finding out Raegan was alive. My brother being far more evil than I ever could've imagined. Everything comes out in sobs that leave me breathless and shaking.

Jackson holds me, despite his own complications.

"I'm horrible," I manage. "Here I am crying on your shoulder when you took a bullet to your gut."

"Rissa… Just because your struggle is with an invisible

enemy doesn't mean it's any less important. Grief is painful. Our minds trap us in the worst hell we could ever know. I don't care what mountain I'm climbing; I will always want to help you climb yours first."

I lean up and kiss him, unable to find the words for how I feel. My heart bursts with so many emotions.

I've never been the mushy kind of girl. I'm focused and dedicated to whatever it is that I'm doing. But as we stop kissing, I say, "I love you."

And the smile on his face is worth the mush.

CHAPTER SIX

Peter

SATURDAY, NOVEMBER 18TH, 2023

I EASE ONTO THE BENCH IN THE CAFETERIA. A FEW other men from my barracks sit here. Jose looks up and says, "You look sore, Daniels."

"I am." I grimace at the slop in the bowl in front of me. It's supposedly beef soup, a collection of leftover beef and vegetables from the week. Although it's not the worst thing in existence, the smell coming from it is questionable. Despite my hesitation, I take a bite. My hunger is far too powerful to resist even this disgusting excuse for food.

Jose frowns at his plate of what appears to be meatloaf. "Any thoughts on what might be in this?"

The rest of us shake our heads.

Seth Jennings, one of the quiet ones of our group, says, "I'm thinking it's some sort of animal protein and veggies. But I haven't figured out how they get it to hold its shape like that. Definitely one of the world's deepest mysteries."

A few others chime in with theories, but I hardly pay

attention. My mind is on the burner phone in my pocket. The one I managed to sneak past the guards when I first arrived. I don't know where I'm supposed to be able to make a call to Mr. Williams. This base is observed tightly during the day.

Night is my only chance.

But night is complicated. The only place I can think of is the cellar that's near my barracks. It's underground, almost like a shelter in case we're under attack. We toured it when we arrived and talked about backup plans in case we couldn't get to the cellar.

It's the only place without surveillance. Getting to it in the night might not be easy. Even though the base has less activity then, I can't imagine being able to stay out of view of the guards or the night patrol.

"Daniels, you look a little green. Too much beef soup?" Jose asks with genuine concern.

"Beef soup? That's hardly correct," Jennings interjects.

I wave them both off with my hand. "I'm fine. Just tired and sore."

I can tell neither of them believe me, but I take another bite to prove my point. When they return to their conversation, I take a breath. I can't let my emotions show like that.

Being readable will only bring trouble. And that's the last thing I need right now.

After dinner ends, everyone is sent back to their barracks. We wait at attention, silent, as Officer Conrad makes his way through the bunks for the day's final inspection. As he leaves, everyone climbs into their beds like clockwork.

I wait, wide awake, for everyone to be asleep. I don't know how long I'm waiting, but once the room is filled with heavy breathing and snoring, I feel safe enough to leave.

Outside, the air is cold. My breath comes out in a fog. I glance around, not seeing anyone. It's almost entirely silent, save for the sounds of the generators around camp, providing heat and power. Voices approach from around the corner. I duck between buildings, tucking myself into the shadows. A couple of soldiers on night patrol walk past, deep in conversation. Once they're gone, I slip back out of the dark space.

I inch my way along the shadows, keeping my back against the buildings. Trying to stay out of the view of all the cameras is hard, but not entirely impossible.

I reach the cellar, leaning over carefully to open the doors. Glancing around one more, I slip in when I'm sure no one will see me. I breath slowly, counting the seconds, the minutes until I'm caught.

When no one descends on me, I figure it's safe enough to make the call. I tuck myself into a corner, sliding to the floor with my back to the wall. I pull the burner phone out of my pocket, staring down at it.

The chances of getting caught brings up my heart rate. Trying to catch my breath feels impossible. The idea of calling Andre doesn't help my case. Maybe it's because I have nothing concrete to report right now. I've talked to Mr. Williams a few other times, but that was when I first arrived. I was stupid enough to do it out in the open field, and I almost got caught. Ever since, I've put off talking to him.

Shakily, I type in Mr. Williams' number. Every ring seems to grow louder, rivaling the beating of my heart.

"Hello?"

"It's me," I say.

"Peter? I'm glad you called. I was just about to head out of headquarters for the night. I was beginning to worry about your lack of contact."

I nod, only to remember he can't see me. "Yeah, it's been hard to get away. But all that's been happening is training and preparing."

I can hear him typing on his computer, likely making note of this call. But I'm calling for a purpose. "How's Raegan?"

"Oh, she's well, last I heard. Her parents say that she's making excellent progress with her healing. Your mom mentioned her as well. She's been taking the dog over to visit with her now and then."

I smile. Gunner will comfort Raegan, which is what I hoped for. Mr. Williams continues. "Spencer's gone to see her a few times as well. He says she's doing great. They're all amazed at her progress."

"That's good," I say.

"Is there anything else to take note of?" he says, all business.

"Not really. Not unless you count the strict training regimen and the fact that new recruits show up almost every day. Not all of them have come from resistance backgrounds, but there have been more. This batch was mostly female."

"Sounds like there is no limit to who they'll draft." There's a hesitation to his voice. "What seems to be the atmosphere between the established soldiers and the new ones?"

"I haven't noticed much hostility. Mostly, everyone's trying to survive the training and do their jobs without getting noticed by any of the commanders or generals."

"Seems fair," he says, and sighs. "How many new recruits do you think arrived with the last batch?"

"Maybe fifty?"

Silence permeates the line for a long time. I begin to wonder if the call has dropped when I hear the clicking of keys on the computer and Mr. Williams mumbling under his breath. "That sounds... strange," he finally says. "I don't know if I'll be able to find anything about that yet.

But most of the drafts so far have been between ten to fifteen people. And I've been aware of every draft. I haven't heard of a fifty-person draft. When did they come in?"

"A couple of days ago. We don't really welcome or greet them. They arrive and start training with us as if they've always been there. That's kind of how they treat all of us. Maybe it just hasn't reached your sources yet?"

More silence.

More clicking keys.

More trying of my patience.

This conversation is going nowhere, and every minute I'm in this cellar, I'm more likely to be caught.

"Perhaps," Andre says absentmindedly. "I can't find anything on it. But keep me updated and I'll see what I can find out about this. Though I'm not seeing any reports from the other rebellions about losing more people."

Other rebellions? Since when does Andre Williams communicate with other rebellions? I almost ask, the question dancing on the tip of my tongue. But when I hear things outside the cellar, I go cold. I pause, not saying a word.

Counting every breath.

When the noises pass after five breaths, I decide now is the time to go. "Okay. Thanks, sir. I'd better get back to my bunk before they realize I'm missing. But I'll be in contact again when I can."

"All right, Peter. Have a good night."

The line goes dead and there's an ache inside of me. The ache of being so alone. I feel it every time I think of home, or of the resistance. It feels defeating.

I rise from the small, dim corner of the cellar. I go to slip the burner phone back into my pocket, but a couple of times lately I've almost been caught with it during surprise inspections. It almost feels as though they're looking for something.

I look around. There are shelves in the cellar, full of canned food in case of emergencies. I slip the phone onto one of the top shelves, behind a row of cans, where no one will see it should they come down here. I climb the few steps of the ladder and pull myself out, shutting the cellar hatch behind me.

I'm careful to stay in the shadows on the way back. I'm nearly to the barracks when I hear someone calling from behind me. "Hey, you!"

I turn to see a female soldier from the night patrol. She slits her eyes at me as she approaches. "What are you doing out? There is a curfew inside the base, too, you know."

"I couldn't sleep. I just needed some air. I'm sorry. I didn't mean to break the rules."

I hate pretending like I'm a scared newbie. But if I act like I don't know the rules, they're likely to go a bit easier on me. Not much, but enough to help me make it back alive.

She seems unconvinced, but says, "Get back to your barracks. Once the commanding officer does the nightly check, you're not allowed out. You'd do well to remember that, soldier."

"I will. Thank you." I quickly set off in the direction of my barracks, knowing she's watching my every move.

Once inside, I get back into my bunk as quietly as I can. I lie on my back, resting my hand on my stomach. I'm breathing heavily, my heart beating loudly in my ears. But I made it.

And Raegan is doing okay. That's all I can hope for. And for the first time, tonight, I don't have night terrors of soldiers breaking into the room and dragging me away. I don't see my mom sobbing on the asphalt as she falls to her knees while I'm being taken away.

I don't see Raegan's mom rushing her back inside before neighbors can see who she is.

I see hope. Tangible and real hope.

SUNDAY
NOVEMBER 19TH, 2023

SUNDAYS ARE CALM. The base doesn't train on Sundays,

giving everyone one rest day. It's kind of strange for a government that's hardly pious to observe a day that's usually set aside as holy.

I'm not super religious. My family stopped going to church when we moved from Texas to California. But I still find some things sacred. For something so evil to give everyone a Sunday to rest feels wrong.

But I don't complain too much. My muscles scream just climbing down the ladder to my bunk. I don't know that I would be able to make it through training if we had it today.

"Daniels."

I startle, glancing over behind me.

"Jennings," I say. "I thought I was the only one still here."

"Sunday morning food isn't good food," is his only response. Seth Jennings has been here longer than most of the men in this barracks. He's a few years older than us, too.

I grimace. "Worse than leftover medley soup that doesn't taste like it looks?"

He grins. "Way worse. On Sundays, they feed you sugary food."

"Sugary? Like donuts?"

"Yeah," he groans, lying back in his bunk. "It's horrible."

"We must have different definitions of horrible."

He smirks. I shake my head, turning away and heading towards the door. His voice stops me. "Hey, by the way, I wanted to ask where you went off to last night."

My heart drops as my hand rests on the cold doorknob. I turn to face him, opening my mouth to speak the lie that rests easily on my tongue. But he rises. "Don't tell me some bogus reason, either. I know you and a bunch of the others are here are from resistances. What did you go and do?"

I don't know how Jennings feels about being here. I don't know if he came as a drafted soldier or as a volunteer. All I know is the tone of his voice is unnerving. I need to be careful about what I share with him.

"I couldn't sleep. I have a lot of nightmares and anxiety," I say, all true words. "I needed fresh air. I didn't get too far before the night patrol found me and sent me back on my way."

Jennings studies me. I can tell he doesn't believe anything I'm saying. But I'm not about to tell him the truth.

"All right." He brushes past me, leaving the barracks.

Even if he tells on me, the night patrol soldier will remember me. She'll remember what I said about being unable to sleep. And nothing will seem strange.

I'm almost thankful she ran into me last night now.

I'll have to be careful around Jennings. He's obviously going to be watching me now. I can't afford to have someone following me or getting me in trouble.

Mr. Williams' question about how the other soldiers are treating the drafted ones replays in my mind. People waiting to take down the new guys, especially those of us who came from enemy lines.

I head towards the mess hall, glancing around often. Paranoia fills my head, convincing me everyone is the enemy.

Maybe they are.

CHAPTER SEVEN

Raegan
WEDNESDAY, NOVEMBER 22ND, 2023

THE WIND RATTLES THE SCREEN ON THE KITCHEN window. I glace outside, watching for a moment the way the breeze caresses the leaves in the trees. My mom moves through the kitchen gracefully, opening cabinets, writing things down on her grocery list, then closing the cabinets again. I pick up the vitamin pill that sits on the table in front of me, rolling it between my fingers. My mom's detailed search of the kitchen repeats a few times before I finally ask, "What are you doing?"

"I'm checking to see what we need for our Thanksgiving meal."

I place the gel-capped pill on my tongue before taking a swig of water to swallow it. The lump forming in my throat doesn't make it easy. I didn't know it was close to Thanksgiving. I glance at the wall calendar my mom keeps near the fridge, my heart sinking lower and lower.

My mom writes something else on her list as she closes yet another cabinet. Without looking at me, she says, "How would you feel about having Michelle over for our dinner? She will probably be lonely, especially since Linley is going to be meeting with her parents that day."

"I think we should have her over. It would be nice."

Nice doesn't come close to what I'm feeling. But I don't know how to convey any of my emotions in words lately. Not when it comes to Peter. Everyone else is either trying to pretend life is still moving or is like me: too fragile to process anything.

I reach for my second vitamin, swallowing it painlessly. Mom seems to finish off her list and sighs. "We should've gone shopping sooner, but I guess we'll have to hope I can find half of this stuff for tomorrow."

"Is Dad going with you?"

"I think so. Will you be okay?"

"Of course." I'm used to being left alone. Last year, I helped with the shopping. Before I was believed dead by everyone I know and grew up with in this town. I've escaped one prison; I'm no longer locked away in Evan's bunker. And I've avoided the bunker Mr. Williams was considering. But my home has become yet another place where I am stuck. I can't leave, no matter how much I wish to.

The world outside keeps moving.

Mine seems to stand still.

When my parents leave, I'm left alone with my thoughts. Too much time to think is never a good thing for me. I consider calling Nicole. Asking her to come over. But then I remember she'll be busy working. Mimi's café has been struggling lately. Workers are harder to come by. Nicole is working a lot of shifts to help Mimi keep it running.

And to distract herself from Sawyer.

I tap my fingers against the armrest of the couch. A wave of anxiety creeps into my chest, threatening to drown me.

The doorbell rings three times.

A code.

I run to the door, checking through the peephole before I throw it open. Nicole saunters in, the cold air brushing my exposed skin.

"It's November, it's freezing, and you're wearing shorts," she remarks as I shut the door. The chill lingers in the hall.

"Because I'm stuck inside this warm house all day. I don't have to worry about dressing appropriately for the season. I thought you had work."

"Mimi closed early. I saw your parents in Main Street Market so I figured you'd be pretty lonely."

I throw myself into her arms, unable to hold back the flood of emotion coursing through me. She holds me close, keeping me steady. In these past few months,

Nicole's matured so much. It's sad that I don't get to see much of her life outside of the walls of my house.

"Come sit down. I'll get you some hot chocolate," I say, finally finding the strength to stand on my own.

Nicole doesn't sit on the couch, choosing to follow me in the kitchen, where she sits at the little nook. I pause, hands resting against the countertop.

"What's wrong?" Nicole asks gently.

I look around the kitchen, searching for the traces of the blond boy who breezed through here three months ago.

"Peter isn't here for the holiday. I don't know how to handle… He's not been here for Thanksgiving for so many years. But he would call me in the evening. I could…"

Nicole's expression is one of sadness. She rises from her chair, guiding me to sit down. "I'll make the hot chocolate," she says.

"You're a guest."

"You're my best friend. I practically live here, anyway."

She gets to work on pouring the milk in a saucepan, setting it on a burner and stirring in the chocolate mix. I rest my face in my hands, looking out the window. Soft rain begins to mist the glass.

I just want to hear his voice.

"He misses you, too, you know."

"I know."

"He'll come back for you."

That's what everyone says. That he'll come back for me. Like I'm a damsel in distress, waiting for her knight to come rescue her from the abyss. But the abyss has its dark, cold grip on me, pulling me closer every day. And Peter feels farther away than ever.

Nicole places a steaming mug of hot chocolate — topped with whipped cream and chocolate shavings — in front of me. I smile, shaking my head. "Dr. Ho says you're a terrible influence."

"Dr. Ho is a vegan who doesn't eat dessert. I think she needs to learn how to live."

I sip the hot chocolate. The liquid burns my tongue, sliding down my throat. Warmth isn't something I have much of. But this helps.

"So, tell me what's wrong," Nicole states, setting her mug down in front of her.

"My mom wants to have Peter's mom over tomorrow for Thanksgiving dinner. I want that, too. She shouldn't be alone. Linley is going to see her parents for the day. I assume they'll try to convince her to go home with them. But Michelle… I want her to be here. But I also…"

"It's hard," Nicole finished for me.

"Yeah."

"No one's expecting you to be okay, Raegan. You know that, right?"

Yes.

No.

"I want to be strong. I want to fight. Peter rescued me, Nicole. When I was out of hope, he came in. He saved my life. I want to do the same for him."

"It's a different situation. The draft isn't something he can run away from. Not without bringing the entire rebellion down."

"I used to be the logical one in this friendship," I remark, taking another sip of my hot chocolate.

Nicole smirks. "Heartbreak has made me logical, unfortunately. But let's focus on brighter things. What are you going to wear tomorrow?"

I shrug, swallowing the rest of my hot chocolate in three large gulps. The warmth spreads through me as I set my mug down. "I don't know."

Nicole rises from her chair, marching past me. "We must fix this immediately."

I smile, following her out of the kitchen and up the stairs. She's already digging through my closet by the time I reach my room. I flop onto my bed, waiting for her emerge with some random article of clothing I don't remember having.

She returns from the closet with a pair of black leggings and an oversized cream sweater in tow. "How about this with those nice brown boots you keep tucked away in the closet?"

"I'm not leaving the house. I can wear a pair of socks

for this event, I think."

"Fine, but they need to be cream or neutral colored to match the sweater."

I mock-salute her as I flop onto my back, staring up at the ceiling. Nicole studies me for a moment.

"You know," she says slowly. "You could ask Andre's nephew if he can give you a way to contact the burner phone. Just to talk to Peter, even if it's five minutes."

I scoff. "Yeah, Spencer isn't going to do me any more favors right now. He wants to win the good graces of his uncle. Besides… there's no guarantee that calling Peter's burner phone would do me any good. He may not be able to answer it. Or I might get him in trouble."

"Yeah… that's true."

"Speaking of Spencer…" I smirk, watching Nicole's face flush slightly.

"What about him?"

"He's single."

She shrugs. "That matters to me because?"

"Because you think he's hot."

She rolls her eyes, but the smile and blush on her face are unmistakable. "I am not looking for anyone right now. I'm working on myself. I can admire someone's appearance and not throw myself at them, thank you very much. I didn't bring him up to be interrogated about him, either."

I laugh. "I know. But since he's your trainer, and you have all of that time together…"

Nicole opens her mouth to argue, but her phone rings. She pulls it from her pocket and answers. "Hey, Mom… Yeah. I'll be home in a few minutes… Okay. Bye."

I frown, siting up. Nicole offers a sympathetic look. "I have to go help with our own Thanksgiving preparations. I'm sorry."

I rise from my bed. "It's okay. My parents will be back any time now. I'll be fine."

I can tell she's hesitating, but I usher her out of my room, walking her to the front door. "I understand. It's a holiday. You need to get home. I'll be okay."

"Okay," she says, tugging on her coat. I close the door behind her, locking it.

I wander back up to my room and sit on my bed.

If the town didn't need to believe my death was real, I could go drive around. Driving always helped me feel free from whatever was haunting me.

I think of Peter driving me while I cried my eyes out. I think of his jacket he made me wear when I forgot my own. The same jacket that was entirely ruined when I was kidnapped by Evan. It was navy blue but similar to the forest-green one I keep on hand when I want to feel him near me. I miss being out there in the world.

Being trapped inside feels like prison, even though it's

in my own home.

It's lonely.

And dark.

It's strange how quickly any light that was inside of me leaves as soon as any reminder of someone is gone. Nicole is one of the few lights that shine in my life. And I'm happy and warm when I'm around her. But when she inevitably leaves, I'm cold and dark again.

It's the same with Linley, or Spencer, or even Gunner. I can be fine when they're around. But alone, I have too much time to think about it. Too much time to reflect on what's missing.

Before I realize what I'm doing, I'm wrapping myself in Peter's hoodie again. I'm inhaling the scent of his pine and woodsy cologne. Or maybe it's because he spent so much time outside that he smells like that. And then I'm sobbing as I pull the hood over my head, curling into the fetal position.

I don't know how I'm supposed to keep going without him. Maybe it's dramatic. Maybe I'm in love. But he's been my best friend for nearly my whole life. And suddenly he's just... gone. And I can't hear his voice or ask for his help or feel him with me.

I hold on to the sweater.

I hold on to how it felt the night before he was taken.

I remember everything I can because that is all I have left.

BUZZ.

My eyes flutter open. I glance around my room.

Buzz.

I reach over for my phone, wondering why it would be vibrating. No one would call me this late.

I sit up, seeing *Private Number* appear on the screen. I'm not sure what to do. But the call ends. Probably a wrong number. Or a spam.

I reach over to set it back down, glancing at the time.

12:44 am.

But then it's vibrating again. *Private Number* calling again. I don't know what compels me to answer, but shakily I bring the phone up to my ear. "H-hello?"

I'm quiet, hoping my parents won't hear me.

"Raegan?"

My heart rushes, beating against my rib cage. "Peter? Is that… is it really you?"

"It's me," he says, and I can hear the emotion filling his voice.

Tears spring from my eyes. "What are you doing?

How are you calling me?"

"The burner phone," he says. "I couldn't sleep. I keep having night terrors and thinking soldiers are busting down the door."

"You've had those nightmares, too?" My heart warms in a twisted kind of way. No one should ever have those dreams. Yet… it feels good not to be alone.

"I asked Mr. Williams how you've been, and he said you've been getting better, but he didn't seem to really know anything."

I rise from my bed and tiptoe into my closet, where I know my voice will be muffled further. That way my parents won't be awakened by me talking. I'm worried they'd want to tell Mr. Williams or take my phone away. If Mr. Williams knew, I know he'd forbid us from talking like this.

"Yeah, he visited once, the day you were taken. That's really it."

"I miss you," he says, and I can hear the heaviness in his tone. "Gosh, I miss you so much."

"I might've stolen one of your hoodies," I confess. "I was able to sneak over to your house once. Your mom let me in and she let me take the hoodie."

He chuckles, and the sound makes my heart beat faster. "Let me guess," he starts. "The forest-green one?"

I twirl my hair around my finger, unable to

prevent the smile. "Perhaps. How'd you know?"

"Because it's like my navy one that you were obsessed with."

"It is. It also smells like you."

There's a silence on the line, and for a moment I wonder if I've lost him. But then he says, "I'm going to come back. This isn't goodbye."

I close my eyes, taking in the sound of his voice.

"You believe me, right?" he asks. There's something helpless and broken about the question.

"Of course," I reply. "I just wish you were here tomorrow."

"I do, too."

There's pain in his voice. The same pain I feel gripping my heart whenever I'm thinking of him.

I take in the silence, his soft breathing, imagining him sitting here with me.

"Promise me you'll come back," I murmur, tears threatening to fall from my eyes.

"I promise," he says firmly.

Another pause.

Another few heartbeats.

"I'm sorry, but I have to go. I don't want to be missing for too long," he says softly. "But… I can try to reach out again at some point. I don't know when. It's a bit hectic getting away to do this. But I will try again sometime soon."

"Okay," I say. "I love you."

"I love you, too. Get some sleep."

And then the line is dead. The cold starts to seep back in. But I hold on to his voice, to his promises. I settle into his jacket and back onto my bed. And for once, I don't feel the need to open the window and numb myself to the pain. I feel light, despite all the heaviness around me.

There's a certain sort of calm, despite the chaos. And even though the ice threatens to freeze over my heart, I let the warmth of my sunshine boy melt it long enough to fall asleep.

For once, there are no nightmares.

This time… this time I dream.

CHAPTER EIGHT

Evan
THURSDAY, NOVEMBER 23RD, 2023

TAP.

Tap.

Tap.

I glance up from the paper in front of me, to the window. Rain pelts the glass pain, reflecting my somber mood. I tap my pen to the rhythm of the rain, finding it nearly impossible to concentrate.

I've not written a letter in a long time. And I've never written one I don't intend to send. But there are thoughts in my mind that I need to be rid of. Memories of traditions and family. Family I'm not part of anymore.

The emperor holds no feast for Thanksgiving, claiming the holiday should be done away with. Of course, he knows that even most of his supporters celebrate the day, so he won't touch it.

I hate to admit it, but I miss my family.

This time last year, I helped my mom cook the turkey

while my dad started on sweet potatoes. My sister worked on string beans and Spencer set up the dining table despite grumbling about all the extra knick-knacks my mom wanted set out.

We didn't have family nearby, and even the ones from out of town didn't come around anyway. It was always just us. We were all we had.

They were my world.

A world I threw away because of a stupid wrong place, wrong time situation.

I crumple up the half-written letter and throw it at the wall. It bounces off, landing on the floor next to my desk. I don't bother trying to pick it up.

I walk over to the window, but it's hard to see beyond the heavy rain.

What I'm looking for won't be out there.

Maybe I don't even know what it is I need anymore. A simple mission to DC changed my life forever. And now I stand here, heir to the entire nation. I'm built on a lie. Lies to the emperor. Lies to my family.

Perhaps I'm a lie.

A knock at my door draws my attention away. I cross my room and open the door, finding Sam on the other side. Her hair is loose around her shoulders and she looks almost disheveled. "We need to talk."

"Come in," I say, noticing the security agents

watching as she enters. I close the door firmly, locking it.

Sam looks up at me; her hazel eyes seem sad. She's not in her usual business attire. Instead, she's in leggings, a white tank top, and a brown cardigan.

"What's going on?" I ask.

"I think we need to make a move soon. I've heard some things about future plans and if we don't do something, we're going to be in a lot of trouble."

I lean my back against the door, crossing my arms. "What have you heard?"

She wraps her cardigan more tightly around herself. "It's just rumors, but I've learned better than to think that some rumors aren't true."

"What's the content of the rumors?" I know she's avoiding my question, which is unlike her blunt, to-the-point demeanor.

She sighs. "He's talking about getting rid of you now that the resistances have been weakened."

I don't want to believe it, but it sounds exactly like something the *lovely* emperor would do. I'm worthless to him now. He can choose anyone to be his successor.

I push away from the door in case any of the agents are outside within earshot. Sam lowers her voice. "We have to do something drastic."

I run a hand through my hair, fully aware of our proximity. "What do you suggest?"

She bites her lip, a nervous tic. Something inside of my

heart skips a little. Finally, she says, "Maybe we could get married."

I know my eyes widen because she says, "It wouldn't be that bad."

"No, I know that. I'm just… shocked. What will that do to prevent him from getting rid of me?" I take a seat on the edge of my bed as Sam begins to pace in front of me.

"Well," she starts hesitantly. "He's always looking for a photo op. Our marriage would be high profile, since our relationship is, too. And he can make it seem like his heir and his legacy are secure because you'll be married. Another heir in his dream world won't be that far behind, at least to his mind and to the public's minds."

"Do you want to marry me?" I ask. Maybe it's a stupid question, since it seems to be our only option. But lately there's so much hesitation in Sam's interactions with me that I'm not entirely sure this is a good idea.

"I told you I'm falling for you, Evan. It's taken time to let myself love anyone again, but I know I'm safe with you."

Safe? She feels safe?

I look up at her, trying to find any sign that she's lying. But all I see is pure determination. Slowly, she comes closer to where I'm sitting, resting a hand on my shoulder. "You shouldn't doubt that people can love you."

I laugh dryly. "Yeah, abandoning my family for the government has left me a little numb to love."

Her hand absently moves to my hair. "You miss them, don't you?"

"Intensely," I say, my words coming out choked. I'm hyper-aware of her fingers in my hair, of her lingering touch and closeness to me now. Electricity rushes through my body.

I swallow and add, "I never meant to get caught up in all of this. I wish I could go back to a year ago. When my life wasn't upside down."

I don't know why I'm admitting this to her, of all people. Maybe it's because she listens. Or because I hold her deepest secrets; it means she won't use mine against me.

"It's okay to miss your old life," she says sadly. "And maybe someday they'll forgive you."

Forgiveness is a concept my father won't even think of. He may have forgiven my sister. But I'm too far gone. I don't bother saying that to Sam. I let her think she's given me some sense of hope.

Her hands come to rest on my shoulders. I decide to take a shot, raising my hands to her slim waist and pulling her closer. Her eyes meet mine before she lowers her face. Our lips brush together softly at first. But I'm desperate for connection and maybe she is, too.

I slide to the floor, my back resting against my bedframe as Sam sits in my lap, arms around my neck. My hands tangle in her hair and we're kissing until we're both out of breath. Her cardigan has slipped off one shoulder, leaving it bare. I place a kiss there, too.

"I'm sorry," she murmurs. "You're struggling right now and I shouldn't have done that."

"I don't mind," I reply too quickly. "Really."

A small, sad smile tugs at her lips as she kisses me again. There's hesitation and a hint of… regret. I wonder if her apology was for me or for herself.

"So," I say as we break apart. She sits across from me, her back against my dresser.

"So," she says, looking more anxious than she did when she arrived.

I sigh, wondering if my face is as red as hers. If my lips are as swollen and pink. I tilt my head back, looking up at the ceiling. "Marriage. How will we get that to happen?"

"You could go to the emperor. And tell him you want to get married. And he'll probably arrange a whole thing for us. At the wedding… we can poison his wine."

"What?"

Sam tilts her head. "We have to move faster than him. Right now, you are legally his heir. You do understand him getting rid of you likely means killing you, right? So, if we poison him first, we inherit the country and can finally make things better."

"We?"

She smirks. "Well, we'll be married. And someone has to help you do it the right way."

I can't help the smile that tugs my lips. Even scarier is how genuine it feels. I could get lost in the idea of marrying this woman in front of me. Everything about it feels perfect. But then reality sets in.

This is a plot.

To kill an emperor.

"How would we poison the wine?"

Sam sighs, rising from the floor and adjusting her cardigan. "I have a special poison that is completely untraceable. It's slow acting. He won't know until around the time he goes to sleep. It won't hurt him. He'll just die in his sleep. The coroner will diagnose him as having had a heart attack because the poison damages the heart; it will appear as though that is the truth. Some agents will have to be fired for show."

My head swims with all this information. She seems to realize this as she heads to the door. "Leave the planning to me. You ask for a wedding. And make sure it's rushed. I don't know how much time we have to act before he starts putting his own plans in motion."

I follow her to the door, resting my hand on the doorframe near her head. She looks up at me, hazel eyes seemingly innocent. But behind them are years of pain and a lifetime of having to do hard things. Things that would require her to know poison concoctions and other lethal methods of getting rid of someone.

Our noses brush briefly before I back away. My heart pounds against my ribcage and my lungs seem to fill with a new kind of air.

When she leaves, I feel less alone than I did before.

I glance at the crumpled letter on the floor. I don't need my family. I don't need anyone but Samantha at my side. And I don't need anything but the country in my hands.

I throw the letter in the wastebasket and head to the shower, trying to figure out how I'll beg the emperor for a marriage. I cast my family away from my mind. They're better off without me.

And I'm about to be better than the rest of them.

CHAPTER NINE

Peter

THURSDAY, NOVEMBER 23RD, 2023

"TWENTY MORE PUSHUPS, MAGGOTS!"

My arms wobble from the constant exertion. But I make it through, jumping up when I finish. As soon as the last soldier finishes, we're dismissed for the night.

"I heard they're going to make a feast," Jose says, rubbing his hands together. "For Thanksgiving. The generals all organized it since the emperor doesn't celebrate."

Jennings marches past us, plowing ahead. Jose frowns, watching him. "He's been acting highly suspect lately."

I haven't told anyone about my encounter with Jennings in the barracks. I don't want the unnecessary attention. It was a blessing that Jennings was on the night patrol last night. I slipped away and called Raegan the first chance I had.

I had been scared to call her, but I have always had her number burned into my brain. And hearing her voice was everything I needed.

But now, as I get in line for a "feast" that consists of turkey and something that resembles stuffing, sweet potatoes, and green beans, I can't help but wish I was home.

I shudder and move along in the line, getting my meal and finding the usual place to sit. Jennings doesn't join us, another strange occurrence. But for now, I'm grateful. I don't know what he's up to and I don't really want to know.

Jose and a few of the others join me at our table. Usually, we can talk at meals. But the security tonight is strict. Part of me wonders if Jennings said something to our higher command about me leaving past the curfew. But he was never one that liked the security being so watchful of us.

I take a bite of the turkey. It's surprisingly good, but it doesn't taste like my mom's.

Reggie, another soldier from our barrack, is the first to break the tense silence. "I miss my momma's home cooking the most right now."

Jose sighs. "Yeah. We didn't eat turkey at Thanksgiving. No one in my family really likes it. My mom would make chicken enchiladas and carne guisada. My grandma would bring her homemade tamales. We'd make chocolate cake together, as a family."

I smile, even though my stomach only aches

further from homesickness.

Reggie smirks. "We had turkey and yams. I hated all the other side dishes, but I'd eat them to make my mom happy. My dad made dessert since he owns a bakery. Or did own it. He had to sell it since everything was kind of…"

We all know what he means. Anyone tied to rebellion had their businesses ruined.

Reggie shakes his head. "My dad would make this cheesecake swirled with pumpkin. None of us liked pumpkin pie, but he felt it was important to carry on the tradition. I don't know how he did it, but we loved that cheesecake."

Jose glances over at me. "What about you, Daniels? What would you do on Thanksgiving?"

"When I was a kid, my parents cooked together and would have my sister and me help them with the sides. Pretty traditional, with turkey, stuffing, and sweet potatoes. But when I got older, I was back and forth between my parents' houses for holidays. At least until my dad realized he could work holidays, too. Then it was just my mom, me, my sister, and her boyfriend."

I take a moment, remembering one Thanksgiving. The one before I went back to Bent Ridge.

"One year," I begin, poking at the rubbery turkey on my plate, "my sister decided to go with her boyfriend to his family's meal. So, it was just me and my mom. My mom was disappointed, so I told her I'd help her with the preparations."

Hot tears prick behind my eyes, but I refuse to let them out. I don't need that kind of attention. "She declared turkey was overrated and we barbequed instead."

My heart aches. All I want is to be home. I really don't care about the complications between my mom and my dad. I don't care that my dad has a new woman in his life, or that I'll have a step-sister. I just want to be home.

No one talks for a while. We're too sad to say anything. Reggie sighs. "What do you think they're doing now?"

Jose shrugs. "My mom is probably trying to keep the family together without me there. My sisters followed me out when I was being taken away. It was pretty devastating."

I look up from the food and glance around at the men of my barracks. We may not be friends or even allies. But we're all greatly affected by this. We miss the people in our lives. The ones who kept us going to this point.

"Let's hope they're still doing their celebrations," I say. "And that they're enjoying themselves despite our absences."

"DANIELS."

I see Jennings off to the side of our building. Jose glances at me. I shrug, but break away from the group. We have fifteen minutes before bunk check.

"What's up?" I ask, crossing my arms.

He sighs, running a hand over his buzzed scalp. "I know I was pretty weird with you the other night. I can be intimidating."

He's not wrong. Even though he's about the same height as me, he has a lot of muscle and never smiles. Or talks much to anyone.

"I accept your apology," I say, taking a step back.

He pins me with a glare and says, "I wasn't apologizing. I need your help."

"With what?"

"I know about your past and I know why you snuck out of the bunks. Same reason you snuck out last night."

Ice seems to take over my veins. He saw me leave the bunks last night.

Which means he has information on me.

"What are you talking about?"

"Don't play dumb with me." He shifts on his feet, not backing down. "I know you're in contact with your rebellion. I know most of our barracks is full of rebels. Look, I wasn't part of any rebellion, but I need your help finding my sister."

Something inside of me softens a little. "Your sister? What happened to your sister?"

He shakes his head. "There's no time to explain now. We gotta get to the barrack. But this conversation isn't over."

He rushes past me to get inside. I don't move for a moment, processing. Could it really be that he sees me as his only way of finding his sister? Or is this a scheme to get me to talk more about who I am and what I'm doing? As I head inside, I decide to be cautious in how I handle this. I can't afford to give anything away.

When everyone else is asleep, I'm awake. Every time I begin to fade into some semblance of sleep, I find myself startling awake at any noise. My pulse shoots up and my breathing becomes shallow.

Something must be wrong with me. Maybe I should go to sick bay. But I don't trust any of the medics here. I don't trust anyone.

My thoughts wander to Raegan, as they usually do. I can only hope her night went well.

Sometimes, when I can't sleep, I think of how it felt to lie beside her. The night had been quiet. And we fit together like two pieces of a puzzle. I could feel her heart beating fast like mine, then slowing down into a gentle rhythm.

Sleeping felt like bliss.

The moment the doors were being busted down, I knew what was coming. I could only hope they wouldn't hurt Raegan in the process of getting to me. I held onto her until I couldn't any longer, until I had to let go.

My heart broke to leave. To see my mom collapse in the street. To see Raegan being rushed back inside.

And to leave everyone I loved behind.

Evan brought me here. There is no other explanation. So many rebel men were drafted this time. It doesn't make much sense to have us all here together, where we can plot something. But maybe that's what they want.

They want a reason to take us down.

I roll to my side, feeling for the keychain under my pillow. Inside is a picture of Raegan and me. I won't be able to see it in the dark, but I open the locket anyway. I run my finger over the picture. The easy days feel so far away. Almost like they never existed to begin with.

How can I survive if the point of my being here is to kill me in the end?

CHAPTER TEN

Raegan
THURSDAY, NOVEMBER 23RD, 2023

RAIN FALLS OUTSIDE, A REFLECTION OF THE MOOD inside my house. Michelle sits in the lounge chair, her mug of coffee sitting on the side table. It's long since gone cold. Gunner lies at my feet, my hands absently stroking his fur.

I can hear my mom and dad in the kitchen, pots clanging, cabinets opening and closing.

I lean back on the couch, hands resting on my thighs. The sweater Nicole chose for me is large on my small frame, but it's comfy and warm. For the first time since escaping Evan, I feel pretty.

I even put on some basic makeup before Michelle arrived. Nothing fancy. I just… want to feel less like a ghost in my own home, haunting the rooms. I want to feel alive.

My conversation with Peter last night buzzes in my mind still. Part of me wants to tell Michelle, to give her hope and maybe calm her. But the nerves are tight in my stomach, and selfishly I want to hold on to the conversation for myself. She is his mom. I should say something.

Yet, I know the loyalty she has to Mr. Williams, even now. If I let her know about Peter's call, I can't be certain she wouldn't tell him. And if she did, what the consequences would be.

So I keep my mouth shut, despite the guilt gnawing at me.

My mom enters the living room, kitchen door swishing open. "It's time to eat."

Michelle offers a small, forced smile as she rises. I rise, too, though Gunner doesn't move. He's fast asleep.

The guilt still eats through me as we sit. My father says grace, but my mind isn't on the prayer. It's on Peter. His words of encouragement run through my head on repeat.

Talking to him last night made me realize I can't treat him like he's dead. I have to treat him like he's coming back. I have to believe in his ability to survive.

Everyone else is murmuring amen to the finished prayer. I lift my fork, shoving a bit of turkey into my mouth while my mom and Michelle try to converse.

The longer this dinner goes on, the more conflicted Michelle seems to become. She's trying to seem normal. Always working, always bright.

Yet, there's a tiredness in her eyes. A sad reflection of my own emotions.

When the first course is over, my dad cuts into the

pumpkin pie, handing slices around the table before cutting his own. We're silent. There's not much else to say. As soon as I finish my pie, I excuse myself. The weight of the room is too heavy, too hard to hold up. I long to go outside, to feel the cold air blowing over my skin. The house begins to feel suffocating, bringing down the weight of everything on top of me.

My breathing becomes shallow, labored. The sun has sunk below the horizon long ago, casting the outside in darkness.

It's a risk, but I need to take it.

I step out the back door, the cold air hitting me immediately. It's dark and cold, and I soak in every bit of it. My feet are bare—save for the socks Nicole carefully picked out to go with my sweater. The cold from the concrete seeps through the barrier to my feet. It feels soothing, calming my nerves. I inhale, finally able to breathe.

I move farther into the yard. Darkness is all around me. No light penetrates the night back here. It's safe enough for me to hide in without being spotted.

I hate keeping up the ruse that I'm dead. Mr. Williams says it's to protect my family. But what more do we have to lose?

The back door opens behind me, light from the living room pouring out onto the patio. I turn to look, expecting my mom or dad. Instead, I see Spencer, hands tucked into his pockets.

"Kind of a cold night to be out here without shoes."

I shrug. "I like the cold."

"Your mom let me in and said you were in your room."

"How'd you find me out here, then?"

"Gunner was sitting by the back door, staring out into the dark. I figured no one else knew you were out here."

I sigh, my breath coming out as a wisp of steam in the air. "They don't want me outside."

"Fresh air is beneficial for healing. But the town discovering you're alive is a little dangerous."

"How is it dangerous? Maybe more people will want to help."

He shakes his head, stepping out fully into the night. I move back onto the patio and lean my back against the house. "What brings you to this side of town anyway? It's cutting it close to curfew, isn't it?"

"Yeah, well… my family is a little insufferable right now. So, I went for a drive. Ended up in Bent Ridge. Now I'm here. I also haven't checked on you in a while and something Peter asked of me was to make sure you're okay."

I consider telling Spencer about the phone call. Even though he tries to act like he's in the palm of his uncle's hand, he's no snitch.

"Can you keep a secret?" I ask. "Especially from your uncle?"

"If you're planning on raiding a military base to free

Peter from the government, then no."

I laugh softly. "I don't have the strength for that. Besides, I'd get us killed. That isn't the secret."

"Then I'm pretty sure I can keep it."

I inhale and exhale slowly, nerves clawing their way through my stomach. "Peter called me last night. From his burner phone."

"How is he?" Spencer seems intrigued.

"He's okay. I've realized I've been acting like he's already dead. And if I plan to ever save him or help him escape… I can't keep moving like this. I have to work on healing. I want to get back to training. With you and Nicole." I turn, facing Spencer now, though all I can see is his outline in the darkness. "Of course, I don't want to interrupt your *private* training sessions with Nicole."

I don't need light to know Spencer is flustered. "What? I swear, I'm teaching her the skills she needs to graduate to the next level. What are you implying?"

"That you like her. I'm not blind."

Spencer grunts. "She's nice. But I'm not looking to date anyone. I'm far too busy for that." He clears his throat. "Anyway, since you're doing all right, I should probably head home. Curfew is in thirty minutes and the drive is forty-five."

"Of course. I'll talk to you later."

"Don't freeze to death. I'd rather not be murdered

by Peter because I let you stay in the cold too long."

I laugh and follow him inside. "I'll warm up now. I promise. Have a good night. And Happy Thanksgiving."

He nods as he lets himself out. I find my parents and Michelle still in the kitchen. Michelle is just rising from her seat and says, "I should probably get home. It's getting late."

My mom rises, too. "I'll walk you home."

My dad gets up as well and begins taking the dishes to the sink. Michelle walks over to me, giving me a brief hug.

"You should get some rest, Raegan," she says. "You've done more today than you have in a while."

"I will rest soon. I'm feeling okay," I say.

The cold still rushes through my body, giving me energy. I help my dad with some of the cleanup. When my mom returns, she wordlessly joins. Soon the kitchen is clean and leftovers are packed into the fridge.

My mom turns to me, smiling softly. "You should get some rest, dear. You look tired."

I smile wryly. "Thanks. It's the fatigue and trauma."

Frowning, she says, "You know what I meant."

My dad laughs, hugging me, too. "Go sleep."

I tell them goodnight and head up to my room. I change into my t-shirt and shorts, then brush my teeth and wash my face. Finally rid of makeup, I can see just how tired I look.

I crawl into bed, feeling the waves of sleep gently take over.

Until more nightmares begin.

CHAPTER ELEVEN

WHEN I SLEEP, I DON'T DREAM.

Which is strange because, in my coma, I dreamed all kinds of scenarios that I thought were real. And when I woke up, they were the only memories I had besides walking up to the warehouse with Carissa.

I attribute my not dreaming to not really sleeping well at night.

I've been moving around the house a little more, much to Carissa's annoyance. She's worried I'll overexert myself. But I feel most alive when I can do something more than be a lazy bum lying in bed all day.

The doctor says I can't do anything super strenuous. It's frustrating to watch all my muscle deplete into nothing.

But the upside is I get to watch Carissa train.

She's hot when she's beating up the punching

dummy. Her movements are so coordinated, so skilled. Light on her feet, she's punching the training dummy from all angles. When she lands a final blow that knocks it over, my mouth falls open.

She grabs her water bottle from the ground and says, "You'll catch flies like that."

I smirk. "Do you know how hot you are?"

"Considering I'm swimming in my own sweat, I'm aware of how hot I am. But I think we have different meanings of the word."

"Very funny," I say. "Do you ever go to sleep?"

"You don't have to wait around for me, Jackson. I know you need your sleep."

I rise from the bench slowly, carefully. "That doesn't answer my question. What's going on? Spencer says you avoid sleeping lately."

She takes another swig from her water bottle. "Nothing's going on. I'm fine."

Fine. The universal woman code for opposite of fine. If a woman says she's fine, it means the opposite. Words never keep their meaning with females.

"Fine isn't fine. I'm not a stupid teenager. Tell me what's wrong."

Carissa sighs, wiping her face with her sweat towel. "All right. I'll tell you. But I don't want to hear Spencer talk about it. I don't know when you two became best friends, but it's weird."

"Your secrets don't leave me. I'll always hold them and protect them."

She sighs again, coming to sit on the bench. "I've been having insomnia. I figured if I could exhaust myself, I'll finally sleep. But… it hasn't been working."

"Insomnia?"

She nods. "Yeah. I start to drift off to sleep, but then I'm suddenly anxious and terrified that something bad is going to happen. I get up, I walk around the house. I drink some water. I go back to bed. And it repeats like this throughout the night. I just can't sleep."

"What if we try sleeping together?"

"Excuse me?"

I shake my head, laughing. "Not like that. I meant… you could stay in the guest room with me. Maybe then you could get some sleep."

Maybe I could get better sleep, too.

"I don't know," she says hesitantly. "My parents won't be very pleased."

"We're not up to anything bad," I reassure her. "I promise you, it's just about sleep. You don't even have to tell them. You could try to sleep tonight, and if you wake up you could come to my bed."

She seems to consider my offer, but I know it's already enticing to her. I would never force her to take it. So, I stand back up and say, "I'm going to turn in.

Offer still stands at any time. Don't worry about waking me up, either. I sleep during the day, too, so I won't be missing out."

I leave her in the training room, knowing she'll go for another round with the punching dummy before she showers and tries to sleep.

MY EYES FLUTTER OPEN as I feel someone settling in next to me, shivering. Realizing it's Carissa, I relax. I cover her with my blankets, leaving my arm wrapped around her. Her fingers absently trace my arm.

"Do you want to talk about it?" I ask softly.

"I don't know."

"Okay."

Somewhere on the ranch, I hear an owl calling into the night. The wind rattles the screen on the window. And sleep has left me entirely in the presence of this woman I love. The woman who shows only her strongest sides, never her vulnerable ones.

"It's stupid," she says after a while.

"Your struggles aren't stupid," I say, locking our hands together.

She sighs, coming closer to me. "I hear screams. In my

mind. Sometimes it's the night I thought Evan killed Raegan. Sometimes it's from my nights on the run. I know they're not real, but I still…"

"You can't be held responsible for your brother's actions," I murmur into her hair.

"Are you smelling me right now?"

"You came to my room, sweetheart. I get to smell your hair."

She scoffs, but I feel her relax a bit more beside me. For a while, we're silent again. Then she sighs and says, "If my dad or Spencer waltzes in here tomorrow morning, you will die by their hands, gunshot wound or not."

"Are you saying your mom won't kill me?"

"No. She loves you. She thinks you're good for me."

Something in my heart warms up. "I'm good for you?"

"She thinks so. I didn't say I thought that."

I pull my hand from hers, hovering it above her waist. "I could tickle you right now."

"Ah, you desire a quick death."

"I desire for my girlfriend to admit that she's obsessed with me."

"Good luck with that."

As her breathing evens, I find myself calming down again. Drifting to sleep is peaceful this time.

Sleep hasn't been easy the past few nights. Some of my memories have started coming back. I don't want to tell Carissa because I know she'll worry even more than she already does.

But I remember confronting Evan and watching Carissa get Linley out of the warehouse. I remember being on the ground outside, bleeding out. The in-between is blurry. I hope it stays that way. I don't want to remember some of the events of that day.

Especially not when I close my eyes at night.

But with Carissa next to me… I feel safer than I have in forever. My eyes fall closed and I'm lost to the darkness of sleep.

CHAPTER TWELVE

Carissa
SATURDAY, DECEMBER 2ND, 2023

I'M IN JACKSON'S BED.

My first thought upon waking up is that I'm not in my bed, but in Jackson's. His arms are around me, holding me firm to his chest.

His heart beats steadily against my back. I shift slightly, more awake than I've felt in a while. It's only one night of sleep, but it may be the best sleep I've had in a while.

I need to get up before my parents or Spencer find me in here. I'll never hear the end of it. And Jackson will end up homeless and caring for himself. I carefully slide out from his arms, not wanting to disrupt his sleep. When I'm upright, I glance back at him. He's still out cold. I can't help the smile that creeps onto my face.

I leave the room silently, walking down the hall to my room to get dressed. It's still quite early. The house is quiet and peaceful. It's almost nice. Too bad there's a war rising between the rebels and the government to put a damper on my mood.

I throw on my training clothes and head downstairs to headquarters. I want to get some training in before breakfast. My dad is there in the lobby when I arrive. He's pouring himself some coffee from the machine behind the front desk.

"Good morning, Carissa."

"Good morning. I didn't think you were awake."

I'm hoping he has no idea that I slept in Jackson's room. Jackson and I didn't do anything bad at all. But I don't need another thing working against me when it comes to getting on my father's good side.

"I couldn't sleep much," Dad says. "Thought I'd get some work done. But I'm actually glad you're here. I wanted to talk to you about something important."

He motions for me to follow him to his office. I hesitate for only a moment, and then trail behind him. His office is the same as it ever was. Dark bookcases behind his desk full of old literature and self-help books. A few are books on how to run a business. None of them looks at all entertaining.

I used to be a reader. Before life got in the way.

"Close the door behind you," he says as he settles into the chair behind his desk. I do as he says before taking a seat in one of the plush chairs across from him.

"What's up?" I ask.

"I had an idea about a contingency plan for the resistance."

"Contingency plan?"

He nods, sliding a flat map over to me. I look down, seeing a red circle around an area in some woods. It's nowhere near here. I don't know if I even know where this is. I take the map in my hands, studying it intently.

My father is a bit of a cartographer. I recognize this as some of his handiwork. The sketching and the colors are his signature touch. The rough, sloping lines forming an almost square shape, the dark greens and blues used to map out earth and water. The map itself is so detailed, it could belong in a fantasy book. The red circle is inside the square shape that seems to mark a clearing—a large one in the woods.

"What is this?" I finally ask, sliding the map back to him.

"This may be the key to all of our problems. It's the location of a base I've been building over the years. I wasn't sure if the resistance could last in such a small location like it has here. It's not much, but the camp is nowhere near complete. I think it could be a good place for people who want to leave society altogether to relocate. Those from the resistance, that is."

"W-what? Relocation? Are we outgrowing this place?"

He tucks the map in his desk drawer, then settles his hands in front of him on the desk. "I've contacted the other resistances. The ones we don't really talk about or talk to. And we all have a common enemy here. Their sons and brothers have been taken."

"So, you want to unite the resistances into one so our forces are stronger?"

"Yes."

It's risky. Yet it may be the best plan my father has had in a while. "How will it work? You lead us, but their leaders are unlikely to give up their own power."

He sighs tiredly. For once, I don't see a rebel leader. I see my father. An exhausted man who's been carrying the weight of the world on his shoulders. He rises from his chair and begins to pace the room. "I've thought long and hard. The end goal is not who gets to play leader. It's bringing down the corrupt government that oppresses us. It's stopping the soldiers that monitor everyone in the stores and schools. It's being allowed to think or say what we want to without being dragged away and killed in the middle of the night."

"Are you saying you're going to step down and let someone else lead?"

"No. I'm saying that I will form a council with all their leaders. We will make decisions together for the good of the united rebellion."

My head is spinning with the possibilities. A lot of the

rival resistances have grown and become louder. They're making some headway. Which means if we all combine our power, we might be the unstoppable force the government fears.

But for every leader to share their power… Could it be too much to hope for?

Dad stops pacing and looks at me. "You are my daughter. We've been through a lot, but I know I can begin to trust you again. Do you think this will work?"

"I think if everyone agrees to form a council, we'd be a lot stronger than we are right now. Where does this new camp come into play?"

He takes his seat again, pulling out the map. "This fortress will protect us. I don't want to move everyone to it just yet. But my last call with Peter a few days ago confirmed that things look pretty bleak. If we have somewhere reliable to go, somewhere with plenty of food, water, and space, it will help to encourage all the rebellions to unite in one place. And it will be safe. Most of the sleeping quarters are underground. But some of the facilities will be above ground, like the dining hall, the training grounds, and some other places. It's all surrounded by a huge wall to keep anyone out if they find it. And to get in is to go through a series of tunnels underground."

"Sounds insane yet… entirely amazing. I think this is a great plan."

"I think so, too. I'm glad I was able to talk to someone else about it. Your mom has been helping me plot it out, so I knew I needed someone who hadn't known about it and would tell me the truth."

I smile, feeling a surge of warmth through my heart.

"So…" he says after a moment. "Let's talk about you and Jackson."

I quickly rise up from my chair. "Would you look at the time? I need to get to training. Especially since I'll have a class here soon."

"Your class consists of just Linley and you, and you are not getting out of this conversation. We will talk about it eventually."

"Oh, I'm sure we will," I retort, opening the door and stepping out of the office.

"I only want to protect you," my dad calls before the door shuts behind me.

It's strange, feeling close to my father again. I've always been my father's daughter. I get caught up in my plans, too focused to notice anything else around me, and then I go past the point of exhaustion, never letting myself truly rest. For all my father's good qualities, I inherited a lot of the bad ones, too.

But my heart warms up to the idea that he's trying to protect me and look out for me. And I think he's beginning to trust Jackson, too. But I don't plan to have a conversation with my father of all people about my relationship with

Jackson. Especially not when I just slept in his bed.

I don't take long to train this time since I'll be getting some more work in later with Linley. I do only a couple of rounds with the practice gym and the punching dummy. Then I make my way back upstairs to check up on Jackson and get some breakfast.

I find him in the kitchen with my mom, who is serving him some food and a mug of coffee.

Spencer strolls past me and follows my gaze. He looks to Jackson, then to my mom and says, "Does it take getting shot to get star treatment? What about your favorite nephew?"

My mom laughs. "Spencer, I make you coffee all the time. Jackson is our guest—and an injured one at that. But no, don't get yourself caught in the crossfire of some war or battlefield. We've had enough near-death experiences this year."

Spencer mumbles something under his breath. I smirk and join Jackson at the table. "How are you feeling?"

He leans over to kiss the top of my head. Then in a whisper near my ear he says, "Never been better. That was the best sleep of my life."

"What the hell are you whispering about?" Spencer says, stalking over to the table.

Jackson leans back, his arm still around my waist. "Someone's a bit grumpy this morning."

Spencer responds with a glare aimed at Jackson.

Jackson smirks. "If you must know, I was whispering sweet nothings in her ear. If you're jealous, I'd be happy to do the same for you."

"Absolutely not," Spencer says, taking a greedy sip of his coffee. "I know it's hard to believe, but not everyone is absolutely enamored by you."

Jackson smirks. "Oh, that's right—you're crazy about Raegan's redheaded best friend. What was her name?"

Spencer sets his mug down a little too hard on the table. Some coffee spills over the top. My mom glances over from the eggs she's cooking on the stove. "Do I need to put you three in time out? I'm not afraid to do it."

Smiling sweetly, Jackson says, "We're behaving, Mrs. Williams. Spencer's mug just slipped out of his hand."

My mom isn't buying it, but Jackson's charm is enough to make her turn away. I clear my throat. "Her name is Nicole and Spencer's been training her. She's very dedicated to fighting for the resistance. Spencer, I had no idea you liked her."

"I don't," he says a little too quickly. "I mean, she seems nice. But I'm not here to find a date. I'm here to get work done. When does your stupid boyfriend move out?"

"*Spencer*." My mom's warning tone causes Spencer to sit up straight.

Jackson tilts his head and feigns hurt. "After all we've been through together. You really want me to leave?"

"That's it, I'm gonna head down to work," Spencer mutters, leaving his half-drunk coffee on the table.

I pinch the bridge of my nose, thoroughly annoyed. Jackson seems to pick up on this, taking his arm from around me and settling it at his side. "I'm sorry," he says softly. "I was just trying to have fun."

"It's okay," I sigh. "Spencer is clearly working through something."

"His best friend was just dragged away to war."

I never thought of my cousin as an emotional person. Despite what life threw at him, he always countered it with logic. But maybe there's more to him than that. Maybe even the strongest of us have breaking points.

My mom sets a plate of eggs, toast, and sausage in front of me, which I gratefully take. Jackson eats a little, too. After breakfast, I search for Spencer, but discover that his truck is missing from the garage. Whatever he's going through, it's not likely he'll talk to me about it.

LINLEY WALKS IN, THROWING her bag on one of the

benches. She huffs as she tosses her hoodie on the ground, marching up to where I'm standing near the training course.

"I see there's a bit of mental anguish about you. Want to talk about it?"

"No, I just want to get to the part where I can punch the stupid dummy."

"I see," I remark. "Well, if you change your mind, I'm happy to listen. Until then, I need to see if you can beat your old time on the course. Press the button on the floor with your foot when you're ready, then go."

Linley nods once, setting up at the starting point. She exhales, pressing the button, then takes off. The training arena is essentially an obstacle course. There's a small rock wall, a platform to jump down from, a set of monkey bars placed high off the ground, and a rope bridge that shakes.

It's designed to work on speed and some agility. Frankly, I've found it to be pointless.

Evan designed it, though. And it's one of the few things in the training program my father kept.

Linley runs back, hitting the button again.

Two minutes and twenty-three seconds.

"Good," I say. "You shaved twenty seconds off your time. I wanted to teach you some defense technique, but I think you'd be better off going straight to the punching dummy. Let off some anger."

"Thanks," she says, and I know she means it.

She lands a few solid blows and kicks. But her footwork is sloppy. I don't say this. This isn't about learning. This is about therapy.

"What happened?" I ask.

"Nothing," she huffs, hands on her knees as she catches her breath.

"I don't believe that."

"I don't either."

She charges at the dummy again, another round. This one less sloppy, but with no form. No technique.

When she throws herself on the ground, exhausted, I know she's done.

"I'm a failure," she says. "What did I learn today?"

"You learned that sometimes focus can't be found in anger, and that the best way to find your focus again is to get the anger out productively."

She sits up, breathing heavily. "How was my form?"

"Terrible. But I think you needed this more than you needed to learn your exact stance. Besides, you're not going out there on missions any time soon. Your punches were without technique. And your kicks were awkward and not well timed."

"Wonderful. Why are you smiling like you're proud of me?"

"Because I am," I say, rising from the bench. "You have always run from your problems. Today, you came here. You put it out there on the field. You worked through it. Maybe it's not solved. Maybe it's going to be there whenever you leave. But you didn't run from it."

It bursts out of her all at once. "I'm tired of running. I'm tired of not feeling at home. I'm sick of my mom trying to win me over as if she isn't the reason I had to leave in the first place. I know she's not replacing my dad or anything, but she didn't even *tell* me she found someone until the day *after* she got engaged. I should've been there. And now she wants me to come back to California."

"And what do you want?"

She looks beyond me, beyond the walls of this resistance. "I want to not feel trapped or afraid."

I nod. "So… what's holding you back?"

Linley's silent for a while. The gears turn in her head until her brown eyes meet mine. "You're right."

I smile. "I know."

CHAPTER THIRTEEN

Evan
SATURDAY, DECEMBER 2ND, 2023

I LET TIME PASS AFTER THANKSGIVING BEFORE approaching the emperor about asking for his permission to marry Samantha. It's a strange thing, asking him to let me marry someone. But I know with the media presence around us, it's important we're all on the same page.

Like a stupid business transaction is about to take place.

I straighten my tie and exhale slowly. My heart is beating erratically in my chest. When Carlos opens the doors for me to come in, I stand as tall as I can. False confidence is my specialty.

Emperor Morgan sits poised and ready behind his desk. His office is tucked deep within the White House. The Oval Office is used only for photo ops and special messages. He used to do work in there as well, but it became too predictable for any assassination attempts. Now, he hides in this dim room with few bookshelves. A portrait of himself hangs behind him, watching everyone who enters.

I bow, a new rule that makes me sick. "Your Majesty, I've come for a special reason. I'd like to ask for Samantha and me to receive your blessing to be wed."

Emperor Morgan's eyes meet mine. I can tell instantly that something is wrong.

"Evan," he says. "You have worked for me for about a year and a half. You were my Agent Specter, a ghost of an agent that no one could trace. You proved your loyalty to me countless times. First by killing a resistance agent, and then by abandoning your family. Giving you my blessing would be simple."

I straighten, waiting to hear the magic words, the ones that will allow Sam and me to do all that we have planned.

"That's why it brings me great pain to place you under arrest."

My blood turns to ice. "What?"

Emperor Morgan motions to someone behind me. I feel the heavy hands of a burly guard on my wrists, pulling my hands behind my back. Once they're locked in cuffs, I'm pushed down onto my knees.

"What's going on?" I ask.

Emperor Morgan rises from his seat and comes around to stand in front of me. "You'll soon learn what happens when you cross me, boy. I thought you knew better than to trick me."

"What? Your Majesty, I don't know what you're talking about, but I'm happy to clear up any misunderstandings. This must be some mistake."

I hear the sound of high heels on marble flooring. The clicking comes closer, and then stops, and I see Sam's signature red heels off to my side.

Emperor Morgan says, "Agent Winters came to me last night and told me everything, including your plot to poison me."

My heart seems to stop beating. Time stands still. The only thing that indicates this might be real is the sound of my pulse hammering in my ears.

"Your Majesty, I have no reason to plot against you."

"Agent Winters has your voice on recording."

Everything inside of me turns cold. My stomach begins turning in on itself. What is she doing? I am brought to my feet and on the desk is a phone. Emperor Morgan leans forward and presses a button.

The recording crackles a little. Then I hear my voice.

"How would we poison the wine?"

I meet the emperor's eyes.

Cold.

Unflinching.

Sam sighs in the recording and it sounds reluctant. "I have a special poison that is completely untraceable."

Then it's cut off. The entire conversation we had at that moment has been cut out. Just me asking about poisoning the wine. And Sam's voice sounding hesitant even though, at the moment, it didn't seem like she was.

I look over at Sam, our eyes locking together. The girl who stands there is not the girl who kissed me a week ago, the one who's stuck close to my side. Instead, I find someone who looks like she's won first prize for a game. A game I didn't know we were playing.

"Sir, please let me explain."

"You will have your chance to explain at a later date. For now, you will be taken to the holding cells beneath the White House. You will be given rationed food. And I suggest coming up with a good argument, because treason is punishable by firing squad. I'm not afraid to let you fall, Agent Specter. I don't tolerate traitors of any sort."

The officer behind me starts to lead me out. I glance back at Samantha one more time. I don't know what I'm looking for, but all I find is a cold-hearted woman ready to throw me to the wolves.

THE PRISON IS DAMP and cold. Mildew grows on the thick stone walls. It's almost like a dungeon.

It's quiet down here, too. I'm the only prisoner. Those who come down here aren't kept long. My fate is practically sealed. I don't know how I'm to fight against the doctored recording.

But what I don't understand is why Sam wants me dead.

I settle onto my cot, my back pressed against the cold wall. For a moment, I'm back in time. It's summer, and I'm a mere agent operating from an abandoned warehouse in Texas. I was on my way to claiming my safety and the safety of my family when I locked Raegan in a bunker similar to this room. Dirty and cold, with mildew on the walls.

Maybe this is the world getting back at me. Some Higher Power having me pay for my sins.

High heels click against the concrete floor. I quickly get to my feet, knowing that I'm about to meet the object of my questions.

Sam stops in front of my cell.

"What do you want?" I snap.

"I wanted to see you."

"Why? Why did you do this?"

She sighs, resting her hand against the cool bars that separate us. I don't come any closer. I don't want to.

"Evan... this world is a cruel one. I never wanted to hurt you. But you're in my way. You always have been. I've worked hard to be where I am. I've lost a lot to get here. I may resent the emperor. But *I* should be his heir. I'm the one he made promises to. You're the one he found in the wrong place at the wrong time. It's nothing personal."

"This doesn't feel anything but personal, Samantha. But there's something I have to know. Did you love me?"

She doesn't answer right away, and her eyes don't meet mine, giving me the answer before she opens her mouth. "I told you from the start, Evan. I can't love you."

"But… you…we…"

"Kissed?" she finishes. "I've been in deep cover situations before. I can play any part I need to. And I got your defenses down enough to get that recording."

"A recording you edited," I say, half-shouting now. Anger rushes through my veins, seeping into my newly broken heart.

"I removed the making out. I didn't think you'd want Emperor Morgan to hear us doing that in your room. And I cut the audio after I spoke. I didn't do anything but make it perfect. I know you'll never understand why I did this. But I had to do it."

I rush to the bars, reaching beyond them to grab her shoulders. The energy and anger startle her. Her eyes search mine. Rage boils beneath the surface of my skin. "You are the worst person I've ever met, Samantha Winters. And I hope my blood stains your hands. I hope the memory of me haunts your sleep. I hope you know that even with me out of the way, he will never give you what you're looking for."

I shove her away and stalk into the shadows of my cell. I hear her heels click rapidly away against the stone floor, a hasty retreat. Then she's gone. My hands shake and I collapse to the ground, sobbing.

I have nothing.

And soon, I will die.

CHAPTER FOURTEEN

Peter

SUNDAY, DECEMBER 3RD, 2023

WATCHING SNOW IS AN INTRIGUING EXPERIENCE when you've never seen it before in your life.

Then, after fifteen minutes of it falling and coating the ground, making everything a sopping wet mess, you're over it.

A few of the soldiers run around, throwing snowballs and playing. I don't join them. I'm huddled up in my bunk, staring at the keychain in my hands.

"Tired of the snow, Daniels?"

I look up to find Jennings entering the barracks. So much for being alone. He walks past my bunk to get to his.

"I want to talk," he says, not waiting for me to reply to his first question.

"About what?"

"About what you can do to help me find my sister."

I shake my head. "Not here."

"Where else are we going to have this discussion,

Daniels? If you're worried about the barracks being bugged, you don't have to be. I check them myself regularly."

I don't know if I can trust Jennings or anything he's saying, but I also know I'm not getting out of having this conversation with him. He seems determined, which makes me question his motives even more.

"All right, what is it you think I can do to help you? I told you before I'm not in contact with anyone from my life back home. I've been here for a month."

A full freaking month away from my family. From my friends.

From Raegan.

Jennings takes a seat on his bed. "Look, I'm not asking you to confirm anything. But if you really are still part of the resistance, I need you to hear me out."

I nod once, not saying anything. I don't know if he's wired to get me to admit something. I don't put it past Evan, and I don't put it past the government to want me to say something condemning. They didn't bring us here to help their cause.

They brought us here to die.

Jennings takes a deep breath. "When I was drafted a few years ago, I was dragged away from being the sole caretaker of my sister. I thought I was safe. I had legal custody of her. My parents were nightmares and

I knew I needed to get my sister out of there as fast as possible. When I was eighteen and she was fourteen, we were out."

He pauses, and for a moment I question whether he is showing me his real emotions now. His face looks pained and if I didn't know better, I'd say he wants to cry. He doesn't meet my eyes as he continues. "I was drafted by letter. I went to the county office, telling them I was the sole caretaker of my sister. They reassured me the letter was sent by accident and that I would not be drafted because my sister was a minor. Two nights later, I'm being dragged from my house. I thought it was another error. But I've been here ever since. No one's offered to give me information on my sister, no matter how much I ask. All I know is she was either taken back to our deadbeat parents or she was thrown into the foster system."

"I'm… I'm really sorry," I say, and I mean it.

Jennings doesn't say anything. He seems genuinely distraught and traumatized. I know how it feels to be so helpless as they take you away from all you know and love.

When he stands from his bed, he says, "But you may be my way of finding information about where she is."

I shake my head, sliding off the side of my bunk and landing on my feet. "I don't know what you think I can do for you. But I'm telling you that I'm not who you think I am."

"Please, Daniels, we both know you *are* who I think

you are. Don't play mind games with me."

"I'm not playing mind games, Jennings. I was part of the resistance. Now I'm here as part of the initiative to break up any rebellion. I don't like being here, but no one really seems to. I know you think I can do something, but I really can't."

Part of me wants to. Something about this seems wrong. Denying him the right to his sister, whom he was legally raising for likely a lot of their childhood. But I can't tell him that. I don't trust anyone here.

He runs his hands through his hair. Emotion seems to be overtaking him. Which is strange. If he were lying, I don't think he'd be so emotional about any of this. He could be acting… but I don't think he is.

"Look," I murmur hesitantly. "I'm not saying I'm part of anything. But if I find a way to get information, I'll help you out as best I can."

Jennings rises from his bed, clapping his hand on my shoulder. "I knew I could count on you, Daniels."

He moves to leave the room, something that strikes me as suspicious. He got what he wanted. Why leave in a hurry? I don't know if I can believe his story, but it doesn't hurt to ask Mr. Williams to look into it. If it turns out to be nothing, then I'll know I can't trust Jennings any further than I can throw him.

I make my way out into the cold snow. The icy air

pierces through my winter clothes. My stomach growls with hunger. The snow will make training tomorrow worse than it ever has been before.

I'm approaching the mess hall, my boots sinking in the fluffy white powder, when the trumpets blare throughout the base.

Evan's convoy is arriving.

I tense, my eyes on the front gates as three SUVs pull through. The driveway has already been cleared of snow. When the doors of the SUVs open, I'm shocked to find myself staring not at Evan Williams, but at the emperor himself. He holds his head high. Unlike Evan, who wears a mask of confidence, this man exudes arrogance and strength. There doesn't appear to be any doubt in his mind that *he* is meant to be here. He knows he rules this place.

"Whoa, is that…?" Jose comes up next to me, staring as well.

"It's the emperor," I manage to say, anger taking hold of me.

"What could he want?" Bryce, another soldier from our group says, joining us.

Jose smirks. "I heard Evan Boy got himself arrested for treason."

I laugh dryly, a cloud of cold fog coming from my mouth. "I doubt that. He kisses the ground the man walks on."

"Yeah, I thought so, too. But someone I know told me.

Someone who has eyes and ears inside."

I glance over at him, wondering if he, too, is in communication with his rebellion. But I don't have time to ask. An announcement begins to play out over the crackling speakers.

"All soldiers to the mess hall for an important meeting."

Jose grunts. "Likely a campaign tour. Not that he has to worry about reelection. But that's the kind of thing that would be happening soon, isn't it?"

I shrug. "I've lost track. He's been in office forever, it feels like."

"Careful," Bryce says. "Let's just get inside and play nice… for now."

I follow them into the mess hall. At once, my eyes lock with Jennings', before he returns his focus to the conversation at his table.

"Seth still out to get you?" Jose asks.

"I'm not sure," I say. "And I'm not worried about it if he is."

We get our food and sit down at our usual table. When the emperor and his crew walk in, Khan on their heels, I can't help but groan in disgust. What could he possibly want?

I assume there will be some announcement, but instead, the emperor goes around the room, shaking hands and greeting the soldiers. I can tell some have to hold back their anger. Others seem enthusiastic about his presence.

I take the time to study him. A man of pure evil. His dark eyes and even darker presence cloud the room. He's in a suit, despite the frigid weather. I wonder if someone with ice in their veins even feels the cold anymore. One of his attendants follows him around, carrying a winter coat and scarf that the emperor presumably will use when returning outside.

Something wicked seeps off him, chilling me to the bone. I don't have to ask the others if they feel it. They're all too wise to say anything out loud. But I see them tense up, too, as the emperor makes his way around the room.

It's strange to me how someone so shrouded in darkness and mystery could look so human in person. I've seen the broadcasts on TV. I know what he looks like.

Being in his presence is different.

He's not as tall as the broadcasts showed him to be. Or as young as they've tried to portray. Though he's still younger than many of the presidents this country has had, this job has aged him. Gray streaks cut through his hair. Wrinkles mar his face.

Maybe dancing with the devil does this sort of thing to your appearance. Ages you. Makes you look weak.

I try to keep low, eating my dinner and staying out of sight. It doesn't matter. He eventually makes his way to our table. He doesn't offer his hand, though, just stares at us for a moment. Jose doesn't meet his eyes, choosing to slurp up his chicken soup and pretend the emperor isn't standing right by our table.

Bryce glances over at me, a worried look crossing his face.

The emperor moves on to the next table down the line, not lingering nearly as long as he did with us. Whatever's going on, I don't think Emperor Morgan's contempt had anything to do with anyone but me. While we all come from the opposing side of the war, Andre Williams has always been the biggest threat.

"Something strange is happening," Bryce says, interrupting my thoughts. "We'd better hope we're not in the crossfire for whatever it is."

CHAPTER FIFTEEN

Raegan

MONDAY, DECEMBER 4TH, 2023

SURVIVING IS SOMETHING I DIDN'T KNOW I'D HAVE to do every single day. I'd never given much thought to what it meant to be alive… to keep moving… until anxiety became a dark cloud lurking in the shadows around me. Now it takes a lot of energy to press forward when the beating heart in my chest threatens to break out. Or when the tremors in my body show up suddenly, sending me into a panicked state of mind.

When it happens in my sleep, I shoot up from bed convinced I'm dying.

Sleep hasn't been my friend lately, though that's really nothing new.

I pull my cardigan around me as I stand near the window, looking out into the bleak, bitterly cold afternoon. I'm tucked away in the living room, staring out through the glass while a space heater near me blows hot air in my direction.

Right now, the storm inside me is calm.

But my mind is on the other half of my heart, thousands of miles away.

I sit down again and Gunner jumps up beside me and lays his head in my lap. Michelle brought him over to stay for a few nights. My parents thought his presence would help my panic episodes. I don't know if they prevent me from having them, but he usually senses when they're happening and comes over to offer himself for me to hold and pet until they pass.

I run my hand over his head, taking in the calm.

The doorbell rings, and I tense. I'm home alone, which doesn't happen often. And I've answered the door before, for Linley or Michelle or Nicole. But without anyone else home, something inside of me is uneasy.

I rise from the couch, move quietly to the door and look out the peephole. A wave of relief washes over me when I see that it's Sawyer.

I open the door, stepping aside to let him in. The cold air sweeps in after him, chilling me more than usual. "Hey," I say. "How are you?"

"I'm doing well. I wanted to come over and see how you were doing. I know I haven't been around in a while."

I know he's kept away because Nicole has been coming over a lot more lately. I'm surprised he'd show up without texting to ask if it was all right. But I'm not mad about it. Sawyer is still a good friend.

I tug the cardigan tighter around me and make my way back to the couch, to the space heater. "I'm okay."

"You look healthier than last time."

"Thanks. My doctor says that I'm healing really well. She has me doing some basic exercise to get my strength back. And she's cleared me for a mostly normal diet."

"That's amazing." He beams at me, sitting down on the chair near the couch.

Despite Nicole's insistence that it's okay if I'm his friend, Sawyer and I have a bit of an awkward dynamic now that they're not dating. Nicole is my best friend. And Sawyer has been my friend for a long time. But he's tense, even around me.

"So," I start, grasping for any conversation. "How's school?"

His smile flickers then fades away into a frown. "I know you and Nicole are best friends. I just… it's hard to see her around school. She's always smiling and laughing, and some guys hang around her now that I'm not there. And she's totally allowed to move on. But… I miss her."

I nod. "I understand how it feels to miss someone, Sawyer. You're always allowed to tell me how you feel about it."

"Does she ever… talk about me?"

I bite my lip, thinking of the nights Nicole has called

me, crying. Or the times she's come over to sit with me and eat ice cream. She's never talked bad about him, even though she felt unsupported and betrayed when he walked out on her that night. But I can't say any of this to Sawyer. It's confidential and she's moving on, though not for another boy. She's moving on for herself.

"Not really." I let the lie slip out. Though she doesn't talk about him much anymore, so perhaps it's not truly a lie.

He nods slowly, sinking further into the chair. "I mean… I didn't expect her to just… be okay. I thought we'd cool off and then…"

"You left her," I say with a little more force than I mean to. When he looks wounded, I instantly regret it.

"I know. And it was the worst mistake I've made in my life. She's a wildfire. I shouldn't have tried to contain the flames."

I can't help my half-smile at that description of Nicole. I shrug. "Maybe when the time has passed, you can see if she's open to trying again. I think she's working on her own goals right now. I haven't heard of any man in her life. The guys at school are probably just hoping for a chance. I don't think any of them truly has one."

"You're right. I just… the resistance is the reason my mom died. I could've died. I don't want that life invading mine any more than it already has."

We both fall silent for a moment.

"Do you need to talk about it?" I ask.

I realize how much I don't want to be alone right now. How willing I am to take Sawyer's company, despite how awkward it gets.

He is silent for a moment, and then the words begin to spill out of him. "My mom worked for Andre Williams when I was young. And Andre was a man with ambition, as my dad calls him. At the time, there was nothing entirely wrong with the government. But… Andre had sources that said things were about to take a turn. He started forming a rebellion based on a what-if. But soon he found that it didn't matter whether we had a good or a bad president. The corruption went deeper than that."

"What do you mean?" I ask, feeling guilty for interrupting.

"Any president is usually a puppet. They do what they're told. Whichever way the wind blows, that's what they focus on. This… *emperor* is different. But at the time that my mom was a resistance agent, she was really just part of Andre's accounting team. She didn't really have anything to do with rebel networks."

Sawyer's face creases with pain. My eyes fall to the scar near his eye. It's a scar he's always had, from the accident he was in as a child. He's never talked about the accident, except to say that it was because of the rebellion and the government war. It's always made my heart ache even more for him.

He runs a hand through his hair and continues. "My mom was driving. I was in the backseat. Government agents tried to run her off the road. She nearly got away, taking a turn they couldn't follow, but she was going too fast and she spun out. Our car careened down a hill, flipping so many times I lost count. She didn't… die immediately."

"Did the agents come back?" I ask softly.

"No. At least, I didn't see them. Our car was hidden from the road at the bottom of the ravine, so they wouldn't have been able to see us down there even if they had tried to. I assume they drove the streets looking. My dad says it's God that cloaked us, but I struggle to believe that sometimes."

I nod slowly. I grew up in a faith-filled home. But lately, I don't know what to believe or think. And doubt isn't usually welcome in religion.

"What happened? After… after the crash?"

Tears form in Sawyer's green eyes. Gunner senses this, shuffling over to offer him comfort. Sawyer absently rests his hand on Gunner's head. "My mom was able to get her cell phone. She dialed 911 and could barely talk. But soon sirens were getting louder and closer. I knew I was bleeding. I panicked about the blood on my hands. But my mom told me to be strong and to look after my dad. Then she… passed out."

He pauses. I don't press for more. I know how the story ends. But he runs a hand over his face and says, "She died at the hospital from all the blunt force trauma. I made it out with a few scratches and bruises. The blood on my hands was because the broken glass cut up my fingers. But it was nothing more than flesh wounds."

"I'm sorry," I say, unable to meet his eyes. "I'm so sorry you went through that."

"That's why," he says rubbing his still-streaming eyes with his sleeve. "That's why I worry about Nicole. I worry about you. And look at where Peter is now. Andre doesn't care enough for his agents. He left you to die. What will he do if Nicole is captured or hurt?"

I don't want to agree with him. I don't want to give in to the thought. I hug my arms over my stomach and say, "He's trying to do better. He's a man of ambition, as you said. And that ambition sometimes gets in the way of his logical thought. But I can assure you Nicole wouldn't be out there doing anything yet. She'd have to train. And she's underage currently."

"She turns eighteen in a few months."

"I know," I sigh. "If you want to win her back, you can't try to control the fire that burns inside of her. Her passion to make the world better isn't one you can contain. You have to let her do what she believes is right. And right now, that's fighting for the resistance."

He shakes his head, rising from the chair. "I can't be with her and let her be a rebel fighter. It's better we stay apart. Even if it hurts."

He doesn't say anything else as he gets to his feet, walks slowly to the door and lets himself out.

When the door closes behind him, I run my hands over Gunner's fur. "I don't know how to do this," I say to him. "I don't know how to help them get what they both want."

Gunner looks up at me with his soft eyes, a smile on his face.

When the door opens again a little while later, I expect to see my mom or dad. Instead, Linley stands there with a leash. Gunner hops down from the couch and saunters over to her, waiting to be hooked up. Her face is tense.

"What's wrong?" I ask.

She shakes her head. "Nothing. I'm just here to walk Gunner. Michelle said to drop him off back here afterward if you still want him here."

"If you miss him, he can go back home."

Linley shrugs. "I'm fine either way."

I don't believe her, but I say, "Well, I'm sure he misses his home. It's okay if he goes back. If I end up needing him here at night again, I'll let y'all know."

Linley nods, then leads Gunner out.

And now I'm truly alone.

I wish Peter would call. It's been a couple of weeks since I heard his voice. And a month since I've seen him in person.

My life is cold without him.

CHAPTER SIXTEEN

Evan

THURSDAY, DECEMBER 7TH, 2023

I REALIZED NOT LONG AFTER BEING THROWN IN here that the emperor would put off my hearing with him. He has no intention of getting me out of trouble in a timely manner. He wants me to rot down here as long as possible.

Food is brought in small portions. And I only get two meals each day.

I've lost all sense of time. Though they say I committed treason, I'm sure this is my punishment for putting a young teenage girl in an underground bunker with similar conditions.

I'm a monster.

Each time the guard brings me food, I ask about my trial. My hearing. Anything at all. Each time, he ignores me. Sometimes he mocks me and laughs at me all the way back to his post.

Today, I don't rise when he approaches my cell. Though I have no concept of time, I know it's not a feeding time.

"Your trial awaits you, *Your Highness*," he says with a smirk, jangling his keys.

I look down at my dirty clothes. "I don't suppose I'll be allowed to change into something more presentable?"

"No. His Majesty the emperor has requested your presence in his office at once. You will not delay."

Two other guards proceed to enter the cell, grabbing my arms roughly and shoving them behind my back. One slaps cuffs onto my wrists, as if I'm some hardened criminal.

I go along with them; the odor of my unwashed body shames me. But I won't delay the hearing I've been waiting for. I need to be on my best behavior if I plan to get back in Emperor Morgan's good graces.

Inside his office, there is no real trial, of course. There's Emperor Morgan, Samantha, and Carlos. Plus, the two guards on either side of me.

Emperor Morgan smiles wickedly at me. It's a sight I wish to erase from my memory.

"Evan Williams, my heir, my champion. You have been brought here to answer to accusations by Agent Samantha Winters that you have been plotting treason by discussing the act of killing me and taking over in my absence. How do you plead?"

"Not guilty."

Sam's eyes fall to me; after a moment, her hard stare gives way to her usual icy, callous expression. I should've known she was not my friend. But it's the way she made me feel that still has me shaken. I thought we had something special.

I trusted her.

Emperor Morgan says, "Then please explain the recorded audio Agent Winters provided."

I clear my throat. "Gladly. I can't deny that the recorded audio captured my voice. But I propose to you that the audio was doctored and edited. As you may be aware, Emperor, I was deeply in love with Agent Winters." My voice nearly cracks on the word *love*. I feel my face turn crimson as the truth of that statement sinks in. Everything inside of me wants to scream to the sky, pour out the agony of my broken heart. But I keep my composure and continue. "Madly, hopelessly, desperately in love. And because of that, I had a lapse in judgment. When Samantha... Agent Winters proposed killing you, I never thought to take it seriously until one night, she came to my room to seduce me. It was only after a heated moment of passion that she spoke of the poison. She spoke of it, Your Majesty, not me. Everything I said was because I was blinded by love. And I didn't think it would go this far. I never would've let her poison or hurt you, Your Majesty."

I bite back every rotten, vulgar word I want to say to him, and instead add, "I owe you my life for all that you've done for me."

The final nail to the coffin my heart is being buried in.

Goodbye to my family.

Goodbye to the Samantha I fell in love with.

Goodbye to whatever remnants of myself I was holding on to.

Everything is shattered and destroyed.

Emperor Morgan seems intrigued by my confession. He stares at me thoughtfully for a moment, and then turns to Samantha. "I do believe, Agent Winters, that you should provide the full recording."

Sam's face pales. "Your Majesty, I assure you the only thing I cut out was our… more intimate matters. I didn't want to make anyone listen to that."

"I understand your hesitancy, but you just admitted to editing the audio, and Mr. Williams here has confirmed that. I need to hear the whole thing, or else we'll have two cases of treason to deal with."

Samantha looks shaky and her face is ashen. An agent outside is dispatched to go find the laptop with the full audio. I admit, I'm not thrilled to have everyone hear what all happened in that room. But if I can twist things enough, I can be found innocent.

But then Sam will stand in my place, meaning she will be sent to die.

I don't know if I want that fate for her. Despite the fact that she betrayed me, I don't think I could live with myself if she were to die.

I don't have time to think about it, because the agent returns with the laptop. She hands it to Sam for the password. Sam's hands are shaking hard when she begins to type. When the laptop goes flying, crashing against the far wall, I jump. There is a gun in Sam's hand, the barrel pointed at the emperor's head. Tears fill her eyes.

"I didn't want it to be like this, but you've ruined my life. Now I will end yours."

The agents all aim their guns at her. "Drop your weapon right now, Agent Winters!" one of them commands her.

I'm surprised no one's shot her yet. This is my chance. I rise up, charging forward, despite my hands bound behind my back. I crash into Sam, sending her gun sliding across the floor. Agents descend upon us. I'm pulled to my feet again, an agent keeping his hand firmly on my shoulders.

Two more hold Sam's arms, keeping her restrained. She doesn't fight. Her eyes find mine.

Empty.

Cold.

She's giving up.

Emperor Morgan rises to his feet, unbothered by any of the events that have played out in front of him. "Clearly, we've got the wrong person. Let my heir go and take Agent Winters to the holding facility. I think we've seen enough here to skip a trial. We'll figure out a day for her execution soon."

Samantha makes no sound. Her face pales further, but she says nothing, only hangs her head as the agents lead her out. The agent closest to me releases my hands from the cuffs. I rub my chafed wrists, turning to face the emperor.

Emperor Morgan nods to me. "You'll be reinstated as my heir immediately."

He gives no apologies for how I've been locked away for days, for how I've been punished. I don't know if I really expected one.

"Thank you, sir. I need to ask one request of you."

"Of course."

I inhale slowly. "Please don't execute her."

He eyes me warily, suspiciously. "Why not? She intended to have you killed in her place and intended to kill me not five minutes ago."

I run a hand through my greasy hair. "I know. And I'm aware that I have been a fool. But I still love her. And if she were to die, especially because of all of this, I don't know that I could live with myself. I just want to see if I can get answers from her when she's settled in the prison."

He seems to consider, finally saying, "I suppose it doesn't hurt to put the holding facility to good use. She may be allowed to live as long as you are in charge of her care. I want nothing to do with treasonous snakes, and I'd be fine letting her rot down there slowly."

I flinch, but he doesn't seem to notice. Bowing my head slightly, I say, "Thank you, Your Majesty. If you'll excuse me, I'm going to bathe now. Thank you for this new chance."

I leave the office, feeling emptier inside than I have in a while.

Maybe it was because I thought someone could love me. Or maybe I'm so deprived of love that I was willing to find it somewhere it didn't exist. My heart still aches, as if it's been ripped out and all that's left is phantom pains.

I may not have answers yet.

But I'm going to get them somehow.

CHAPTER SEVENTEEN

Peter

I'VE BECOME PRETTY WELL ACQUAINTED WITH THE cellar. It almost feels like a hideaway for me. I plan to ask Mr. Williams if he can dig up information on Jennings and his sister. I need to know if any of this is legitimate or if I'm being watched.

I look at the phone in my hands, my one connection to my old life.

Old life.

It's only been a little over a month and I'm already so far removed from all I used to know.

I dial the number and wait. Part of me wishes to call Raegan instead, but this has to be done. I've put off talking to Mr. Williams long enough.

"Peter, I'm glad you're finally calling. Anything new to report?" Mr. Williams sounds peppy.

"Not really. I need you to look into something, though."

"What is it?"

"There's a guy from my barracks named Seth Jennings.

He wants me to find out where his sister is. He was her guardian before he was drafted four years ago. I didn't agree to anything, but he thinks I may have a way to find her. I thought maybe you could find out if this is legitimate or if he's trying to sell me a story so he can spy on me for Evan."

"Interesting," Mr. Williams mumbles.

He's hardly paying attention.

"Sir, I'm serious."

"Oh, I know. I'm writing it down on my to-do list for tomorrow. It's late here, you know."

I bite my tongue, even though I could argue that he's up right now. That he always works late into the night, which is why I knew I could call.

"Anything else?"

"There are rumors that Evan has been arrested for treason."

"Highly unlikely."

I nod, then remember again that he can't see me. "I thought so, too. But then the emperor came and was sizing us up."

There's a pause on the line. Then Mr. Williams mutters, "Firing squad."

"What?"

"Treason means death by firing squad. Publicly. He could've been seeing if any of the new soldiers would be fit to do it."

My stomach turns quickly at the thought of that. "That's sick."

"But why would Evan commit treason? That doesn't make any sense."

"I don't know. I don't know if he really did or not. This was almost a week ago. I haven't heard anything else on it. And no one's been selected for anything. You're probably right… rumors are vicious around here. But that's all I really have to report."

Mr. Williams sighs tiredly. "All right. I will let you know what I find out about this Seth person next time you call. Try to keep personal attachment low. You can't trust anyone there. Even the other rebel agents would be willing to betray you if it brought them their freedom."

"I know," I say. And I do know it. But the longer I've been here, the less I feel like they're all out to get me.

"Have a good night, Peter."

Then the line is dead.

I rise from my little corner of the cellar. I sigh, looking down at the phone. I'm tempted to try calling Raegan. There's a rattle outside the door, then voices. I quickly stuff the phone in my pocket and brace myself for whatever is about to happen as the doors fly open

The female patrol agent and another soldier are at the top of the ladder, looking right at me. I jump back slightly, then say, "I can explain."

"Oh, you'll have to. You're coming with me," the

female agent says.

I climb the ladder and she grabs my arms. "I told you not to be out here, and where do I find you? In the cellar? What could you possibly need down there?"

"I'm sorry," I say, trying to play the role of innocent, dumb soldier. "Sometimes the barracks get super loud with all the snoring so I go sleep in the cellar. I didn't know I'd get in trouble."

She tugs me harder along the gravel path. "If you think I'm believing that, you're a fool. Don't you know we're careful to watch those of you with troubled histories?"

Troubled histories?

I try another tack. "All right. You caught me. I needed to get away to just think. I didn't want to be in the barracks."

"Think about what? You don't need to think about anything. We tell you what to do and when to do it."

I wonder if she realizes how messed up that is. Or maybe she thinks that's normal. "How long have you been here?" I ask, my tone calm.

"Nine years. And if you think I want your pity, I don't. I *chose* to be here when I turned eighteen. I understand the draft is rather frustrating. But you don't own this camp. Now you'll be talking to your barracks supervisor."

I'm not worried. Officer Conrad will likely believe

me if I'm convincing enough. Even so, I know the target will be on my back more than ever. I'll have to tell Andre somehow. The contraband phone feels heavy in my pocket.

Every officer in charge of a barracks has their own building near their wards. Officer Conrad stands outside of his, likely alerted to the trouble before the agents came to grab me. He looks down at me, arms crossed. "Care to explain?"

I nod once, standing firm. "I needed to get away from everything. I'm in a new place, dragged from my home. I just wanted some time to myself to sit and think."

The female agent scoffs, interjecting. "I told him he doesn't get to think—"

"I asked for his statement, not yours," Officer Conrad says, holding up his hand to the agent. Her grip is still firm on my arm.

She scowls, but shuts up. To me, he says, "We don't let the soldiers wander around at night unless they are on patrol. Seeing as you've been spotted many times, perhaps we should put you on night patrol so you can have all the time you want away from your bunk at night."

"Sir," the agent says, clearly annoyed. "He's only a month into his training. He can't be on patrol. He has five more months before he's even allowed to set foot outside of camp."

"Oh, I'm aware," Officer Conrad says. "He won't be

setting foot outside. He'll patrol inside, keeping watch. Then he'll get to sleep until breakfast. He'll train in the afternoon and evening just like before."

The agent is stewing beside me. Her grip falls from my arms as she plants her hands on her hips. "You can't be serious."

"Are you talking back to a commanding officer?"

This shuts her up fast. She salutes, gives him a strangled "No, sir!" and then quickly turns, stomping off back to her squadron.

Officer Conrad points to my building. "Go to sleep. Tomorrow night you will begin your new job."

My heart sinks slightly. There's no way I'll be able to sneak away and use my phone now. This isn't going to work. I'll have to tell Andre when I can. And then I'll call Raegan for a final time.

Most importantly, I'll have to destroy this phone and any ties I have to the resistance. Tonight's close call could've landed me in trouble. And not just me… everyone I love. I refuse to the be reason they're targeted or hurt.

I climb into my bunk. The rest of the room is full of heavy breathing or snoring. I roll to my side, feeling the keychain beneath my pillow and rubbing it with my fingers. I don't like that I have to do this. But what choice do I have?

WEDNESDAY
DECEMBER 13TH, 2023

I'M SHOCKED AWAKE BY the sound of horns blaring. I inhale sharply, choking on the smell of… cologne?

I look over the side of my bunk to see Jose standing already. His hair looks gelled and shiny. For a moment, I think of Jackson and his infatuation with his hair.

"Jose… what are you doing?"

Reggie yawns, sitting up in his bed a few rows down. "Smells like preening."

Jose grunts. "Birds preen. I sparkle and shine."

I blink. It's too early for this.

Jose struts out of the barracks. I look over to Reggie, who just shrugs.

Brendan from the bunk next to mine hops down. "Bet you he found a cute girl he's trying to impress."

I shake my head, finally climbing down from my bed and slipping into my boots. The others follow suit. We have to be at training in five minutes. We have ten minutes once the horn sounds, but Jose wasted our time.

The air is cold out, but it's a little warmer than before. The snow has even melted, which is good. I hate training in the snow.

Out on the training field, my eyes meet Officer Conrad's for a brief, fleeting moment. He's talking to

General Kahn and a few others I've never seen before. Kahn glances at me and gives me his usual scowl, stroking his dark facial hair.

As Officer Leland begins to yell at us, I feel the group of officers and generals watching me specifically. I catch their eyes from time to time. I'm assuming they're checking in because of what happened last night. I try to ignore their stern gazes.

The others seem to notice, too.

Jose nudges me as we stand in line to go through the training course. "Those guys seem to be watching you."

"I know."

"Is it because you keep leaving at night? Caught traipsing around with a girl?"

Anger pricks beneath my skin. "I have a girlfriend back home."

"I know. But we've been sent here to die. Might as well have a little fun."

My fists clench at my sides and I bite the inside of my cheek to center myself. "I'm not that kind of guy."

It's my turn to go before I can finish this conversation. It's better that Jose doesn't know what I've been doing. But I won't let anyone believe that I could ever love anyone besides Raegan.

The training course is not at all like the one back at Williams' ranch. It has tires laid on the grass that we have to hop and march in, a rope net we have to army-crawl under where the grass cuts at our skin and stains our clothes, a large wall we have to climb despite it being muddy and slick. Then it's a long-distance run across the field, made harder by the ground being wet from melted snow.

But I've always been one for fitness and challenges. I take off, blocking out the eyes that watch me, blocking out Jose's words and my irritation that he could even suggest something so vulgar, blocking out everything breaking me down.

I have to cut off the people I love if I want to protect them.

I jump from tire to tire. I crawl under the rope net. I climb the muddy wall up, then down. I run the distance, pumping my legs harder than I ever have. I reach the end, out of breath. I inhale deeply, doubling over. My hands rest against my knees to keep me standing.

"Peter Daniels."

I look up to see Officer Conrad, Officer Leland, General Kahn, and few others watching me. They all look mildly shocked as they stare at me. Kahn's frown lines deepen as Conrad smirks.

"Did I…do something… wrong?" I gasp.

Officer Leland holds a timer to my face. "You made it through the course faster than anyone we've ever seen."

I finally stand up straight, my lungs still burning as my

legs throb. "I did?"

Officer Conrad laughs, "I think this guy could move up to advanced training. Keeping him here is a waste of potential."

Officer Leland nods. "I agree. Kahn, what do you say?"

"I suppose we can't keep him back here if he can be used elsewhere. We'll advance him, which will give him opportunity to do the night patrol as you wish, Conrad."

Conrad nods once, claps a hand on my shoulder, then walks away towards the center of the base.

Officer Leland goes back to the field, waiting for the next person to finish the last sprint. Kahn crosses his arms.

"I've got my eyes on you, Daniels. I don't trust you."

I smirk, despite knowing that could get me in trouble. "If it's all the same to you, I don't trust you, either."

He mutters something under his breath, then storms off. I head back to the start of the course, but Officer Leland says, "Head back to your barracks until breakfast. You don't need to stay here."

I don't argue, feeling weak and exhausted from pushing myself so hard. I'm wondering if I should've held back. What will advanced training look like? And why me?

When I arrive back at the bunks, no one is there. I realize it's now or never.

I pull the burner phone from inside my pillowcase. It's still early. I know Raegan won't be awake. In fact, I'm counting on it. I want to leave a message. I don't want to hear her voice when I tell her what I'm doing because we'll both break apart.

I'm relieved when her phone goes to voicemail. After the beep, I say, "Raegan, it's me. I want you to know that I love you, I miss you, and I will always love you. But the other night I almost got caught. I can't risk everyone's life anymore. I'm destroying my phone and cutting off my connection. I promise I'll see you again. I love you. Keep fighting."

The voicemail cuts off just in time. Tears prick at my eyes, but I refuse to let them fall. I inhale again, then slowly exhale as I dial Mr. Williams' number. I'm hoping he's not in the office yet. Unfortunately for me, he *is* an early riser.

"Peter! Calling so soon?"

My heart drops. "Uh… yeah. Look… I don't have a lot of time. I was almost caught and there's a lot going on here. I don't think I'll be able to contact you anymore. I'm not putting anyone else at risk."

"Peter, you don't have to call when you're not able to. Let's talk about this rationally."

I sigh. "I am being rational. I'm sorry, but I can't keep

doing this. Just tell me if you found out anything about Jennings or his sister."

"I haven't had time to look. What do you plan to do, then? If you sever ties with us, how do you plan on coming back?"

"I don't know," I say, running my hand through my hair. "I really don't. But I know this isn't working. They're watching me closely. They're putting me in situations to test me."

"You do what you see best, Peter. But just remember I can't help you if you destroy the phone."

The line clicks and I know he's hung up.

I glance around, seeing that it's almost time to go to breakfast. I don't have a choice. I drop the phone to the ground and crush it under my boot. It takes a few stomps before it's fully destroyed. I pick up the pieces and toss them in a trash bag, tying it up. When I step back outside, I throw the bag in the dumpster on the side of the building. I don't plan on being caught.

As I walk away, I feel my heart crack, like the phone under my boot moments before. My last connection to everyone is truly severed and broken.

Now I'm truly alone.

CHAPTER EIGHTEEN

Raegan
WEDNESDAY, DECEMBER 13TH, 2023

BIRDS CHIRP OUTSIDE MY WINDOW. I BLINK THE sleep from my eyes a few times. It's early, the sun just beginning to rise. I sigh, sitting up in bed. For once, I got a good night's rest. So why do I feel more exhausted than ever?

I swing my legs over the side of my bed. My phone sits on the charger on my nightstand. I reach for it and find I've missed a call. I'm slightly confused, but then I realize it's Peter's burner phone.

He called two hours ago.

My heart drops. I missed his call.

The voicemail notification sits on my phone, and I quickly hit it. I want to hear his voice, even if it's a short voicemail saying he'll call again later.

There's a crackle, then Peter's talking.

"Raegan, it's me. I want you to know that I love you, I miss you, and I will always love you. But the other night I almost got caught. I can't risk everybody's lives anymore. I'm destroying my phone and cutting off my connection. I promise I'll see you again. I love you. Keep fighting."

My phone slips from my hands as tears cascade down my face. "No," I whisper.

I try to call back, but there's nothing there. It rings and rings and rings but never picks up. I call again.

And again.

And again.

Nothing.

He must've destroyed the phone already.

I'm sobbing into my hands, quietly so as not to wake my parents. I never told them Peter reached out. I still don't want to tell them.

My last connection to him is shattered.

When I finally calm down, I listen to the voicemail again.

"Raegan, it's me. I want you to know that I love you, I miss you, and I will always love you. But the other night I almost got caught. I can't risk everybody's lives anymore. I'm destroying my phone and cutting off my connection. I promise I'll see you again. I love you. Keep fighting."

Keep fighting.

He doesn't want me to give up, despite the pain. So, I won't give up. I *will* see him again. I refuse to let this break me.

I rise from my bed and head to the bathroom. I splash my face with cold water, trying to soothe my swollen red skin. It doesn't do much, but it's sort of calming.

I study myself in the mirror—really study. Unlike the characters in the novels I used to read, or the movies I used to watch, I don't pick out my flaws or point out the imperfections in how I look.

I see *strength.*

I've gained weight back since being so malnourished. My eyes are brighter. My body is stronger. I've even begun mild exercise, approved by my doctor. The only thing that truly bothers me is how pale I've become without the sunlight. But even that isn't enough to shake me.

I'm getting better.

And I will fight. For Peter. And maybe for myself.

"ALL RIGHT. WHAT'S GOING ON?" Nicole enters my room.

I texted her that I'd need her to stop by early today. Wednesday is our day.

I hand her my phone. "Listen to the most recent voicemail."

Nicole takes my phone, typing in my password, which

she knows, and brings the phone to her ear to listen. I watch as her face goes from happy to sad. When the message is over, she looks at me. "Oh, Raegan."

I nod, but no tears escape my eyes. I've cried them all out.

"You know he wouldn't do this without good reason."

"I know."

"He's smart and knows what he's doing."

"I know."

But knowing these things doesn't change the fact that he's gone. If they're closing in on him, how can I know if he's okay?

Nicole sits down beside me. "Trust him. He said he'll see you again. You know nothing he says is meant to be taken lightly. If he's making that promise... he means it."

"You're right," I say, but my words lack conviction.

I need a distraction. "Tell me about what's going on in your life lately."

She hesitates. "I don't know. This is pretty heavy. I don't want to brush your pain aside for my own feelings."

"You're not. I need to get my mind off this. I need to think of other things. Peter isn't dead yet. I can't treat him like he is. I've said this before. So tell me about your day."

Nicole groans as she flops onto my bed. "Why is it so hard?"

I tilt my head, looking down at her. "Why is what so hard?"

"Seeing him at school. Why do I miss him?"

"Sawyer? You did date for two years."

She covers her face with her hands. "That's not the point. And I've realized it's not even the fact he disagreed with me. We disagreed on a lot of things. It's the fact that he stormed out and left me as if my thoughts didn't matter enough to hear me out. I had never seen that side to him before."

I bite my lip, feeling mildly guilty. I set my book aside and say, "Sometimes Sawyer visits me."

Nicole turns her head, her blue-green eyes finding mine. "I knew that. I've seen his truck here sometimes when I'm about to stop by. I usually leave when he is. But it doesn't seem to be too often."

I shake my head. "It's not."

"Raegan, you don't have to feel bad. He was your friend, too, before I dated him."

"No, I know," I say, though some relief washes through me to hear her reassure me again. "But he told me about his mom."

Nicole sits up. "He never told me about his mom. She was a topic I wasn't allowed to bring up."

"He was with her in the accident that killed her. She

was in the resistance. And he feels like her involvement is what brought about her death, what led to her being run off the road."

I can see the thoughts running through Nicole's mind; her face is like an open book to me. Some pain, a little sadness, but mostly numbness. Her fists clench as she rests them on her knees.

"I know he mentioned that. And I understand he worries. But why leave me like none of it mattered? Why let it come between us?"

A few tears well up and roll down her cheeks. I hand her a tissue, which she gratefully takes. "I'm sorry," I say, unsure if that's the right thing.

But Nicole rises from the bed. "He will always be an important part of my life. But I'm not going back to him. Not if that's the way it's going to be. I understand the trauma and the pain he must've gone through. But I can't just sit here and pretend like I don't know the truth."

I nod. "I know." I decide to change the subject. "Any updates on Mr. Williams accepting your request to join?"

"Yeah. I'm officially a member now. My training will start soon. I just hate that I'll be coming here less."

I smirk. "I know. My company is the best you'll ever get."

She rolls her eyes, but smiles.

"Don't worry," I say. "I'm going to ask Dr. Ho to clear me for some mild training. I want to get back into the game."

I need to.

Peter wants me to. But more importantly, *I* want to get back into it. I want to fight again. And feel like I'm ready to make a difference.

"Then we'll be training together."

I smile. "That's the plan."

"Raegan," my mom calls from downstairs. Her tone is… strange.

Nicole senses it, too, and follows me down the stairs.

Mr. Williams and Spencer sit on our couch. My mom sits in the chair, my father standing next to her. I'm a little confused.

"What's going on?" I ask.

Mr. Williams rises from the couch. "Raegan, I've lost contact with Peter."

My stomach turns in on itself, despite the fact this isn't news to me. I'm going to have to come clean and explain what I know. But before I can speak, Mr. Williams says, "I had access to the call history of the phone. It's part of the security features that I had Spencer install so I could keep tabs on Peter, but it said he called you before he called me. And that he's called you before."

My parents' eyes are on me intently. I've told them nothing. Spencer and Nicole know everything.

I exhale slowly. "He did contact me. Once, the night before Thanksgiving. And then early this morning, before I was awake."

"What did he tell you?"

Nicole touches my wrist. I glance over to her. "Show them the voicemail," she says softly.

I put my phone on speaker as the voicemail plays. "Raegan, it's me. I want you to know that I love you, I miss you, and I will always love you. But the other night I almost got caught. I can't risk everyone's life anymore. I'm destroying my phone and cutting off my connection. I promise I'll see you again. I love you. Keep fighting."

My knees go weak at his voice.

So broken and lost.

I can't look at my parents. I know they probably feel betrayed by the fact I didn't tell them this had happened.

I've played it cool all day. I only broke down when I was alone and when I was with Nicole.

Mr. Williams shakes his head. "There's nothing I can do for him now. But I don't think he's thought this through."

"It's Peter," Nicole says, her voice steady and strong. "He knows what he's doing."

My chest starts to tighten, my heart picking up speed. Suddenly all the voices in the room are too much. Mr. Williams talking to Spencer about what their next steps are. My parents whispering to each other, probably about me.

The room around me seems to close in. I clutch my chest, then my head, and collapse to the floor.

Peter is gone.

He's unreachable.

There's nothing to be done.

Tears blur my vision and I can't breathe.

"What's happening?" Nicole almost screams.

Spencer is the one to kneel next to me, but I can't acknowledge him. Not right now.

Everything is racing.

My heart.

My mind.

I must be dying.

Somehow, I must've overdone it. My body can't take it. My heart is giving out.

Death is imminent. It has to be. My chest tightens more and more, my heart threatening to burst out from under my ribs. My palms begin to sweat.

This is death.

I've escaped it too easily before.

"She's panicking," Spencer says, gently bringing a hand to my shoulder. "Give her space. She needs to breathe. Raegan, breathe. In and out."

What is air? How do you breathe? I can't voice these

questions. Not right now.

Peter's going to die.

I can't reach him.

"Raegan." Spencer's hands on my shoulders are firm. "Breathe in for four seconds, hold it for four seconds, then exhale."

It sounds stupid.

It's not going to work.

In-in-in-in.

Hold-hold-hold-hold.

Exhale.

Repeat.

Slowly, my heart seems to calm. My body aches; my jaw is clenched so hard I have to massage it to make it release.

Nicole is staring down at me. My parents are nearby as well, but they've stayed back as Spencer instructed them.

"More panic attacks?" Spencer asks me quietly.

I nod, not strong enough to speak.

Spencer helps me stand. "She'll probably need to rest," he tells my parents. "That was pretty severe."

"Thank you, Spencer," my mom says, wrapping me in her arms gently.

"No problem, Mrs. MacArthur. My uncle and I will head out now. But we'll be in touch about everything soon."

My mom lets me go. Nicole looks uneasily at me, afraid I might break.

"Are you okay?"

"Yeah," I breathe out. "I'm fine."

I can tell she isn't buying it. That's fine—for now. But my parents and I have to talk about everything. They deserve to know. Nicole hugs me briefly before leaving. I take a seat on the couch, finding comfort in the plush cushions.

My dad sighs. "You know you can tell us things, right?"

"I know. But I didn't want Mr. Williams to try and take that away from me. I needed to hear Peter's voice. And I didn't know he was planning any of this. I don't know what happened. He called early this morning."

And I wasn't awake to hear him one more time.

Knowing him, that was why he called so early.

Dad heads into the kitchen. As he goes, he turns and says, "All I know is Mr. Williams is suspicious of Peter's sudden need to cut all ties."

My mom frowns. "If he tries to contact you by other means, you let us know, okay?"

"Okay."

I don't like the implication that Peter is a traitor.

Mr. Williams doesn't know what happened. Even I don't know what happened to Peter.

All I know is he's gone and I'm going to fight for him.

CHAPTER NINETEEN

Carissa

WEDNESDAY, DECEMBER 13TH, 2023

GROCERY SHOPPING ALWAYS PUTS ME IN THE worst of moods. Too many people crowd down aisles, refusing to get out of my way. Or they look at me like *I'm* the problem.

I push my cart to the bread section, surprised there's only one other person on the far side of the aisle I grab the loaf my mom likes to use. Music beats against my eardrums from my earbuds. I entirely refuse to deal with stupid grocery store music. It's like they take the worst pop hits and gather them to play on the overhead.

I look down at the paper list my mom gave me, tapping my foot impatiently. I hate being away from home.

From Jackson.

Spencer promised to take care of him. But can I trust *either* of them with each other?

I grab the milk and the eggs, then move down a few aisles for paper plates. When I'm done, I book it to the checkout, reluctantly removing one of my earbuds to talk to the cashier.

I load my few items on the conveyor belt. She pops her bubble gum, scanning items fast.

"Your total is going to be thirty-two dollars and sixty-five cents," is all she says, bored.

I hand her the cash my mom gave me. She sighs as if this is really putting her behind. Despite her mood grating on my nerves, I can't imagine working at a grocery store. It's probably annoying.

She hands me the change and says, "Have a good one."

I can tell she doesn't care if I have a good one or not. To be fair, I don't quite care if she does either. I grab my bags and set them in my cart. I'm ready to get out of here.

Driving home is safe. I'm away from people. All the back roads are usually empty. And the way to the ranch is all back roads. I pass a couple of cars here and there, but never many of them. The air starts to cloud a bit the closer I get to the house. I'm a bit confused. It's strange for there to be any haze. The sun is out, despite the chill air outside.

I notice smoke rising in the air. Probably another fire in the woods, set by stupid people who don't know how to properly handle a campfire.

But who would want to camp in this weather? The wind is wickedly gusty and the air is cold with a bitter chill.

I turn onto the gravel road that leads to the ranch, and the realization creeps over me. It's not a forest fire.

Our house is on fire.

"No," I say to no one but myself. My heart is in overdrive. I speed down the gravel road, reaching for my phone sitting in the cupholder. My hands shake as I get closer. Now I can see people outside the house, firefighters working on putting out the fire. Police, paramedics, and my parents stand away from the danger.

I pull up inside the gates, not bothering to shut off my truck when I hop out. Adrenaline takes over as I march up to my parents.

"What the hell is going on?"

My mom's eyes are puffy and red. She's holding onto my father like she never has before.

When they don't answer my question, I realize two people are missing. "Where's Jackson? And Spencer?"

My dad says, "They're okay."

His voice is shaky. I realize his eyes are red.

He's cried a little, too.

"They're both sitting in my truck further down the road," he continues. "Spencer helped me get Jackson out. I didn't want him out in the cold, and he can't just stand around like this for too long. And Spencer has a few burns and cuts but refuses to go to the hospital.

The paramedics are taking care of his injuries."

"What… how did this…?"

My dad's voice drops, even though we are a safe distance from anyone hearing us. The police have wandered closer to the firefighters, closer to the danger. "The headquarters suddenly blew up. I barely made it out. But because it exploded, everything is gone. And the house caught fire."

"Is everyone out?"

He nods. "No one was here today. I've been having a lot of agents work from home instead of here at HQ because it was starting to be too suspicious, having all these people here at one time. I was worrying about unwanted attention. I don't know if anything can be salvaged down there. I can't check until the fire is fully out. Even then, I don't know if the headquarters is on fire. It probably is, given the explosion. And if it is, there's no way for them to put it out without finding out it exists. It's not good."

"Who could've…"

My brother.

Evan is the only one who would have the means and the motivation.

"Did Peter say anything that indicated Evan had plans?"

My dad stiffens. "Peter chose to cut his ties this morning. He says it was too dangerous. But considering he cut his ties right before this happened, I'm thinking he did know about this."

Peter left? "That doesn't make sense."

"None of this ever makes sense, Carissa. That's just how our life is now."

I watch as the flames eat up our home.

My home.

My childhood home.

I grew up here. We have never lived anywhere else. This place has seen everything. And just like that… it's all ash and flames and burned-up memories.

Everything is gone.

"What will we do?" I ask, my breath creating a fog when I speak.

"I have my backup plan. I didn't expect to enact it so soon, but maybe this was the push we needed."

This is more than a push.

This is a shove.

A way to force our hands. Whatever Evan is planning, I don't like it. How could he burn our family home?

Something inside of me breaks. Everything we had is gone.

Despite the heat from the fire reaching where we stand, I feel cold. Numbness begins to seep its way into my heart again. Slowly, the ice had been melting. But this has frozen over whatever progress I had made in letting my heart beat again.

Evan is making his plot for a war.

"We'll just have to go into the woods," my dad says, bringing me from my thoughts.

"The woods?"

"I've built an incredibly secure base. It's time we put it to use. I didn't want to use it in the winter because of the cold. But if this is what it's come to, then so be it. I'm not losing this war, not against my own son."

I'm not so convinced.

Everything is broken.

And there's nothing I can do to fix it.

I cross back over to my truck, hopping in and pulling away from the burning house, from my parents who I watch in the rearview mirror, from all that I know. I drive until I reach the place where my dad left his truck and Jackson. Spencer must be in the ambulance parked a bit further up.

I park behind my dad's truck and walk over to see Jackson in the passenger seat. I climb up in the driver's seat, closing the door to keep out the cold.

Jackson doesn't look at me at first. His eyes are fixed on the ambulance doors. But I know that's not really what he's looking at.

"I thought we were going to die." His voice is hoarse.

"I'm so sorry," I say, though it's a lame response.

"What will we do?"

"I don't know. My father…"

Jackson turns his head, meeting my eyes. I see the haunting in them. The absolute agony. His hand rests on his abdomen and I know he's in pain, but he won't admit it.

Not when Spencer is in pain too.

Not when my house is on fire behind us in the distance.

The smoke is still visible in the air. It's not safe to be even this close, but we don't care.

He takes my hand and says, "Whatever Andre has planned out there beyond what we know, we have to do it. This isn't a game. It never was. But this is a new low."

"Do you think Evan did this?" I ask, though I already know the answer Jackson is going to give me.

"He had to play some part in this. It was too coordinated. Only someone who knew how to get in would've been able to plant the explosives."

"Why do you think he did that?" My voice cracks as tears threaten to spill. I won't let them.

"I don't know." Jackson sighs, running a hand through his hair. "But this isn't something forgivable or justifiable. This is evil. Whoever your brother was before this, he's gone. And we can't let it continue."

I may miss my brother.

But the man who burned down our house, who destroyed all that we have left... he's not my brother.

Not anymore.

And I will not stop until he pays for what he's done.

CHAPTER TWENTY

Evan

THURSDAY, DECEMBER 14TH, 2023

THE DOOR SWISHES OPEN BEHIND ME, BUT I DON'T address Carlos. Not yet. I've gone lower than I've ever gone before. And if the mission was successful, I'm not sure I want to know.

"Master Evan?"

"Yes, Carlos?"

"The team you dispatched has reported back. They've returned to their home base."

Time to face the demons I've created. I turn to look at this whiny, insufferable servant of the emperor. I hate him. I hate the emperor.

Yet I'm one of them.

"And what were the results?"

Carols clears his throat and begins to pace in front of me, a habit I find irritating. From a paper, he reads, "'The team successfully infiltrated the base undetected using the secret back door that His Highness provided information about. The files and records needed were retrieved and will be sent to the White House immediately. The team placed bombs in key points at the base. The explosion resulted in a fire at the above-ground residence.'"

He pauses, giving in to a coughing fit. I roll one of my pens back and forth on the table, keeping my calm as carefully as I can.

"Survivors?" I ask, trying not to sound hopeful.

"All residents made it out of the house safely. There were no rebels within the base at the time."

I don't know if that's a blessing or a curse. Facing the emperor and presenting what I've done will not be difficult; I've done that before. But the fact that my mission caused no casualties won't be viewed favorably.

But at least my conscience is still mostly clear.

My home is gone. I don't know what my father will do now. Maybe they'll finally throw the white flag up, and I can stop worrying about them meddling in the business of overthrowing the government. I'll do it on my own. No one has to die.

"Thank you, Carlos," I say, and hold out my hand for the report. "I have a meeting with His Majesty in ten minutes."

"I shall prepare the tea," Carlos says, rushing out of my office.

I rise from my chair, leaving the report on my desk. I'll

need it to meet with the emperor, but I have one place I need to go before I see him.

I cross the room to a bookcase. The White House is full of tunnels and passages, made specifically to protect the people inside who are in danger from outside attacks.

But I've discovered that the tunnel from my office leads to the prison underground. I enter the tunnel, waiting for my eyes to adjust to the dim light that spills from my office. When the bookcase closes behind me, I am in near-darkness. The only lights are on motion sensors; they glow faintly and then blink off, one by one, as I move through the corridor. The stone walls are cold, but I keep my hand on them, trying to steady myself as I descend the ever-spiraling staircase. When I reach the bottom passage, I hesitate uneasily. I don't know if I really want to see what waits for me behind this door.

The lights shut off and I'm trapped in the dark again. I fumble for the handle and pull the door open silently. The light is very dim here too; the last cell of the prison is across from me. I keep to the shadows, not wanting to be seen. I want to observe.

Sam sits on the floor of her cell, her arms crossed as she shivers. The only light comes from a single bulb hanging farther down the corridor.

"Are you going to stand there and keep staring?" Sam asks.

I step forward. "How'd you know I was here?"

"I could sense someone out there. I assumed it must be you. No one else would bother coming down here to see me. So what is it? Here to mock me?"

"No. I want answers."

She rises, turning away from me. "I'm not offering any of those."

I glance at my watch. I've got five minutes before the emperor expects to see me. I scoff. "Fine. You don't have to answer anything. But did I mean nothing to you?"

"I told you I wasn't capable of feeling something for you, Evan. You shouldn't act surprised."

I don't bother giving her a response. I turn on my heel and head back down the corridor into the tunnel, closing the door behind me with more force than is necessary. I make my way briskly back to my office. I don't have time to beg for her to answer me. I already know she won't tell me anything. All I can do is prevent her death. I don't know how long the emperor will be patient about that.

I grab my papers and quickly move through the halls of the White House. When I arrive outside the emperor's office, Carlos says, "You're late."

"I had things to take care of." I brush past him hastily.

"He's waiting for you."

I enter, finding the emperor sitting behind his desk.

"Nice of you to finally show up," he says, rising from his chair. I don't find the action a means to welcome me.

He's trying to intimidate me into feeling bad for my tardiness. I hardly care.

"I apologize, Your Majesty." I bow slightly, as a means to placate him. "But I have good news."

"I do, too."

I already know whatever he thinks is good news will not be good in my eyes. Still, I'm curious. What else can he have done to ruin my life?

He gets straight to the point. "At our training base, one of the newer recruits has already surpassed the basic training requirements in both skill and ability."

My stomach twists. "Oh? And what does that mean?"

"It means he's being moved to more advanced training. But because he's gaining this attention, I think it might be good to interview him. See if he can be used as a special agent for our purposes regarding the resistance."

"Who is it that has accomplished so much already?"

"Peter Daniels."

The emperor watches me, waiting for a reaction. I give him nothing. "I will interview him. I'm sure he can be of use to you, Your Majesty. In the meantime, I've received word of progress. The resistance headquarters has mysteriously exploded. While there were no casualties, the base is ruined and so is the home of Andre and Maya Williams."

I almost choke as I say those words. My childhood home is gone. The emperor looks intrigued, surprised.

"Any indication of what could've caused the explosion?"

"Nothing yet, Your Majesty."

I didn't tell the emperor of this mission I devised to destroy the resistance. I know the details don't truly matter to him. It's all about the outcome.

"Well, then this is perfect timing, isn't it? We'll have Peter come in and you can speak to him about what we're expecting of him."

"Yes, Your Majesty. I will get right on that."

"One more thing, Evan."

Emperor Morgan slides a small stack of papers toward me. I pick it up and quickly scan them.

Names, ages, and states are listed here.

"What's this?"

"All currently active resistance members across the country. Slowly, we're drafting them one by one, as you know. I want you to pick the next batch of drafts. Five from each resistance."

As I'm scanning the names of people in my father's resistance, I stop when I see Raegan MacArthur's.

"I thought you said these were all active members."

"Indeed."

"But Raegan MacArthur is listed here. She's dead."

Emperor Morgan laughs. There is something terrifying, wicked even, about it. "Oh, Evan. You know that isn't true."

The blood in my veins becomes ice. "I…but…she's…"

"I know you didn't kill her. If you think I ever believed you killed that girl, you must believe me to be a total fool."

"I can explain," I say quickly. "I did capture her, and I did intend to kill her. But I thought maybe I could get more information."

The lies come easily. "So, I locked her in a bunker I had built for the warehouse. But when Jackson defected, he helped her escape. I tried to search for her, but it was too late."

The emperor regards me quietly, a small smile playing on his lips. "You're wise, Evan Williams. This is why I chose you to be my heir. I see a lot of myself in you. Your potential to continue my work should something happen to me is strong. I've known from the beginning you didn't kill the rebel girl. I've always known the truth. But you pulled off the entire scheme. However, we now have a girl who is alive but is legally listed as dead. And that will not do."

"I'll file for her death certificate to be revoked."

"Excellent. And then we can use her as a pawn to get Peter Daniels to do what we ask."

As always, the emperor always thinks ahead. "Yes, Your Majesty. I will get everything set up. You don't have to worry."

"I'm not worried. Now get to work."

I bow, though I hate to do it. Then I take my leave, barely catching my breath. I don't bother with the tea Carlos offers me.

"Have Peter Daniels brought to my office," I tell him.

"Yes, Your Highness," Carlos says, rushing off.

Returning to my office, I light a fire in the fireplace. Flames dance and crackle against the wood, burning it up. I wonder if this how my house looked.

Helpless.

Broken.

Deep inside me, guilt gnaws in my gut. But I shove it down. I can't feel guilt for this. I don't have time for such emotion.

I made my choices.

"SIR, THE SOLDIER YOU wanted to see is here."

I turn away from the fire to see Carlos standing in the doorway. His fingers twitch at his sides before he clasps his hands together behind his back.

"Send him in," I say.

Carlos steps out and in comes Peter.

Despite the heat of the fireplace, I feel cold.

"I hear you've done well in your training," I begin.

Peter stands tall, his eyes not really meeting mine, only staring ahead. "So I've been told."

"You don't have to pretend to be modest, Peter. You were always one to excel at whatever you were assigned."

"Is that why you called me in here? For fake congratulations?"

I laugh. "I don't have it in me to congratulate you for anything. I'm supposed to, of course. But I think we both know how fake that would be, as you say."

"So why am I here?"

In two strides, I'm at my desk. I reach for the single sheet of paper I need to make him react. I thought about just telling Peter the news. But watching him read it will be more fun. I hand him the paper.

"What's this?"

"Read," I say.

He looks down, skimming the paper. His eyes stop. His eyes scan over her name once. Twice.

"What is this?"

"Part of a list of all the active rebels across the country. That one is obviously from my father's rebellion."

"Why is Raegan on this list?"

"The emperor is fully aware that she is alive. And if you intend to keep her alive, you're going to do what we need of you."

Peter looks slowly back up at me, his eyes full of rage. He seems to be holding himself back from lunging at me. I'm not concerned. He'd be killed the moment he laid a hand on me. I take the paper back from him and say, "This morning, Andre Williams' resistance headquarters unexpectedly blew up. His house caught fire and burned to the ground. All that remains is ash."

"What?" he almost yells.

"Fortunately, everyone made it out alive. But that will put quite a damper on the resistance's plan to unite as one, won't it?"

I'm not sure if Peter is aware of my father's plans like I am. He doesn't react, but I don't read anything into that; he's obviously skilled at subterfuge. And whether he's aware of my father's plans or not isn't important.

"Your progress and skills are not going unnoticed by the emperor. He wants to use you. And if you plan on protecting everyone on that list, then you'll do as we say."

"You don't know where Raegan is," he retorts.

"She's home. You were dragged from her bed. I've heard the story."

His fists clench at his sides, his jaw tight. "What do you want from me?"

"Obedience. For now, you'll keep on with your advanced training. But when the time comes, you'll do what we want. Do we have an understanding?"

He glares at me, not saying a word. I take that as his agreement. I smirk. "Good. Now that that's settled, you are dismissed to return to your base."

His eyes narrow. "Do you enjoy being like him?" he says coldly. "Is the power worth any of this?"

I don't give him the satisfaction of answering that question or even acknowledging that he's said anything. Instead, I repeat, "You are dismissed to return to your base."

When he's gone, I finally breathe.

None of this has been worth anything. I've lost my family. I've lost a girl who I thought loved me. I've gone too far to go back now. I have to keep up this act until I figure out how to kill the president and take over. Then maybe I can undo all the terrible actions I've committed and get back all the things that have been taken from me.

I crumple up the list of rebels and throw it into the fire.

Poor souls.

They have no idea what's coming.

TWO
YEARS
LATER

CHAPTER TWENTY-ONE

COLD RAIN BEATS AGAINST MY EXPOSED SKIN.
I adjust my raincoat, pulling the hood over my head. I duck into an alley, catching my breath for only a moment. The industrial district of Cyrus isn't one for rest. Many soldiers patrol here. When they're not on patrol, they spend their leisure time at the illegal curfew-breaking parties held by the more unsavory people in the city.

The ones that can afford to get away with it. Kids of parents with big money who can buy their way out of trouble.

On the side of the building, I find the ladder that leads to the fire escape. It's just out of my reach. But I've dealt with worse odds. I back off a few paces, take another breath and get a running start. My feet nearly slip out from under me on the slick ground as I run and leap up to grab the ladder. My fingers scrabble to get a grip on the rungs. I dangle only for a moment as I work to gain footing against the wall.

It's not entirely graceful, but I'm up. I climb until I get to the top of the building. Once I have clear view of the streets, I stay in the shadows.

The rebellion has three main rules for missions like this one.

Rule number one: If you can see the soldiers, they can see you.

Rule number two: Keep a knife on your person at all times.

Rule number three: Don't get caught.

Keeping low, I pace the perimeter of the roof. A party across the street leaks flashing lights and pounding music into the streets.

I pull my coat closer, though it does nothing to keep me warm considering I'm wearing jean shorts. Probably a poor choice on my part. But it's hot and humid.

I kneel down out of sight, fixing the laces on my boots. I rise again slowly, glancing over the edge of the building.

"Quite the meeting spot."

I turn quickly, gasping.

I calm down when I see who it is. "Noah, you scared the crap out of me."

Noah smirks, staying in the shadows. "Andre sent you?"

"Of course." I dig in my satchel, pulling out an envelope. I hand it to him, and he tucks it into his jacket, shielding it from the rain.

He's dressed in dark clothing, helping him to blend in with the night. His hair is still long, almost to his shoulders. But he doesn't have it in a ponytail anymore.

I haven't seen him for about a year, when he went to help one of the other branches of the rebellion. After every rebellion in the country united forces, a lot of us spread out, working to even the odds as much as we can.

I stayed with Andre's branch. Noah and Stella moved on to a different Texas branch, somewhere north. But when it comes to exchanging information, we meet in places like this. Secluded. Dark.

Noah tilts his head. "You shouldn't be out at night like this. It's not safe for a woman."

I scoff, rolling my eyes. "I'm stronger than I look. I've worked hard to get where I am."

"Soldiers will find you on the streets and try to take advantage."

"They'll end up with problems if they try to mess with me. Anyway, my home base isn't that far from here. I'll be fine. You, however, have a long drive ahead of you, and it's after curfew."

He pushes off from the wall he's leaning against. "No, I'm staying at a friend's place for the night. He's down the street. As soon as curfew is lifted in the morning, I'm heading back north."

I begin heading towards the ladder. "Well, good luck and safe travels."

"How's Jackson?" he asks abruptly.

"He's doing fine," I say stiffly. Jackson and Noah aren't exactly the best of friends. The question feels odd coming from Noah.

He nods, not saying anything else about his stepbrother. Instead, Noah says, "Be careful. The soldiers have been relentless lately."

"I'll manage," I say, beginning my descent down the ladder.

I don't wait to see if Noah is coming down. I pull my hood over my head and start towards the woods at the end of the road. As long as I make to the trees, I'll be fine.

The sound of my footsteps echoes off the concrete; the rain has made it slick, so I walk carefully. Suddenly I hear voices behind me, growing steadily louder, and an icy shiver runs up my back.

Soldiers.

It has to be. Even though the party is still happening, no one is stupid enough to wander these streets.

No one but soldiers and rebels.

I dare to glance back over my shoulder. Sure enough, it's a small platoon of soldiers. Their flashlights are shining in my direction, though the beams don't quite reach me. A patrol truck follows closely behind them, its headlights off. The rumble of the truck drowns out the sound of their voices, but I can see they're getting closer.

Keeping my head down, I pick up my pace, hoping the dark of the night will conceal me. The edge of the forest is within sight. The rumble of the truck has stopped, and I hear the voices more clearly now. Meaning if I can hear them, they can hear me. I have to be careful.

Just a bit farther…

"Hey, you!" the deep voice of a soldier yells from behind me.

I don't dare look back as I take off in a full run. I won't lead the soldier to the base, of course, but the forest is my domain. I can lose him in the trees and then make my way back home. Most soldiers are rotated, never patrolling one area for more than a month. They won't know the layout of the forest as well as I do.

At least… that's what I'm betting my life on.

I keep running until I find myself in the trees.

"You're breaking the federally mandated curfew, a violation of the law," the soldier calls. "I command you to stop where you are."

That voice… so familiar and desperate.

I duck under branches and weave around bushes, coming to rest behind some shrubbery. I'm breathing deeply now, trying to be quiet as I peer through the leaves to watch him.

The soldier's boots crunch in the dead leaves as he approaches. He's panting, but his stamina seems to be intact.

"Where are you? I know you're in here. You're making this harder than it needs to be."

I'm out of breath from all my running, but I don't have time to linger here. He's close. And he'll find me if I don't keep moving. I burst out of my spot as quietly as I can and begin to run again, but some twigs break under my boots, alerting the soldier.

My legs and lungs burn, but I don't let up. His footfalls are not far behind me. I'm capable of running for long periods of time, but all the training in the world doesn't prepare you for a real-life situation.

"Stop running or I'll have to do something we'll both regret!"

That voice…

The one-second distraction is all it takes. My foot catches on a tree root, bringing me to the ground. The soldier is above me in an instant, rifle aimed at my chest. I look up at him, the hood falling off my head.

Eyes, one's that I know, widen as they look back at me, the moonlight reflecting in them.

"Peter," I say.

He takes a few steps back. I'm panting harder now, my heart pounding in my chest as I rise to my feet. He takes a few more steps back before suddenly turning and taking off, back in the direction we came from.

"Wait!" I call after him, but he doesn't answer.

My chest aches; my knees and hands are burning from the fall. I'm still trying to catch my breath. I shouldn't waste any more time standing here. He's not coming back.

He's long gone.

I start off in the direction of the tunnels, looping around a few times in case I'm being followed. But I don't think I am. I sort of wish I was.

Peter…

After a few minutes, I make it to the tunnel entrance, an above-ground pipe that leads down into a deep darkness. I descend the ladder, jumping down when I reach the final rung.

A flashlight shines in my face. I raise my hand, shielding my eyes.

"It's about time you showed up."

Spencer.

He lowers the flashlight and says, "You look terrible."

"Thanks," I mutter, pulling leaves out of my braided hair. Wet blades of grass stick to my jacket. He's probably not wrong. That fall left me pretty sore. I can already feel the bruise forming on my thigh.

"No, seriously. What happened out there?"

"I fell in the woods. I tripped over a tree root while

being chased by a soldier."

"*What?*"

I tuck a loose strand of hair behind my ear. "I was caught near the edge of the woods. But I got away."

"Are you sure you weren't followed?" Worry taints Spencer's voice.

"I'm sure."

"Do we need to send out a counter-patrol? I can talk to my uncle."

I shake my head, not sure how to tell him what happened out there without crying. The cracks in my heart are deeper now, all because of a chance encounter.

"Raegan?" Spencer asks. "What happened out there?"

I inhale slowly. "The soldier was Peter."

Time freezes. My heart threatens to escape my chest as anxiety closes in. My vision clouds, but I blink the blurriness away.

"We need to tell my uncle."

I follow Spencer through the tunnels, every twist and turn, every long corridor. My mind doesn't stop replaying what happened in the woods. *Peter's here.* But why did he turn and run? After two long years of not really knowing if he was even alive, why didn't he say something?

There's so much to say… But he ran.

Leaving me behind again.

I blink back tears as we arrive at the ladder that leads up to the base. Spencer motions for me to climb first. I move slowly, my hands burning as I grip the metal rungs. Once at the top, Spencer says, "You should probably go to the medic. You've cut your hands pretty bad."

I stare down at them as though they belong to someone else. "I want to talk to Andre first," is all I say.

I let him lead the way, still trying to slow my pulse, calm my breathing. Still trying to numb the pain of my cracked heart.

The darkness of the night doesn't cover the camp entirely. Lanterns burn here and there, and I can see that there are other people around. Carissa and Jackson sit on the edge of the fountain in the center of the courtyard, looking up at the stars.

Linley plays with Gunner in the grassy corner near the mess hall. Andre stands outside his office with his wife, her hand in his as they speak.

Spencer walks up ahead of me. I let him, even though I should probably be the first to speak to them. I don't have it in me to recount all the details yet. I didn't think seeing Peter would evoke such a reaction in me. But everything I've worked to strengthen about myself feels like it's on the verge of breaking again.

I catch up to Spencer. Andre studies me for a moment before saying, "What happened?"

Before I can stop him, Spencer says, "She had a run-in with a soldier who turned out to be Peter."

Not much shocks Andre these days. But this does.

His eyes widen and his mouth hangs open slightly. "Well, we need to make a report."

Despite myself, tears well up in my eyes and spill down my cheeks. I wipe at my face with the back of my hand. "Actually," I say, fighting to keep my voice steady, "let's do this tomorrow. I'm in pain and I think I need to see the medic."

Spencer gives me a look that says *I already said that*. But I ignore him. I thought I could handle making a report to Andre. But I'm suddenly too weary.

"Of course," Andre says. "I'll meet with you tomorrow. Go get your wounds looked at. I'm glad you made it back safely."

I make my way through the camp towards the medical building, a small, wooden shack. The door is wide open when I approach. "H-hello?" I call inside.

A short Native American woman steps out into the light. She smiles warmly. Hannah, Spencer's ex-girlfriend and our resident medic, says, "What's wrong?"

"I fell in the woods. I know I cut my hands and scraped my knees."

"Come in, Raegan."

She flicks a switch and the lights turn on. I shiver, despite the humid air. The ache in my heart is cold, familiar. It's nothing I haven't felt before in the past two years. But seeing Peter was a reminder of everything I've endured since he's been gone. I can almost feel the cold air

I had let in my room that November two years ago. When I'd hold on to the bitter, fragile hope that I'd see him again someday.

That day has finally come. But as quickly as he came, he left me again.

Hannah moves gracefully across the room. She grabs an antiseptic spray and has me hold my hands out as she douses my wounds and washes out the grit and dirt. She's silent as she works to bandage my hands. When she's done, she treats my knees as well. But they aren't as bad.

"Go easy on training tomorrow," she says. "I'll tell Andre to give you lighter loads for the next couple of days."

Usually, I'd argue with that. But I nod, accepting her recommendation. "Thank you, Hannah," I say before heading off to the sleeping quarters. These are all underground for added protection.

I move through the tunnels to the girls' sleeping quarters, finding my room at the end of the second hall. Nicole is nowhere to be found; she's most likely on night patrol. I shut the door behind me to block out the light from the hallway.

After changing into my nightclothes, I climb into my bed. I should shower, but I've already had my hands bandaged. And my heart is too heavy for showering.

When I close my eyes, I see Peter retreating.

Leaving me behind.

CHAPTER TWENTY-TWO

Peter

SATURDAY, AUGUST 9TH, 2025

I STARE UP AT MY CEILING, LIKE A CLICHÉ OF someone who can't get his life together. Seeing her was everything I didn't know I needed. Running from her was every crack in my heart breaking apart, shattering it into a million pieces.

I should've said something. It's been two years and I said nothing to her.

Sunlight pours into the room. Usually, I'm not awake long enough to be bothered by it. Having a night patrol shift means sleeping in the day. But after seeing her, I've been unable to focus. Every beat of my heart aches for her. I see her running when I close my eyes. The past two years, I held onto the hope I'd see her again. The only driving force I have left inside of me has always been her.

Tossing and turning, I reach under my pillow for the keychain. I don't open the locket, or look at the picture. Holding it in my hand is enough.

Sleep isn't coming to me this morning. I sigh, kicking off my covers and climbing down to the ground from my bunk. I'm careful not to disturb the others in the room. I slip out the door, taking in the warm air. A few soldiers run past me, doing their laps around the base. I find myself walking around the camp, looking for nothing in particular. My mind is so clouded with thoughts of Raegan that I can't relax, never mind sleep.

Jose runs by, stopping when he sees me. "Daniels? What the hell are you doing still awake?"

"I can't sleep."

I haven't told anyone what happened. Not even my commanding officer, when he questioned why I ran off the way I did. I was able to play it off with a lame story about needing to the use restroom. Jose has become one of my closest friends within the base. I'm thankful we were transferred to Texas together. But I still don't trust anyone enough with my secrets.

"You should try. I heard you're on patrol again tonight."

"I know. I'm walking to clear my mind. Then I'll go back to bed."

He nods once before taking off again in a run, trying to catch up with the rest of the soldiers. I don't stay out long. The sun beats down on me; the air is unpleasantly humid.

When I go back to bed, it doesn't take me long to crash.

My body is finally exhausted enough that I can sleep.

"TURN LEFT ON MAIN."

I grunt and turn the truck down the street for patrol. Jennings sits next to me, holding his holographic map. I don't need it, but it gives him something to do. I don't really trust the maps, either. They're a rather new development that the soldiers have just begun to use. But they're too futuristic and strange for me trust.

I know these roads. I know how they curve, how they rise, how they fall.

You don't forget Bent Ridge, no matter how long you're gone.

"It hurts to see it like this," I mutter.

"You been here before?"

"This town was my home," I say.

"Oh."

Jennings doesn't say much else. He never does.

I see the old shops of Main Street. I'm too hardened to cry, but everything is gone. Boarded up and broken down. The movie theater is a crumbling ruin. Mimi's is long gone. There's no sign of Tucker's

Barbeque ever existing.

It's all gone.

My childhood. My home.

As we pass the park, the familiar, aching need to find the tree tugs at me again. But I can't go there now. Not with four other patrol trucks in the area. Not with Jennings riding with me.

I keep going, driving through the town and pretending none of this is shattering my already broken heart.

"I'm sorry," Jennings says, startling me.

"Why?"

"Your home looks like it's been hit by a bomb. I doubt it looked like this when you left."

"It was everything to me," I say, my voice faltering with emotion. "I'd even take stupid small-town gossip over seeing it destroyed like this."

"Where did you live?"

"Maple Drive."

"I have bad news, then," Jennings says.

I exhale slowly, turning right onto Maple Drive. I'm not scared to see my home, oddly enough. It's seeing Raegan's. It's knowing she's not there, that she's somewhere in the woods with the rest of the resistance, somewhere I can't find her.

I glance at my house. It looks empty. My mom's car is gone. Wherever Andre is hiding people, they must have their cars with them. I shake my head. I don't point out to

Jennings where I lived and he doesn't ask. I don't talk about Raegan, even though her name dances on the tip of my tongue. Her home is vacant, too. All the vehicles are gone. It's like the town is half empty.

"I guess tonight's easy," I say. "There's hardly anyone left."

"Is it always this empty?" he asks.

To an outsider, this would feel barren. We've driven through a lot of towns, places smaller than Bent Ridge. They were never this deserted. I know what it's supposed to look like at night. Tucker used to be up in the early hours, smoking the meat for his barbeque. Mimi would be heading in to her café with her family at five a.m., making sure they get everything set up for a busy day.

This isn't right. But nothing's been right for years.

"What do you see when you look around?" I ask Jennings.

He looks up from his holographic map, the faint glow illuminating the sharp edges of his face. He shrugs. "I don't know. It looks like a small town."

I shake my head. "I know this place like the back of my hand. It was never like this. Even at this hour of the night."

"You *knew* this place," he corrects me. "It's been a long time since you've been here."

"I left for six years to live in California when I was

young. It hadn't changed at all when I came back."

He sighs, shutting off his map. The only light now comes from the glow of the control screen on the dash. "I don't think the town is what you remember it to be because it's been a long time and there is a very silent civil war being fought right now between rebellion and government."

They've all fled with the rebellion I used to be a part of, I think but don't say. Instead, I take a turn onto the next street and keep my mouth shut.

The rest of the patrol is uneventful. I pull into the base just as the sun begins to rise. I'm shaky on my feet when I finally leave the truck. A whole night of driving has left my legs numb. A few soldiers run by, doing their morning sprints.

The Texas base is large, perhaps larger than the one in DC. And while it's full of strict generals and no-nonsense officers, it has one crucial benefit: Evan Williams isn't here.

And neither is General Kahn, for that matter.

As I walk to my barracks, I hear the officers talking about this evening's patrols. There'll be another one through Bent Ridge tonight. Tomorrow, we'll go back to Cyrus, to the road where I saw Raegan. I wonder if I'll see her again. Or if she'd even let herself be found again. I left her behind on purpose, running before anyone else could find us.

I know it was the right thing to do.

So why does it feel so wrong?

"I THOUGHT ABOUT what you said."

Jennings bumps into me as he rounds the truck. It's his night to drive and my night to hold the map. Not that we'll need one; we're going through Bent Ridge again. I could guide him through the town with my eyes closed.

I slide in and buckle up as he pulls himself into his seat.

"What did I say?" I ask.

"About the town being more empty than usual. I overheard a conversation. I think I might know the reason."

I wait for him to pull out onto the road before asking any questions. "What do you mean you overheard a conversation?"

He runs a hand over his buzzed scalp. "Overheard, eavesdropped. What more do you want?"

"What did you hear?"

"That the rebels have a new base. And that it's bigger and more advanced. Apparently, a lot of known rebels have disappeared off the face of the earth, but it's suspected that they're hiding out in this new place."

"A new rebel base?" Panic grows inside of me. If the military is aware of this, there's no way they aren't looking into it already.

He nods. "All the rebel leaders have united, forming a council with one another and joining forces, as well as finances. I'm sure a lot of the funding came from your old boss, Andre Williams. He's the richest of any of them."

I rest my helmet on my lap and run a hand through my hair. "Why would he abandon his old base?"

Because of Evan Williams.

I know the truth. Evan destroyed his own family's headquarters. But no one else knows that and I'm not about to tell them.

"Don't know. There wasn't talk about that. But I think what we're doing is searching. See, there have been rumors that soldiers were closing in, ready to take Andre Williams and his family into custody. But they were gone when the soldiers arrived, and there's been no sign of them since then. These patrols are about seeing what looks strange. Your hometown is empty, at least according to you. So now we can start to figure out who's all involved by looking at our reports."

Our mission over the past few months was going from city to city, town to town, with a list of ever address. We've been making note whether it's occupied or empty. Getting a headcount of how many people reside in a home. A seemingly simple task—for a census, they said.

But they lied.

They always lie.

I feel both the chill of the truth and the heat of anger rise up inside of me. "I can't believe it."

"I don't know for sure," Jennings says quickly. "Like I said, I was eavesdropping. But I think it adds up. It could be a coincidence, though."

"I don't believe in coincidences," I say, my fists clenching. Besides that, it checks out with everything else I know about what happened two years ago and about why Andre left his original base.

This isn't leading anywhere good.

We're silent for a long time. When we reach Bent Ridge, my mind is made up. "I need to find them."

Jennings glances over at me. "What?"

"I need to find them," I repeat, this time sure of myself.

"Have you lost your mind? How do you plan to do that?"

"I don't know. But I know that whatever is being planned, I'm going to be used for it. And if I don't…"

I don't finish the sentence. I don't have to. Jennings knows enough about my past life. About my true loyalties. Everyone thinks I'm this super-soldier. A warrior with amazing strength and unusual stamina.

I'm desperate.

That's all I am.

Desperate to keep her safe.

To keep *all* of them safe.

To the detriment of my own conscience, morals, and values. I do things I don't want to. I listen to every command. It protects them all.

I guide Jennings through town. He doesn't mention the resistance again. Not until we're heading home, trying to beat the rising sun.

"When you desert, I want to come."

I stare at him. "Who said I was deserting?"

He laughs. "Why wouldn't you? If you find them, they could be your ticket out of here."

"My cutting them off two years ago doesn't look good. I doubt they'd even speak to me. What do I do about that?"

"You cross that bridge when you get to it. But first, you make an escape plan. And I'll be right behind you. I have a sister to find, in case you forgot."

I look down at the small disk in my hands. "I didn't forget. Not for a moment. I regret not getting answers first. But I was in a hurry."

"I know. Don't think you're getting out of helping me just because you have a valid reason for now. When you leave, I'm coming, too."

I smirk. "Deal. But you have to help me figure out what's going on. Get more information if you can. We can't just run off with no idea where we're going."

He nods once.

The conversation is over.

But there's hope ahead of us now. We're not going to be here forever. And I may have a chance to protect the ones I love before it's too late.

CHAPTER TWENTY-THREE

Raegan

SATURDAY, AUGUST 9TH, 2025

EVERY MUSCLE IN MY BODY ACHES AS I ROLL OVER in my bed. I'm only aware it's morning because of Nicole's alarm clock chirping three times before she silences it. She yawns, and I hear her shuffling across the floor towards the bathroom.

I don't usually get up this early on Saturdays. But I don't think I can sleep any longer. The ghost of Peter haunts my dreams. My heart hurts as much as my body does… maybe even more so.

I sit up, glancing at my bandaged hands. The cuts beneath the wrappings still sting slightly. Whatever Hannah put on them has significantly reduced the pain, though. I wonder if she has anything for the rest of my body.

Nicole reemerges from the bathroom, dressed in yoga pants and a sports bra. Her red hair is pulled back in a ponytail and she looks ready to head to the arena. She looks at me, seeming surprised that I'm even awake.

"Why aren't you sleeping?" she asks as she pulls a purple tank top over her head.

"I'm in pain. Sleep doesn't help."

"Physical or emotional?"

Obviously, someone told her when she returned from patrol last night. Most likely Spencer talked to her.

"Can't it be both?"

She sighs, taking a seat on the edge of my bed and flopping onto her back. "Andre's gonna want to talk to you today."

"I don't want to think about that." Tears begin to well up in my eyes again. I've never thought of myself as much of a weepy person. I'm sensitive, but it takes a lot to make me cry. At least it used to. Now it seems I'm reduced to tears pretty often. My heart has been through so much.

"What do you think Andre will say?" Nicole asks.

"I don't know. I'm hoping… I'm hoping Peter finds a way to reach out again. We have to get him out of there."

Nicole sits up, pushing off from the bed and getting back to her feet. "Does he want to get out at this point? He's been gone for two years."

"Why wouldn't he? I saw him, Nicole. I saw the way his eyes searched mine, even if it was only one second. He's not there because he wants to be."

"No one wants to be drafted," she admits. "But… two years is plenty of time to brainwash someone."

I stifle the urge to let my thoughts out. Nicole is my best friend. She's easy to talk to. But when we don't agree, it's not always pretty. Of course, we do find common ground. But I'm not awake enough for this right now, and she's trying to get to the training arena before everyone else does.

"I don't know," is all I say. "I guess I want to hope for something better."

"I know. I'm heading to the arena. Maybe you should go walking or something. It might loosen the aches."

"Maybe."

She's out the door without another word. I'm left to my own devices. I suppose I should get ready. Andre *will* want to talk to me. I can't push it off again.

I slide off my bed, the bones of my feet popping with every step. I shake my head. I'm too young to be this achy already. I grab my shorts and tank top, taking them into the bathroom. I do my usual morning routine of brushing my teeth and splashing my face with water before I dress in my clothes.

Five minutes later, I'm emerging above ground from the tunnels. The morning is warm, humid. A few others mill about the courtyard of the base. I see Spencer sitting at one of the few picnic tables under the great oak trees. He's obviously working, but I still make my way over and sit down across from him. He glances up, offering a quick smile.

He pulls his headphones down and says, "My uncle wants to see you."

"I know. Where is he so I can avoid this conversation?"

Spencer points to the mess hall. "You can't avoid it. He wants to make a report. It's not going to hurt you."

"It might," I mumble under my breath. With a wicked smile, I say, "I'm surprised you aren't working in the training arena so you can ogle Nicole while she trains."

Spencer's face goes red as he coughs a couple of times. "First of all, I would never do that. Second of all, we don't have to be together all the time. We're both busy people."

I smirk. "You wish you weren't."

He rolls his eyes. "Enough about that. You have a meeting and I know my uncle isn't going to let you get around it. Might as well get it over with."

I rise from the table, sighing. Not many people speak of Peter's name anymore. Not since he cut off all ties to us in an effort to protect everyone. Meaning the gossip is probably running rampant through the camp. I shiver, despite the heat. I make my way over to the mess hall. It's mostly empty, but Andre sits alone at a small table, nursing a cup of coffee.

"Spencer said you wanted to see me?" I say, approaching reluctantly.

"I did. I'm glad you're here. We have a lot to talk about concerning what happened last night."

What's there to really know? Peter is somewhere out there, not far from here. We can save him. But I know this conversation won't be so simple.

"Raegan," Andre says, pulling out a piece of paper and motioning for me to seat down. I comply, only because my bones still hurt.

"Tell me everything that happened last night," he says, a pen poised over the paper.

"I met with Noah on the rooftop of the old dog food factory. I gave him the message for his branch leader. After that, I left." I leave out the way Noah frustrated me. It's not relevant and I don't want to relive it.

"After I left, I was near the edge of the forest when I was spotted," I say. "I began evasive maneuvers, like we're taught. The soldier kept up pretty well. He was slightly winded. But so was I. I kept running. When he called out to me, his voice made me stumble. That's why I fell. When I rolled over, a rifle was at my chest. The soldier was Peter and when he realized it was me he was aiming at, he took off. I still did a few twists and turns through the woods to make sure he wasn't pursuing me."

This story is so raw and real. It almost feels wrong for anyone else to know. For anyone else to understand what happened between me and Peter in that moment.

I wrap my arms around myself, despite the mess hall being warm. The coldness comes from within. The ice that's covered my heart for the past two years is seeping through the rest of my body, taking over my bloodstream.

"We're going to save him, right?" I ask, my stomach churning with the tension that's in this room.

"Save him?" Andre repeats, looking up at me now. He's bewildered, eyes wide and confused. This doesn't bode well.

"Yes," I say firmly. "He's back in Texas. Now would be the best time to try and make contact again."

"Do I need to remind you that we weren't the ones that cut off the contact?"

"No," I reply coolly. "But I'm the one he called and left a message for before he did it. I know it's been two years. I know everyone thinks he's a brainwashed soldier. But he's Peter. The guy you always turned to after your son lost his mind."

Bringing up Evan is a low blow. But the notion of leaving Peter behind is one I refuse to live with.

"I know it's hard, Raegan. We've all lost someone to this war. Peter was like a son to me. I wish I could've found a way to save him sooner. But now… I have to protect my people."

"He *is* your people. There's no way in hell he's evil now. I know him. I saw it in his face when he realized it was me at the end of his rifle. I saw it in his eyes before he ran off. I know Peter's still in total control of himself. Why can't you at least try?"

"My people are all within this camp or in the other branches scattered throughout the country. Peter is no longer one of us. You need to accept that, Raegan. He let you go because there's no questioning what you mean to him. But I don't doubt he'd be ready to betray us all in a heartbeat."

His words are like a blow to my chest. But I'm powerless to fight. He has the whole camp agreeing with him. I have no one. Everyone thinks Peter can't still be the same person we knew. And maybe they're right. But I refuse to believe he's not on our side still.

"You've been wrong before," I finally say, pushing up from the seat.

"I have. And I've learned from my mistakes, Raegan. I don't enjoy this any more than you do. But I can't sacrifice us all in the hopes that one person who's now in the government's hands is still good. What about all the other resistance agents that have been taken? If I bring Peter back, what about the others we know nothing about?"

"That's not fair—"

"It *is* fair, because I know every single man on my

council who led those resistances before we all united will ask. Their men are important, too. We've all suffered loss in this war. I truly hope Peter makes it out on the other side and that, someday, you can be reunited. But this isn't the time or place."

I turn and march towards the door without another word. I gave my statement. I don't have anything left to say. But I've made up my mind: every night I'm out on errands or on patrol, I'll look for him. I can't trust anyone else to help me. I'm on my own.

"'EVAN WILLIAMS, HEIR TO THE UNITED STATES, IS now the most eligible bachelor in the world.' Who reads this garbage?" I scroll through the gossip site on my hologram screen.

Emperor Morgan glances up at me from his own screen. "It's gossip. Your relationship publicly fell through when Samantha Winters was put in prison. Now, countless women would love to be yours. Some for power. Some for money. Others for fame."

I scoff, shoving the holodisk away from me. "Some think they can fix me."

Emperor Morgan doesn't react. "Those magazines mean nothing. They publish articles for entertainment. We have a team that heavily screens everything before it goes to print. Nothing bad will ever be published."

Nothing bad? I hardly agree, but I don't say that out loud. There's nothing worse than finding out I have a group of deranged fangirls wanting to marry me. The only girl I've truly loved is beneath the very building I live in.

Love.

A truly weak emotion.

"I've received some reports lately on the census we've been taking."

"What's been discovered?"

Emperor Morgan pushes a stack of papers over to me, but says, "Many people from the town of Bent Ridge are missing. Andre Williams lived in between Bent Ridge and Cyrus. However, his home mysteriously burned down two years ago."

Mysteriously. Of course.

I can't reveal all my secrets to the emperor.

"So," he continues, "that leaves a very strange gap. We lost sight of Andre Williams and his family about a month after his home burned down. Other resistances and their members also disappeared. Not every person of every resistance. But slowly, the numbers have grown."

My fists clench. Whatever game my father is playing, I'm not sure I like it. It's unpredictable. "What will we do about this?" I ask.

"I want to find the new resistance base. Clearly there has to be one somewhere. And if he's really pulling people from society, one by one, he has to be somewhere hidden and safe."

Hidden and safe. I've never been my father's son. My mind was never as creative as his. My sister was much better at thinking like him than I was. But I've spent time studying my father. I know his habits. He's somewhere out there, somewhere he thinks will be safe.

The wilderness that exists between Bent Ridge and Cyrus.

That has to be it. It's the only place he could have built something.

"Peter Daniels… he's stationed at the Texas base, isn't he?"

Peter Daniels. His name boils my blood. "Yes, sir."

"Send him into the wilderness. If anyone can find them, he can. He's rebel scum, isn't he?"

"Yes, sir, but wouldn't it be better for me to go search for the resistance base?"

"No. It would be too dangerous. You will need to go to the Texas base to assign him to this mission. And you'll need to stay until it's complete. But you won't be in on the search."

"Of course, Your Majesty. When do you want me to leave?"

"Soon. Within the next couple of days, if possible. The sooner we find where the resistance is, the sooner this can all be over. We don't need threats to our rule."

Emperor Morgan's words echo in my head as I head to my room. Once I'm inside, I lock my door.

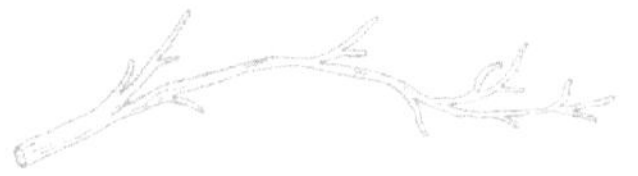

I'M CAREFUL WHENEVER I use the secret passage to the prison.

All the way there, I quietly curse myself. It's just more of the weak emotion leading me here, anyway.

To the girl who broke my heart.

She sits on the cot in her cell. The ratty prison clothes hang off her thin frame. I stick to the shadows. I don't want her to know I'm here.

It's a weak of me even to want to see her.

"Your eyes aren't quiet," she says softly. Loud enough for me to hear, quiet enough that no one else will know I'm here.

I step out where she can see me fully. There's hardly any light this far into the prison. Just the dim overhead bulbs that are next to useless in the dark. I wonder if her skin has taken on that sickly pallor that people have when they're deprived of sunlight.

Are her lips still as pink as her cheeks usually are?

I shake my head.

"What do you want now?" she asks, disinterested.

"The same thing I've wanted since I first came to see you."

"I'm not telling you anything, Evan. You've been doing this forever. Why do you waste your time?"

Because of a weak emotion called love. I don't say this, though. Love makes us weak. Declaring it makes us vulnerable. Vulnerable is easy to manipulate.

Easy to kill.

"You are the one wasting my time by not giving me the answers. I merely come here to do my job."

She rises from her cot, coming up to the iron bars that separate us. She grips the cold metal in her hands as her eyes meet mine. "If it was still your job, you'd use the front entrance, not the secret passage you found that connects to somewhere in the house. You wouldn't hide in the shadows and flinch at any noise coming from down the hall. You wouldn't whisper so the guard on duty doesn't hear you."

I don't give her the satisfaction of addressing that. Instead, I say, "I suppose you think you have it all figured out. But you know nothing."

She laughs. "Evan, I know everything. I know you come down here because you've deluded yourself into thinking I might actually love you. I can get rid of those feelings quickly. I don't desire you like you wish I did."

"I don't come here for that."

I'm a liar.

But lying is the least of my sins. It's not like she'll believe my words anyway. Not when she's onto every single feeling that courses through my veins.

I don't understand how she knows these things about me, but I ignore that she does. I don't have to admit to any of it.

Instead, I slip back into the shadows and say, "Maybe your food rations could be increased if you cooperate more."

"You'd like that, wouldn't you? For me to get more food. To not be under threat of torture here. You think you can be the hero who saves me and I'll fall into your arms. Well, I'm not a damsel in distress and you are no hero."

The words strike something that already feels broken inside of me. I turn away, not giving her a response. I won't fall to her level of mockery. Instead, I retreat back up to my room, cursing the love that somehow exists in my heart for this woman.

A woman who tried to have me arrested for her own crimes.

For crimes that still weigh on my shoulders.

I sit on my bed, staring at the wall, wishing I'd never gone to see her. Wishing my ever-beating heart would stop longing for the short time I was hers.

I'm not here to find love or be loved, I tell myself.

I'm here because I'm protecting my family. Perhaps I'm destroying the very fabric of the resistance, but at least they will be safe from all this.

I remain in my room until evening, staying within the walls of the prison I've made for myself. Creating plans and wondering where on earth my father is hiding.

Too many resistance members who had been clearly marked for our attacks are suddenly gone. And I know my father has something to do with it. He's a man of caution, after all; he'd likely gather everyone and put them somewhere hidden, somewhere safe. After I destroyed our home and what remained of my childhood.

This has to be his handiwork. No one else could garner such attention. At least, no one in the rebel community could. I know practically all of them at this point. No one has the charisma and charm of my father.

Although I suppose I'm biased. He *is* my father.

Or maybe he *was* my father.

Past tense.

I threw away everything.

The articles say I'm cold, ruthless. And that's not just gossip; other people see it, too. Either way, those rumors keep people pleased and entertained.

For some, it will make me the most eligible bachelor in the country.

For others, it will make me more hated than I've ever been.

I clutch my head in my hands. A dull ache throbs in my temples. It's too much. I fall to my knees, wondering what Emperor Morgan would think if he walked in right now.

Weakness.

All I am is weakness.

I love Samantha and it makes me weak.

I love my family and it's put me here.

I.

Am.

Weak.

Tears spring from my eyes before I can stop them. I'm the heir to this country. I don't cry. I don't let meaningless emotions get the best of me.

Yet, here I lie on my office floor. Falling apart. I disgust myself.

I sit up, wiping my face with my hands. There's still a dull throb in my head, but it's subsided enough that I can breathe.

Inhale.

Exhale.

Inhale.

Exhale.

I try to remember the breathing my sister would do. She always knew how to calm the mind. My heart aches now, thinking of my sister. Of my family. My greatest weakness. Yet they hate me. I'm fighting for their lives and they don't even know.

Perhaps that's the irony.

I've gone through all of this for them. And now they want nothing to do with me. I want to prove my true loyalties someday. Maybe they'll take me back.

Or maybe I'm too far gone.

CHAPTER TWENTY-FIVE

Carissa
FRIDAY, AUGUST 15TH, 2025

THE HEART NEVER MAKES SENSE TO ME.

Love exists inside of it. So tender. So unbreakable.

But anger rests there, too. Pain. Grief. Jealousy. Lust. There are so many emotions that come from the heart. People will say trusting the heart is a fatal mistake. Yet we fall in love. We feel all these emotions and we lean into them.

I land a blow on the training dummy.

More complex emotions exist within the heart. How does one hate someone and love them all the same?

I kick the dummy, knocking it a few feet back. Sweat drips down my face, landing on the blue mat beneath my feet.

Another punch.

Another kick.

I lose all form, all technique, and give in to the

emotions, let them control my fists. I close my eyes, tears mixing with sweat. At last, I collapse on the mat, on my knees, head in my hands.

"Rissa?"

Jackson's voice is soft, caring.

My spine stiffens.

"I'm fine."

"You're clearly not."

I don't look at him. Tears won't stop falling from my eyes, the product of every fragile emotion inside my traitorous heart. His footsteps come closer. Shoes on the training mats, breaking my rules. I don't care, though. He can get away with it this time.

He settles next to me, pulling me into his arms. I resist. "I'm disgusting and sweaty."

"You're never disgusting. And besides, you're just sparkling."

I don't force a smile like I usually would. I just let him pull me into his lap. I feel weak like this, yet protected and safe all the same.

"Why... why do I miss my brother?" I ask, my words choked by emotion.

"Because your brother loves you and you love him. I truly think he has moments of missing you, too."

I scoff, rubbing my eyes dry with the backs of my hands. "I highly doubt that. He's not even my brother anymore. I don't recognize the man they show on the TV screens. Whoever that is… it's not my brother. There's no warmth to his eyes and no charisma to his smile. It's just… a stranger in my brother's body."

And maybe that's what hurts.

I'm grieving someone who isn't dead.

Someone who actively has tried to kill us by blowing up our home.

Our childhood home.

Jackson cradles me until I shift to move away from him. I'm calm now, no tears rushing to the surface and no pain constricting my heart.

Jackson leans forward, kissing me softly. He backs up an inch and says, "You should eat something. You missed dinner last night."

"I'm never hungry anymore. There's so much going on. Who has time to eat?"

"You *make* time to eat. I will not have you not taking care of yourself. I know it's hard. Even if it's a small snack, at least it's something."

I sigh, closing my eyes as our foreheads rest together. "I know. I'll eat something at breakfast. I promise."

His hand finds mine and he lifts my fingers to his lips.

Jackson is one of my only comforts these days. He holds me when I'm down. He calms me with just a simple touch, a quick kiss, or by sparring with me so I can take my anger out through my fighting.

The arena is my pride and joy. I train the other resistance members here. I'm in charge of getting them ready for any type of confrontation. Jackson and Nicole help me, but I'm in charge of it. And when no one else is here, I train. I let loose on the training dummy.

But sometimes the comfort is just in being here.

Especially with him.

He stands up from the mat, offering his hand. "Come on, let's go on a starlight walk before anyone else is awake."

I take his hand, letting him pull me up. "Why are you up this early anyway?" I ask.

"I couldn't really sleep and I figured you'd be here anyway. You never sleep anymore."

"How can anyone sleep these days? We live in a time of war. Besides, I need to train as much as possible."

I let him lead me out into the pre-dawn morning. The air is crisp, but not all that chilly. It's August in Texas. This is the coolest it will ever get. Still, the sweat on my back is enough to make me shiver.

I glance up; a few stars are poking through the treetops. We're pretty sheltered here under the big oak trees, hidden from anything above. But sometimes I wish I could just see the sky, the stars and the darkness of the night. I always found them oddly comforting. But I take what I can get now, peeking between the branches of the trees.

Jackson takes my hand and we walk in silence. When my pace begins to slow, Jackson says, "Let's get you to bed."

"I need to shower."

"You need to sleep. You look like you're running on fumes."

"That's because I am."

He shakes his head. "I need you to take care of yourself."

"What's the point? We're all going to die."

"Wow, how positive."

"Thanks. I get it from Spencer."

I can tell I'm starting to annoy him. It always annoys Jackson when I'm being reckless. But I can't help it. Not right now. I'm sleep deprived and I hardly know what I'm saying.

Jackson leads me to the tunnels and down below the ground. We pass the sleeping guard who's supposed to watch for intruders. We don't make a sound.

When we reach my room, Jackson says, "You're going to bed now. You can shower when you wake up again in a few hours."

"No, I need to shower now. I'll take ten minutes."

I don't give him time to respond. I slip into my bathroom and turn the water on. I strip my sweaty clothes off and throw them in the hamper. The water is cold as it passes over me. I let it run through my hair and down over my skin, rinsing every inch of my body. I run shampoo through my hair, then conditioner.

Fifteen minutes later, I walk back into my room. I'm purposely late, wanting that extra five minutes to frustrate the man likely waiting for me. As expected, Jackson sits on the edge of my bed, still here to make sure I sleep.

"Linley could be back at any time from patrol," I tell him, "and if she finds you in here—"

"If she finds me in here, I'll bribe her to keep quiet. We're not up to anything… yet." He waggles his eyebrows as if he's said something charming.

I roll my eyes and collapse onto my bed, despite not wanting to.

I don't remember much. Just Jackson draping the blanket on my head and kissing me softly one more time. Then he's gone and I know I feel empty, but sleep overtakes me before I can register the loneliness.

When I wake again, I wonder if it was all a dream. But it couldn't have been. Linley still isn't in bed, but the night patrol sometimes doesn't come back until dawn.

I glance at the alarm clock on my bedside table. It's just about five a.m. I slide out of bed and grab my usual attire—black athletic tank and jean shorts. I quickly change in the bathroom, staring at my reflection when I'm done. Dark circles have begun to form under my eyes. I consider using light makeup, but decide against it. My time is spent in the training arena. I'll only sweat it off. I sigh tiredly, turning away from the mirror and leaving the bathroom.

Some days are worse than others. I feel the range of emotions, from missing my brother to hating him to a mixture of both. Truly what I miss is our childhood, when war was confined to the storybooks our mother would read to us. When kings and queens were kind and loved their people.

When the world was normal.

I run my hands through my hair as I take a seat in the plush chair. It's shoulder length again, but I've let my natural color grow out rather than keep dyeing it silver like I used to. I miss the silver, but I don't feel like venturing out into the world in hopes of finding a store that still sells hair dye.

Hair dye isn't a commonly found item anymore.

Every store that still stands is regulated to sell just the basic needs: food, clothes, some extras. Everything else has been shut down.

Besides that, our camp is truly far removed from every city and town, from any vestiges of life outside of our own little community. As I begin lacing up my boots, Linley is entering. She looks exhausted. At seventeen, she's one of the youngest to be assigned to a unit. But she's trained since she joined almost two years. My father decided since she'll be eighteen this year, she could join the teams that patrol around the camp. She collapses onto her bed, groaning.

"Long night?" I ask.

She sighs. "We patrol the same paths. There's nothing out there. We're in the middle of nowhere. No one's looking for us."

I cross my arms, leaning my shoulder against the wall. "You'd be surprised who's out there waiting for us to be vulnerable. You're the first line of warning, a defense against what could show up. Trust me. They're looking for us. They just don't know where to look."

Linley sits up, kicking off her standard brown boots. "I know. But it's boring out there. And my commander is so strict. We're not allowed to talk to each other unless we see something."

I smirk. "Talking is dangerous, you know."

She rolls her eyes. "Yeah, yeah, yeah. I'm going to sleep for a while. Are you leaving?"

"Yeah. I have to set up the arena for today's classes." *And maybe get in some practice of my own.*

"Okay. I'll see you at lunch… maybe."

I turn off the lights, grabbing my boots from near the door before slipping outside into the hall. Doors line both sides. The girls' sleeping quarters house a lot of the unmarried women. I lean my back against our door to slip on my own pair of brown standard-issue boots.

I quietly creep down the hallway, knowing most of the

world still sleeps at this hour.

The exhaustion from sleeping only about three hours threatens to overtake me, but I shake it away. Sleep is for people who don't lie awake at night overthinking their every move. It's for those who can afford to ignore all that goes on around them.

I cross the courtyard. There's no light except for that from the lanterns that are scattered around it. They glow dimly during the dark hours of the night and morning, lighting the way for any returning or exiting patrol. Or people like me who don't sleep.

Usually, I find myself alone out here. But to my surprise, I see my cousin at one of the picnic tables near the great oak tree. He's furiously typing away at his computer. I think of going over there to greet him. I haven't seen much of him lately. But his headphones are on and he seems focused. Instead, I cross over to the training arena. My sanctuary. The one place I control entirely. I kick off my boots just outside the door, following my own rule for everyone who enters. I keep the socks on my feet and quietly pad through the front hall to the main room.

The training dummy still lies flat on its back from my breakdown a few hours before. I right it back on its stand before going to shake out the training mats. I put all the weights back up on the racks and wipe off the few seats that are off to the side.

"Wow," a voice says from the entrance behind me.

I startle, quickly pivoting on my heel. Jackson stands there, smiling.

With his shoes off for once.

"I see you finally decided to follow my rules."

"Well, I'm here to get a workout in, so I kind of have to. Why are you awake so early?"

"I could ask the same of you." I tilt my head and smirk.

He shakes his head, a smile creeping onto his face. "Fair enough. I knew you'd be here already."

"I just wanted to clean up a bit, then set up for this morning's classes. I'm heading out. I want to walk around a little bit before I start my own training."

"You hardly need to train. You know everything."

"I don't know everything. And it's good to keep practicing. Besides, this is my only sanity these days."

At least most days. I don't always have a breakdown like I did last night. I feel the heat of embarrassment redden my face as I remember how Jackson found me. If he notices my unease, he shows no sign of it. He just presses a soft, lingering kiss onto my cheek as he passes me.

"Enjoy your walk. It's a rather nice morning. Maybe you can convince your stubborn cousin to sleep."

"I doubt that anyone could do that, but I suppose it's worth a shot."

I exit the arena and slide my boots back on. I stretch my arms above my head as I walk, shaking out the stiff feeling aching inside my muscles. For now, all is quiet. There's no one rushing around the camp. No agents bouncing between buildings. Just the silence of the early morning as the sun begins to rise. The soft dawn light filters through the breaks in the tree branches. I take it in, inhaling the August morning air.

I glance over to where Spencer was a few minutes ago, but he's gone. Maybe he will sleep on his own. Or maybe he didn't want me to lecture him about being up and working already.

I head off through the courtyard, walking and stretching my arms as I do. Alone with my thoughts is a dangerous and beautiful place to be.

CHAPTER TWENTY-SIX

Jackson
FRIDAY, AUGUST 15TH, 2025

SWEAT DRIPS DOWN MY BACK AS I RAISE THE weights above my head one more time. I set them down carefully, not like the gym guys who can't handle a little more lifting and throw them down.

I'm not a gym bro. I'm better than that.

I take a few sips of water, some of it escaping the lip of my bottle and sliding down my chin. I hardly care.

I don't know how long I've been training, but now a few others trickle in, rubbing sleep from their eyes and hoping to get in some of their own training before all the newer recruits come for Carissa's classes.

I clean up after myself—hearing Carissa's voice lecture me in my head is enough to make me actually clean.

When I'm done, I step out of the arena, still chugging water. I slide my boots on and head out into the morning light. A few people are out and about in the courtyard, but I look around for Carissa. When I don't find her, I know she's either back at her room or with her dad going over plans. I head off to my sleeping quarters, where I'm surprised to find Spencer crashed in his bed. I quietly slip into the bathroom so I can shower.

Spencer and Carissa—in fact, *all* of the Williamses—share a rather unhealthy habit of not sleeping when they should. I don't get how they run on fumes.

Last night, I couldn't sleep. But most nights, I have to get my beauty rest. It's when I dream that I have to wake up. Night terrors are my only obstacle when it comes to sleep.

I rinse off quickly, changing into a fresh uniform and spiking my hair with the gel I've snuck into camp.

Only necessities. I can hear Andre lecturing me now. But my hair is a necessity.

Spencer is still asleep when I leave the bathroom, so I let myself soundlessly out of the room. It's not often he gives in to sleep, so I don't want to ruin it. Even though it would be so easy to annoy him.

My stomach begins to growl and I sigh. I suppose it's time for food. Again, I don't find Carissa anywhere in the courtyard or the arena. So I give up and head off to the canteen. It's mostly empty, but that's where I find her and Andre. I saunter over, sliding into the seat next to Carissa.

"How's my darling?" I overexaggerate for

Andre's sake.

Carissa looks like she might murder me. I wouldn't be surprised if she did.

Andre looks like he might find us humorous, but doesn't want to laugh lest Carissa unleash her anger on him. Instead, he clears his throat before sipping his black coffee. "Good morning, Jackson. Seems you slept well."

"Not entirely. Night terrors are fickle things. But I feel fine."

"How do you feel about a recon mission?"

Recon missions aren't all they're cracked up to be. It usually involves checking up on Williams' ranch and all the places we used to take up space. It's about gathering information from the public.

We don't get much information out here. Most of the resistance exists within these walls. Very few still live out there among the regular people. And they do it for information.

"I'm down for it," I say, despite not being all that enthused. I hate recon. There's never anything new happening. The world is falling apart. Everyone either hates Evan or wants to have his children. The general public is full of gossip. But there is one consolation to going on recon and that is wearing normal clothes.

Like my precious leather jacket.

"Good. Carissa, will you accompany him this time? I'll have Nicole take over training today. Spencer's sleeping and Linley was on a late patrol; otherwise, I'd ask one of them to go, too. But I think you could use some getting out of here."

Carissa clearly doesn't agree with her father, judging by the look on her face, but she says, "Yes. I'll go."

I don't blame her for being less than enthused. Even Andre knows it's boring out there. But at least we won't be stuck within these walls.

We eat our meal of oatmeal and fruit. I chug some more water and then follow Carissa out. When we're out of earshot, she sighs.

"He thinks I'm spending too much time in the arena. But that's my safe place. Where else am I supposed to go?"

"I know. It's okay. It will be fun to go out there together. Just like old times."

"Yeah." A flicker of a smile passes over her face.

I break away from her side and say, "I'll meet you in ten minutes in front of the canteen."

She nods and heads off to the girls' quarters.

I quickly change into my civilian clothes, eager to feel the familiar leather jacket on my arms. It's hot out; the jacket is hardly necessary. But any weather is leather jacket weather.

What I love about Carissa is she doesn't take long to get ready. When she reappears, she's got a backpack slung over one shoulder; she's dressed in jean shorts and an oversized tee that's tucked into her waistband. And her sneakers are just plain white. I've dated a few other girls who all took an hour at minimum to look half as beautiful as Carissa does in ten minutes.

Or any time, for that matter.

I take her hand in mine and say, "We could take my bike."

"I'm not getting on your motorcycle, Jackson. Besides, you've been itching to drive your Mustang."

"I have, but I drained the gas out the other day. That car is too obvious, especially if Evan's men are somewhere out there."

"True," she sighs. "What are we driving, then?"

"Probably the Corolla. It's not really attention-grabbing."

"Your leather jacket is attention-grabbing," she says, nudging my ribs playfully.

I feign hurt by clutching my chest with my free hand. "That's rude. I'll have you know this leather is not going to grab any attention. Except for some girls who like bad boys. But don't worry. My girlfriend will give them her evil eye and it will scare them away."

"Very funny. I don't have to give anyone an evil eye. Whenever a girl tries to flirt with you, you run away."

"I'm happily taken."

She rolls her eyes, but smiles.

We head into the garage where Andre keeps all the vehicles. It's large and underground with a ramp that leads up into the open. The design of this base is advanced. A lot of money had to go into it, but the Williamses are very rich. This didn't even put a dent in Andre's pocketbook.

I find the Corolla parked near the back. Next to my prized, all-black Mustang. I run my hand over the hood before walking around the Corolla to open Carissa's door. She smiles.

"How chivalrous."

"I can be charming."

"Oh, really? Since when."

"Ha-ha. Funny. Look who has jokes now."

She smirks as I close the door. I walk around the front, making a dramatic show of sauntering over to the driver's side before getting in. Carissa sighs.

"You entertain me. I think that's why I keep you around."

"Oh, good. For a moment there, I was worried you might actually have feelings for me."

"I hate you," she says, laughing.

It's nice to hear her laugh again. It's not a regular occurrence, especially these days. But when it happens, it warms me from the inside. Especially when I am the cause of her laughter.

I drive up the ramp and out onto the paved path

in the woods. Once we're out on the main road, I take one hand off the wheel and rest it in hers, on her thigh. We drive in a comfortable silence. There's no need to fill the space with useless words when all we need is this.

Us.

Like old times. Driving down the road and not needing anything or anyone else but each other.

"Remember when I asked you out?" I say after a few minutes.

"Yeah. You weren't my type, but something about you was different from the typical f-boy."

"So you *did* think I was interesting at first."

"Maybe a little. But I was fully committed to my job of being a rebel then. And you were my brother's friend."

"I regret corrupting you to come to the dark side. You always deserved better than what we did."

I feel her look up at me. "Jackson… we've come a long way from that. You didn't corrupt me. I love you."

The words still have an effect on my heart. "I love you, too."

Her hand tightens around mine. "I remember the café I took you to for our first date. You kept saying this would never work."

"Yeah. I thought you weren't my type."

"Turns out I'm your soulmate."

She leans her head back, looking out the window as the world passes by. "I don't know that I believe in soulmates.

But if they exist, you're probably mine."

I feel my heart constrict at the sound of those words.

This woman is the love of my life.

WHEN WE PULL UP in front of William's ranch, I tell Carissa, "You don't have to get out."

But before the words are fully out of my mouth, she's already unbuckling her seat belt. "I want to. I need to see it again."

We walk onto the property, Carissa a bit ahead of me. The trees are all still standing, the only reminder that this place once was a front yard.

The house is gone. What remains is the condemned structure, mostly burned down except for a couple of walls that could fall any moment. It's amazing they haven't yet.

Carissa hugs her arms around herself as the breeze shifts, fluttering between us.

"I miss this place sometimes," I say.

"Me too," she says. "We should try to see if we can get beneath it. I know my father wants to get his safe."

"Would it even still be there?"

She nods, walking around towards what used to be the back of the house. "It was indestructible. Even the explosion wouldn't have destroyed it or whatever he's hiding inside."

"How big is the safe, though? The car doesn't have a lot of room."

"I know the codes. We'll empty it and take what's inside."

We've tried coming here before. Not often, since we don't know whether Evan has eyes on the place at all times.

But the first time we came, Carissa nearly collapsed, completely overcome by her grief. The second time we made it out here, there were soldiers crawling all over the place. It was a strange sight.

Third time's the charm, they always say.

Carissa leads the way to the door that once led downstairs.

"Is it safe?" I ask her doubtfully.

"Probably not," she sighs. "But we have to try."

I stop her before she enters. "I'll go first. Wait for my signal."

She doesn't argue, though I see the worry in her eyes. She bites her lip as I reach my hand into the ruined doorway, trying to feel for the ladder that used to hang in the emergency exit. It's not there anymore.

"We'll need a rope," I tell her.

Carissa drops the backpack she brought to the ground.

She digs inside for a rope so I can rappel down. "What will we even tie this to?" she asks.

I look around. Everything is shaky and unreliable. Finally, I find a metal pole lying on the ground. I wander into the half-burned garage, finding a mostly uncharred mallet. I pound the pole into the ground near the entrance. Once it's sturdy enough, we tie the rope around it a few times.

It's not the safest, but it will have to do.

I throw the remaining rope down the hole, and Carissa digs into the backpack again and pulls out a flashlight, which she hands to me. I tuck it into my back pocket and take a deep breath before lowering myself in, easing down the rope slowly. It's not hard, even though the tunnel down is rather narrow. But it's dark. Holding onto the rope with one hand, I reach my other hand around and pull the flashlight out of my back pocket, resting my back against the wall of the tunnel to support myself.

When I'm down all the way, I aim the beam of the light around. The place is destroyed. Some of the roof is caved in; pieces of the foundation are scattered on the floor now.

"Are you safe?" Carissa calls down.

"Yeah," I say. "Let me look around first before you come down here."

It's pitch black, save for my flashlight. I don't trust

it in here.

"Too late," Carissa says, appearing next to me.

I shake my head at her. "I wanted to make sure it's safe so that we don't die down here."

She ignores me and wanders off down the hall somewhere before I can stop her. Suddenly, the whole place lights up. Ahead of me, I can see Carissa smirking. "I was seeing if the emergency lights worked," she calls.

I glance around; the destruction is immense. Dust lingers in the air. It's probably not safe to breathe.

"How is there electricity?" I ask. "The house was condemned. The only thing your father was able to do was convincing the local government to not tear it the rest of the way down."

Carissa shrugs. "Backup generator. My father has every backup plan you could possibly imagine. I figured it would still work, since it was untouched by the fire."

I slowly make my way over to her, picking my way through the rubble on the floor. "Let's hurry up. This place could fall on us at any moment."

She nods once. "You're right. The safe should be over…"

She trails off when she realizes it's hard to know where anything is now that it's all destroyed. But we don't have to look too long. The safe stands firmly in the center of what was likely Andre's office.

Carissa climbs over the dirt and chunks of concrete to

get to it. I follow suit. She squats in front of it, inputting a code and twisting the handle. It opens easily.

I'm expecting something big or important, but all that exists inside this indestructible safe is an envelope and a stack of cash.

"That's it?" I ask, mildly disappointed.

"I guess so…" She sounds as puzzled as I feel. "I'm… not really sure why my father keeps talking about his safe if this is all that's in there."

She grabs the envelope and the cash and rises, not bothering to close the safe now that it's empty. We head back towards the rope. Carissa climbs first, and I follow close behind. When we're at the top, she tucks the envelope and cash into her backpack.

"Let's head back and say we did recon," she says. "We know there's nothing new to see or hear in Cyrus anyway."

I pull the rope up and close the covering to the hole. "Yeah, but first we could go get some food. I'd pay."

Carissa turns to look at me. "Jackson, are you asking me on a date?"

"That depends… Are you accepting my offer?"

I can see the hesitation in her eyes. We've found something important to Andre and we should take it back to him immediately. But going back feels like a wasted opportunity. It's not often that we're free from the confines of the camp. Of course, being in the camp gives us all far more freedom than people on the outside are given, thanks to the government. But it's not the same as being out here, outside the walls, out of routine.

"Okay," she says finally. "Let's get some lunch. Then we can go home."

CHAPTER TWENTY-SEVEN

Evan
FRIDAY, AUGUST 15TH, 2025

PATROL AFTER PATROL, CITY AFTER TOWN AFTER city… No matter where it is, the report is the same. It's emptier than usual. It's less busy. Businesses closed down. Homes boarded up. People not around for the headcount, even in the night hours when they should be safely in their homes after curfew.

"Oh, Father, you are a clever one."

I've taken up talking to myself when I'm bored or tired. I've heard it's part of the descent into madness, but I'm too self-aware for that.

I shuffle through the patrol reports, passing the time of my flight from DC to Texas. I don't need more evidence than this.

The plane begins its landing. I buckle into my seat, packing away the papers in my duffel bag. I don't plan for this to be a long trip. I have other business to attend to back in DC.

I go through the talk I have planned in my head. Not only will I send Peter out into the woods, but Raegan will be out there, too. Somewhere, she's fighting for the resistance from wherever my father has them hidden. And when they find each other out there, they'll team up, hoping to save the resistance before it's too late.

But instead… they'll lead me right to where I need to go.

A car takes me to the base, where I'm met by generals and officers whose names I don't bother to remember. The benefit of being at the Texas base is that General Kahn is not here.

"I need a private room to meet with one of the soldiers," I tell the closest officer.

He nods at me once and leads the way. "Who are you meeting with today?"

"Peter Daniels."

He tells me that Peter's team has not yet returned from their overnight patrol, but should be arriving any moment now. Once he leaves to fetch him, I pace the office. Getting Peter to listen will be a struggle. But the true problem will be leverage. He'll never agree to look for the resistance. And threatening Raegan will be empty and useless since she's with everyone else. I don't know her location, so there's no way he'd feel motivated to move by anything I say.

I need to give him something he wants.

I need to make it seem like he's in control of the situation.

Just as I hear the alarms go off throughout the camp, signaling the return of the patrol and the waking of the soldiers still on base, it hits me.

Peter is brought before me by two other officers, who salute me and then exit the room.

He stands at attention, though he doesn't bother to hide his hatred.

"Do you know why I'm here?" I ask calmly.

"Because you love to torture me with your presence?"

"You should watch what you say. I could have you arrested for hating me."

"I'd probably enjoy prison more than being your soldier."

Touché.

"I am here because you have a new mission."

His shoulders relax slightly. I smile inwardly; this should be easy, simple, and perfect.

"What is it?" he asks.

"We think we've pinpointed where Andre has run to. We want you to find them out in the woods. Then you'll report back to me on their location."

Peter's fists clench. "You realize I've worked for you and obeyed you for this long because you promised they'd be protected. Why the hell would I do this when it completely destroys everything I've done?"

"I'm offering you your freedom, Daniels. You're going to desert your post and go out into those woods. I won't know anything until you report back to me."

He doesn't seem convinced. "That sounds too good to be true."

I shake my head. "It isn't. You'll tell me where they are, and then you can let them take you back in and fight for their cause again."

"But it will be pointless. You'll know where they are."

I sigh. "I need to know where they are so I can get the president off their tail. I have fought for so long on the wrong side of this war to *protect* my family. The president is getting too close to this one area, and I need to make sure everyone there is safe from his plans. Do you understand me?"

Peter goes silent, his eyes wide. "You've... been protecting them this whole time?"

"Yes." The lie slides out easily.

I wanted to protect them. I really did. But now this war has to be won by playing dirty. I have enemies on all sides. If I want to take down the emperor and finally end this whole thing, I have to make sacrifices.

"I don't believe you," he says finally. "I don't believe you want to protect them. Not after everything you've done."

"I know it's hard to believe, but why do you think I let

Carissa go? Why do you think I've prevented any attacks on them when we *did* know where they were at? I need to know, Peter. I can't let my family die because of me."

The clock on the wall is the only noise in the room.

Tick.

Tock.

Tick.

Tock.

"Okay. But I tell you on my terms."

"Of course," I say. Another lie. "Pack your things. Get ready. You desert tonight. I'm going to help you. And you'll tell no one of this. Not even my parents. It's better they not know anything yet."

I know he thinks he's tricking me. Peter isn't stupid. He'd never agree to this. But I'm offering him his freedom. Something he thinks he can take advantage of.

Just as he turns to leave, I say, "Here. You'll need this burner phone to get in contact with me."

He takes the simple phone from my hand, slipping it into his pocket.

He'll likely destroy the phone and anything else that comes from me. I fully expect that. But what he doesn't know is that there's a tracker inside his body that I can see at any time and know where he is. Like every soldier that has been drafted or voluntarily joined, he had the tracker implanted on his first day. None of the soldiers has any idea it's there; the device is tiny, hidden in what we tell them is an immunity booster shot. They're not given a choice on getting the shot. But it attaches to the inside of their arm and stays in place until it's deactivated.

I smile as I watch him go.

Phase one is complete.

CHAPTER TWENTY-EIGHT

Peter

FRIDAY, AUGUST 15TH, 2025

"*DO YOU UNDERSTAND THE PLAN?*"

I roll my eyes, throwing my canteen into my pack. "Yes. We've been over it a hundred times."

Evan crosses his arms and looks out beyond the door. "You only have one shot. If you get caught, I can't save you. And I can't save everyone else, either."

He's laying it on thick. I don't trust his words about protecting the resistance. Not when he has so openly worked to destroy them.

But I don't say any of this. Instead, I nod once. "I understand." There's a lot of weight going into this.

The night air is oddly chilly as I conceal myself among the shadows. The gate is open, just like Evan promised. I don't know how he managed to leave it open without anyone noticing, but I don't have time to question it. All I have is about five minutes during the guard change, and I need to focus on staying out of their line of sight.

I watch, waiting for the shift change. With my back against the wall that surrounds the base, I can see the gate moving gently in the subtle breeze. Somehow, as the guard comes down the ladder of the watch tower, he sees nothing. The new guard is approaching just as the one leaving sets his feet on the ground. They begin talking, the old guard telling the new one what's been going on for the night. From the few snatches of conversation I can hear, it isn't much.

I'll only have seconds to slip out when the new guard climbs the ladder. Once he's up there, he's going to see the gate isn't shut. Most likely, he'll think the night patrol left it open by accident. Then by morning, when they realize I'm gone, I'll be far enough away in the woods that they'll have no hope of catching up with me. I'll need to hide if they come looking for me, but Evan promised they wouldn't. I don't know that I believe him on that count. Just like *he* shouldn't believe that I'll actually contact him if I find the resistance.

I'm hoping the resistance will take me back and hide me, despite what I've done. Abandoning them almost two years ago has probably caused a lot of hard feelings among them. But if I'm given the chance to explain everything, I know they'll believe me. They're my family.

I watch the old guard disappear and the new guard climb up the ladder. This is my chance. The only moment I have. I quickly race through the shadows and slip out the gate, my backpack rubbing against my back as I run through the streets. I'm not too far away when I hear the gate slam shut.

It's done.

I'm out.

I pull a regular compass out of my pocket, letting it guide me. North of here is the woods where I found Raegan. So that's where I'll go.

THE NIGHT IS DARK and I don't like wandering alone like this so late. But I can't stop now. I'm not far enough away yet. Just in case the officers do a surprise bunk inspection and see me missing before the morning comes, I have to be long gone.

My feet drag on the soft earth, the pack on my back getting heavier with every step. Finally, I take a small break to drink water and collect myself. My heart is racing and every step feels like it could be my last.

I've never thought this would be possible.

That I could be this close to freedom, yet so far. The woods surround me, providing enough protection that I can afford to take a break. It was harder when I was out in the open, wandering through the city while dodging patrols. I didn't see any night patrol in the area I was at. I'm sure Evan had something to do with that as well. But I can't rely on his plan alone to make it to where I need to be.

Spending nearly two years working as a government soldier has made me more cautious and careful. I don't trust anything or anyone.

Something behind me makes a noise. I look all around, finding nothing out in the open. I decide it's time to keep moving. I'm not far enough away to stop for sleep. My mind races with thoughts of what could be out there. Something wild. Or perhaps someone in charge of dragging me back.

How can I trust this wasn't some test Evan was giving me to see if I'd really run away? For all I know, he has already assigned someone to hunt me down and drag me back to the camp, where I'll be executed. Maybe this was all a stupid idea.

I keep plowing ahead; the path gets rougher and darker as the night goes on. I finally stop again, needing water and a plan.

A branch snaps somewhere to my left. I quickly pivot, shining my flashlight in the direction of the sound. Someone is there.

I see the shadowy outline of someone standing just out of range of the light.

"Who's out there?" I say confidently. "I'm armed."

"Calm down. No need to get your panties in a twist, Daniels."

The figure comes out into the light, a pack on his back.

Jennings.

"Jennings? How did you…?"

"Escape? Well, I saw you throwing all your stuff together and figured you were getting out of hell. I decided to follow you. Heard you were on some mission or something."

"Jennings, you shouldn't be here. I don't want to see you get caught."

He laughs as if this is the best joke he's ever heard. "I won't get caught. Thanks for caring, though. But I'm done with that place. Rumor has it the resistance is somewhere south of here. I'm assuming that's where you're heading, too."

"Yeah," is all I say. I don't know if I should tell him about the deal. What if this is all part of Evan's plan to test me?

But what if Evan isn't testing me at all?

Jennings marches ahead of me and says, "Well, let's get moving. We'll have to get up over this hill if we plan to find any decent shelter around here."

I follow his lead, not daring to question how he knows where we should be going. We walk in silence;

the only sound is the wind around us and our packs swishing against our backs.

I don't know what time it is or what's going on, but suddenly Jennings stops and says, "This is good. We can camp here."

"Are we far enough away for that?" I ask, hesitant. "I don't want to be caught. I feel like we haven't been walking for that long."

He shrugs off his pack, setting it on the ground. "Whether we're far enough or not, they won't know to look for us until morning. Besides, we'll only be getting a few hours of sleep before we continue on again. We won't be here long."

He has a point. My feet are throbbing and I'm beginning to feel the ache of exhaustion in my bones. I let my pack slide off my back, taking a few sips of water from my canteen.

The weight of the burner phone is heavy in my pocket. I could destroy it now, get it over with. Especially if Evan is using it to track me. But getting rid of it now would be too suspicious. I need to hang onto it a bit longer so he doesn't see it sitting still and figure out what I've done.

I leave it in my pocket for now. I can't let anything look suspicious, especially now that Jennings is also with me. It's not just my life at stake anymore.

Jennings falls asleep fast, but I don't. The ground is hard beneath me and my backpack doesn't make a good pillow for my head. Besides that, my mind is spinning; anxiety makes my heart thunder in my ears. My muscles are rigid with fear, no matter how much I try to breathe deeply and force myself to relax. I listen to the sounds of owls hooting in the trees and crickets chirping in the foliage nearby. My eyes begin to fall closed, but it feels like I've only slept for five minutes when Jennings is shaking me awake, telling me we have to keep moving.

I groan; my head is pounding from exhaustion. I rub my temples and rise to my feet. The sun has yet to come up, but the sky has begun to lighten ever so slightly. In less than an hour, they'll know we're missing.

I shoulder my pack and we're off again, trekking through the wild. A light layer of fog hangs above the ground as we walk. When the sun begins to rise, the air grows steadily hotter and hotter, gradually burning the fog away.

Jennings stops for a moment, taking a long gulp from his canteen. "We need to refill. There should be a river running through these woods somewhere. I remember hearing about it. I have a filter in my bag."

"You came prepared," I say, following his lead.

"You didn't? I'm surprised. How long did you expect to be out here?"

I shrug, though the movement is awkward and

clunky. "I don't know. I didn't really… have time to think about it."

"My grandfather was a survivalist," he says, stomping down some brush with his feet as he walks. "He taught me that even if you're only planning on a day, expect the unexpected. Always come prepared for whatever nature might throw at you."

"I didn't think too much about it. I… was told what to do." The words are out before I can really stop myself. But if I'm going to be out here in the wild with Jennings, I have to know if I can trust him.

He pauses, turning back to face me. "What do you mean you were told what to do?"

I rub the back of my neck. "Evan Williams told me to desert my post."

I explain everything to him now—from my past, to Evan's blackmail to keep me in check, right up to when I deserted. When I finish, Jennings is silent. Finally, he says, "We need to get rid of the burner phone, but not in a suspicious way. He might be using it to track you. When we find the river, we should bury it near there. The ground will be moist and easier to dig."

"Good idea," I say. "But what do you make of the strange orders?"

"I don't trust a word that comes from Evan's mouth. Whatever bullshit he's telling you is to make you listen to him. He's offering you an idea of freedom, but for what gain? If he wanted to protect his family, he wouldn't have done any of the things he has as heir to the country. He's up to something bigger than this. It's up to you whether you trust him or not."

I shake my head. "He made everyone believe my girlfriend was dead. He tortured her, and he has always had it out for me. I don't trust him. But I don't know what to tell the resistance when we find them. *If* we find them out here. For all I know, this is how he's sent me to my death."

Jennings smirks. "Well, I'm a survivalist, just like my granddad, so we're not dying anytime soon. But we do need to find that river. Water is most important. If we have water, we can survive for days."

He closes his eyes and goes quiet. I wait, unsure of what he's doing. Then he motions towards the trees. "Do you hear that?"

I look over, seeing nothing. "Are the trees talking to you?"

He smacks the back of my head. "No. There's water. That way."

I let Jennings lead since I'm already in over my head. The closer we get to whatever he heard, the more I start to hear the rush of a river. Moments later, we step out onto the bank.

The water is rushing rapidly downstream, white foam coming up onto the shore. Jennings drops his pack on the dry ground and digs out a filter and two extra canteens.

I clearly came unprepared.

Jennings goes to his knees on the riverbank, using the filter to fill both his canteens, then hands me the filter so I can do the same with my own.

We set off again and walk mostly in silence. There are no signs of anyone trying to find us yet. Maybe they won't come at all. But that's probably wishful thinking.

As night begins to fall all too quickly, Jennings stops in a small clearing. "This should be good for the night."

He begins digging through his pack and takes out two packages of dried meat. He hands one to me. I don't argue with him, taking it gratefully. It's some form of sustenance that I didn't know I needed. My stomach growls loudly.

Jennings rips open his own bag and says, "Usually, I'd hunt some rabbit or something and cook that up. But starting a fire right now is asking for attention. We'll have to eat our supply of dried foods first. Hopefully, we'll find the resistance soon. They're probably our only hope for survival after we run out of supplies."

I nod solemnly. All we have is hope.

Hope that Andre will let me back in, and, subsequently, let Jennings in, too.

Hope that we can even find them out here.

That this isn't a wild goose chase in the middle of nowhere.

As I chew my dried meat, I hold onto that hope as if my life depends on it. Because it does.

CHAPTER TWENTY-NINE

Raegan
SUNDAY, AUGUST 17TH, 2025

MY BOOTS CRUNCH LEAVES BENEATH MY FEET AS I walk through the woods. Close range patrol is rather boring. Nothing ever comes through these woods. Not even random drifters looking for spare change in the dirt. It might seem surprising that such a thing happens, but desperation leads to strange behavior.

I'm far enough away to be out of sight of the others, but still well within earshot. I'm not worried, though. Not tonight. The only sounds in the forest are the crickets chirping and cicadas singing their lovely tune.

I lean my back against one of the tall, established oak trees. I hear a snap as, nearby, a branch is broken underfoot. I jump slightly, startled and alert. Probably one of my teammates. I see no sign of them near me, though. I glance around and see movement: two shapes are coming towards me. I duck behind a tree to observe.

"We're almost out of food," says a male voice. "I can hunt, but I don't know if a fire is a good idea still. We're far from the base, but close to civilization. They could report the fire."

Survivalists, maybe? I've seen a few here and there. Not this close to camp, but perhaps they're passing through.

They keep talking, but I'm hardly paying attention to the words. One of the voices is familiar.

I move closer, keeping low, staying hidden in the shrubbery and ducking behind trees. One of the guys is tall, with buzzed hair. He looks intimidating, even from here. No smile lights his face or even his eyes.

But the man I heard talking before… I need to know if it's Peter.

There's no way it could be. Escaping the military camps is impossible. They'd have to be on a mission. Yet they look like they're trying to survive. They don't wear the uniforms of soldiers. The only things that appear remotely military are their packs and their boots.

I study the blond one. Even from behind, it looks like Peter. Everything in my body and my soul screams at me that it's Peter. But my brain is cautious, uncertain.

I know it has to be him. And his voice as he talks to the other man with him is warm and comforting. My pulse picks up speed. I inch closer, trying to get a better luck.

It has to be him.

It *can't* be him.

Then he turns around, looking out into the forest.

Something inside me cracks and suddenly I'm running out from behind the tree, racing toward him.

Peter's eyes widen as I leap into his arms.

"Raegan?" he breathes out, stumbling back slightly.

Hot tears pour down my face. Peter pulls me closer, his own tears mixing with mine as he drops his bag to the ground.

The man with him clears his throat. "You must be the girlfriend."

I turn my head and step reluctantly out of Peter's embrace. "I am. And you are?"

"Seth Jennings. Everyone calls me Jennings. I prefer it that way."

I wipe at my face with my hands. "It's nice to meet you."

Jennings smiles. "Can you take us to the resistance?"

I look to Peter. He's grabbing his pack from the ground. "We've deserted."

"Deserted?" I repeat. "How? That's… impossible."

Jennings opens his mouth to speak, but Peter quickly says, "It wasn't easy. But the important part is we're out now."

I stare at the two of them, from Peter to Jennings and back to Peter again, uncertain. Something about this doesn't sit right with me. I take a couple of steps back. "I

can't bring you to the base. At least, not right now…
Andre won't be easy to convince. I'll have to meet with
him first and hope that he'll be willing to try." I see
Peter's face fall. "But stay in this area, okay?" Peter
nods. "I'll work on making something happen."

Jennings nods now, too. "Fair enough."

I give Peter a quick hug and then retreat quickly
so that I can return before I'm missed. I'm hoping that
Andre will hear me out this time and let them come in.
Even if they have to be watched closely, it's better than
them trying to make it out there on their own.

But something about Peter's unwillingness to tell
me how they got out strikes me as odd.

He's probably tired from the long journey, I tell
myself.

I'm silent as I move through the woods, careful to
keep watch behind me. But Jennings and Peter don't
follow me. Part of me wishes I could bring them with
me. The other part of me is relieved they're staying in
the clearing. There's a tug between the connection
Peter and I have, drawing me close, making me wish I
wasn't walking away from him right now. But I can't
ignore the unsettling feeling that's sinking into my gut,
either.

I'm back at the tunnels before the rest of the patrol.
I don't know how I'm supposed to bring this up to
Andre. He's not going to like it.

Spencer startles when I drop down. "Dear lord, I thought you were going to be gone at least another hour."

"Something came up. Where's your uncle?"

"I don't know. Probably in his office. What happened?"

Telling Spencer seems like a bad idea. He might find his uncle first and tell him everything before I have time to make a case. Still, I can't lie to him. "Peter and another soldier are near the camp. They don't know where we are exactly, but they deserted from the base in Cyrus and have made their way here."

Spencer stares at me for a moment in disbelief, then slides off his stool and sighs. "You can never go out there and have a normal night, can you?"

"You're telling me."

"What are you going to tell my uncle?"

I cross my arms. The tunnel suddenly feels cold. "I don't know. I know he's not going to like it no matter what I say. But we can't leave them out there."

Spencer starts through the tunnels and I follow behind him. He runs a hand through his messy brown hair as he turns back to me. "Why not? If they deserted, they can clearly survive for a while on their own. What do they need us for?"

"This is Peter we're talking about," I say. "Why wouldn't we let him back?"

"He could be a traitor. A spy. The whole thing seems suspicious."

I can't help but agree with that, given Peter's strange behavior.

Spencer and I search for Andre, finally finding him in the mess hall with a mug of tea and a mountain of paperwork. The man never sleeps.

"Andre," I say, approaching his table. "I need to talk to you."

He looks up from his papers, his eyes red from exhaustion. "What's up?"

I inhale, gathering all the strength I have left inside of me. "I ran into Peter. In the woods. He says he's deserted, and he's with someone. I didn't make any promises, but I thought maybe you'd want to reconsider…" I trail off.

Andre's face is a mixture of emotions: anger, curiosity, pain. He is silent for a few moments, thinking. Finally, he rubs his face with his hands and sighs. "All right. I will send a team to retrieve them. But they will not be brought here to be rebels. They'll be prisoners until we can interrogate them thoroughly."

Somehow, this is a relief to me. "Fair enough. Can I go with the team?"

I can tell he's about to say no, but Spencer says, "It might help them come calmly if Raegan's there."

Andre pinches the bridge of his nose. "Fine. Now go before I change my mind."

I'm ecstatic but I do my best to keep the excitement at bay. "Thank you, sir."

Spencer and I exit the mess hall hastily. Once we're out of earshot, he says, "You know we have to get Carissa and Jackson to come with us, right?"

"Why?"

"Well, Carissa is kind of in charge of all patrols in and out of the camp. I mean it's kind of her job."

I roll my eyes. "I know that. But Carissa usually sides with her father when it comes to the topic of Peter. And since there's another soldier with him, I know it looks... suspicious."

He shrugs. "She still has to be told, or we'll have hell to pay in the morning."

I sigh. "Fine. Send Linley to get her."

I stand in the center of the courtyard, counting every breath and waiting for the rest of the patrol to return to the camp. They still have no idea what's about to happen. My heart beats erratically in my chest, anxiety creeping in.

I've fought so long for Peter's return that the idea of him being here should be as exciting as I've imagined for the past couple of years. But the doubts in my mind are getting in the way of any hope or happiness. I sit on the edge of the fountain in the middle of the courtyard. The water splashes up and mists on my arms, but I don't care. The night is warm, humid, and it's soothing on my skin.

Spencer returns as the rest of the night patrol files in.

"Linley's been sent to wake Carissa. And I already got Jackson up, too."

Mira, one of the girls on night patrol approaches. "Raegan, why did you leave patrol? What happened?"

"I came across... people. I came to get Andre. We're bringing them back in, but first we're waiting for Carissa and Jackson."

A few people murmur among the patrol, but I can hardly hear them over my pulse in my ears. Spencer places a steadying hand on my shoulder. Concern etches his face.

"Are you okay?"

"I... I don't know."

Okay doesn't describe the mix of emotions coursing through me. And I don't have the energy to build up some sort of lie about being tired. Because I'm not tired. I'm anxious. Energy rushes through every inch of my body. The quiet of the camp only amplifies my own doubts and fears.

What if Andre is right about Peter? What if I've been wrong this whole time?

My thoughts are interrupted by Andre approaching. Spencer turns to face him. "Uncle Andre? What are you doing?"

"I've decided I need to be here for this. I assume you're waiting for Carissa and Jackson?"

We both nod once. Andre turns to the rest of the

patrol and says, "You're all dismissed. I think we've got this incident handled. I'm sure you're all tired."

No one argues with this. The rest of the night patrol disperses towards tunnels. Once it's just the three of us, Andre says, "I've realized that this needs to be a private matter. We don't need a lot of gossip among the rest of the soldiers. I want to know Peter's true intentions."

I want to argue that they're good. But I find I'm unable to speak up. Fear controls my heart. I'm at a loss as to what to do or what to believe anymore.

IT'S NOT EVEN DAWN WHEN LINLEY SHAKES ME awake.

"Whazzgoinon," I say, my words running together.

"The night patrol just returned, and Raegan came in before them saying there are people camping nearby. And since you're in charge of the patrol teams, they want you to come check it out."

"They're perfectly capable," I grumble, sitting up in bed and rubbing my face with my hands.

"Yeah, but it's kind of in your job description."

I rise from the bed, fumbling through my drawers for a pair of shorts and a black athletic tee. My usual attire. I slip into the bathroom, where I change quickly. I reemerge to find Linley sitting patiently on the edge of her bed. I soundlessly cross the room to sit on the small chair we have, lacing up my boots. I pull my short hair into a ponytail behind my neck.

Grabbing my pistol, I shove it in my back pocket. I don't want to deal with putting on my vest and all my gear when it's probably just some homeless people hiding out in the woods or random citizens trying to get away from the government. It happens more often than one would think.

But of course, the night patrol freaks out every time. And I lose precious sleep.

Linley leads me out of the tunnels and up the ladder to the courtyard of our camp. My father, Jackson, and Spencer are already waiting.

"Dad, why are you awake?" I ask.

"I was already awake, catching up on some paperwork. But I decided I needed to take part in this one."

A disconcerting feeling settles into my gut. Jackson takes my hand as my dad leads us to the garage.

"What do you know about this?" I ask him softly, so that my dad won't overhear.

"From what Spencer told me... Peter is the one out there, and he's with another soldier. They're saying they deserted a couple of days ago. But what strikes me as odd is Raegan's lack of excitement. I haven't been able to ask her what's up. But I can tell she's not feeling particularly happy about this."

Despite my own personal feelings about Peter, knowing Raegan's uncertain is even more troublesome.

We load up in the truck— Jackson behind the wheel, me in the passenger seat, and Spencer, Raegan, and my father in the back—and head off in the direction Raegan tells Jackson to go. We don't have to go far. Jackson shuts off the truck when we get closer, letting it coast slowly.

I squint into the darkness and see something move in the underbrush at our approach. Whoever's out there is alert to what's going on. Two men, from the looks of their shadows. They don't move far, though. Seems they're unafraid.

I hop out of the truck first, with Jackson following suit. The pistol in the back of my pants feels heavier. I won't have to use it tonight. No matter how I feel about Peter, I refuse to shoot him unprovoked.

The others climb out of the truck behind us. Raegan doesn't rush up to them like I assumed she would. Instead, she stays back with Spencer.

I take a mental note, filing that away for now. Turning to the two runaway soldiers, I say, "State your business."

Peter smiles. "Carissa! I can't believe you're here."

"That doesn't answer what I just said."

Ignoring me, Peter says, "And Jackson. And Spencer. I can't believe you're all here."

I look to Jackson. He smirks. "Well, it makes sense you'd miss me, Daniels. I am the light of your life."

I roll my eyes. "All right, then. I guess we're not going to do this the *right* way. Peter, what are you doing here?"

"We escaped from the base near Cyrus. We've been looking for the resistance after hearing rumors of it being located in these woods. And I have information that I'm willing to give you about the government."

Information could be helpful. I glance back at my dad, who seems intrigued despite probably not wanting to be.

"Wait, wait, wait. Jackson Maverick?" the other soldier asks.

Jackson points his flashlight at the guy at Peter's side, who's smiling like he's won some prize. Jackson smirks. "Seth Jennings, is that really you right now?"

The other guy approaches us, hands clearly visible, and then claps Jackson on the shoulder. "Maverick! I never thought I'd have to see your ugly face again."

"I see you're still jealous."

"No way. A face like that is too high-maintenance. And you still use all that hair gel."

"At least I have hair."

I step forward, quickly breaking this up. "Okay, enough of that. We have serious matters to attend to."

"Peter Daniels, you do understand that your actions have made you highly suspicious." Dad says, coming forward. "You won't be brought in as a rebel or a lost member of the resistance. We have to bring you in, both of you, as prisoners until we know your intentions."

Peter's hurt is visible as he opens his mouth to speak. "I understand you can't trust me. I know I cut ties and that I may have jumped the gun, but… I did it to protect everyone. And I know you aren't blind to that, Andre. There seems to be something else that's causing your anger against me. What else did I do wrong?"

My father stares him down. "Don't play dumb with me," he says coldly. "You know *exactly* what happened. Why do you think we're in these woods now?"

Peter hangs his head. "I… I know the timing was… horrible. I know I've always said coincidences aren't real. But I promise you, I didn't know of Evan's plans to destroy everything like that. I didn't know it had even happened until later. He used the information to make me obey his orders, do everything he wanted me to do. Raegan…" He begins stepping towards her. "You believe me, right?"

Raegan doesn't move or meet his eyes. "I want to believe you're telling the truth."

"What do you mean, you *want* to believe?" Peter asks, visibly hurt.

I cross my arms defensively as I study his face. "The day you cut all contact and ties with us, our home was set on fire. The original headquarters was destroyed. And we were left stranded. That doesn't leave a lot of room for trust, Peter."

He doesn't say another word. Instead, he says, "If you don't want to take us in, I understand."

Seth Jennings shakes his head. "Speak for yourself, Daniels. I'm not dying at the hands of the bastards in that hellhole, or out here in nature. Mr. Williams, sir, I'll come as a prisoner. I don't care. I'll answer any questions you have. And I hope that, in return… you can help me track down my sister?"

My father's eyes light up with recognition. "I remember Peter asking me about that before… before the incident. Prove yourself trustworthy and honest, and maybe I can help you with that. For now," he looks from Jennings to Peter, "coming back with us as prisoners is your choice. You can come… or you can stay out here."

Jennings smiles gratefully. "Thank you, sir."

All eyes fall on Peter, who doesn't look up at anyone. "I'm coming with you," he says at last. But he still looks wounded. I don't think he's hurt by our distrust. He's hurt by Raegan's. I glance back at her. She looks nearly ready to cry.

Dad says, "Let's get loaded up. First things first: we need to make it look like no one was ever here. Spencer?"

Spencer nods once and walks over to the small campsite Peter and Jennings set up, helping them load up their gear and remove any traces of their presence. When they're finished, Raegan climbs back in the truck, closing the door without a word.

Spencer throws Jennings' and Peter's bags in the bed of the truck and says, "You two can ride back here. There isn't enough room in the cab. I'll ride back here with you for security reasons."

Both men wordlessly climb into the bed of the truck. Jackson walks around it, checking to make sure everyone is secure.

"Still wearing your goth jacket, I see," Jennings says.

"This is imported leather. It's hardly goth. It's emo."

Dad grumbles under his breath, pinching the bridge of his nose before getting in the truck.

Jackson and Jennings exchange a few more words before Jackson finally gets behind the wheel again. The five-minute ride back to camp is silent, almost unnerving. I can feel my father's tension, but Raegan's is stronger. And her reluctance to even look at Peter has me questioning what she knows.

Once we're in the garage, I hop out of the truck immediately. Peter and Jennings hop out of the back with Spencer's permission. Spencer hands them their bags as Dad and Raegan get out of the truck.

Peter's companion saunters over to me and sticks out his hand. "I don't think I've properly introduced myself. I'm Seth, but everyone calls me Jennings. But you can call me anytime."

I eye his hand for two seconds, my left eye twitching. Jackson rounds the front of the truck and smacks Jennings in the back of the head before wrapping his arm around my waist a little more possessively than he usually would.

Normally, I'd lecture him for that, but I've never seen him get jealous. It's quite an interesting sight.

"Jennings, I see you've met *my* girlfriend, Carissa. My love, this is Jennings. We used to hang out back when I was on the wrong side of the tracks. Before you redeemed me."

"Laying it on a little thick, aren't you?" I mumble so only he can hear, rolling my eyes but almost smiling. *Almost.*

Jackson smirks before saying, "Well, darling, you should go get some sleep."

"Not so fast," Dad says. "One of the buildings above ground can be used to keep Peter and Seth for tonight. Tomorrow, we'll sort out the sleeping situations. We'll do interrogations with the full council present and figure out what we need to do."

The full council is the panel of rebel leaders my father gathered together when all the rebellions united as one.

They're rough, stone-cold to get through, and hardly agreeable at any time.

Peter and Seth exchange a look. I can tell the latter of the two is less than thrilled to be treated like a prisoner. Peter smiles, though it's pained. "That sounds fair, sir.

Thank you for giving us this chance."

Raegan has yet to look in his direction, or even talk to him. We all make the journey above ground. Dad unlocks the door and motions for the guys to walk in. Peter says, "Can I have a minute with Raegan? Alone?"

Raegan shakes her head before my father can say anything. "I'm really tired. Maybe we can talk tomorrow?"

The heartbreak is written on Peter's face, but the suspicion grows in my mind. Raegan would never avoid him like this… not without good reason. It seems I may have one other person to interrogate.

My dad clears his throat. "You'll have plenty of time to talk while you're here. I won't restrict you two from seeing each other or even speaking in private. But the night is late and Raegan has been on night patrol for a few months now."

Peter nods and enters the small cabin, not looking back. Raegan leaves, heading towards the tunnels to the sleeping quarters. Jennings winks at me as he walks by, but it seems forced, as if he's trying to remain calm by acting as if he feels in control of the situation.

My dad controls the pieces of the game. No one else does. The sooner Jennings realizes that, the better.

Once they're locked in, my dad gives me a brief hug. "Go get some sleep, okay? Don't be like your old man."

I don't smile. I feel incapable of smiling when the weight of the world suddenly feels heavy on my shoulders. But for once, I listen to him. I hug him quickly back and then head off.

"Hey," Raegan says as I drop down into the tunnels.

I gasp, clutching my chest. "I thought you already went to bed."

"I was going to… but then I remembered… The cabins don't have electricity running to them. There's no air conditioning."

"Yeah. What about it?"

"So will they get some way to keep cool tonight? Or will they be stuck in a hot cabin, locked up like prisoners because Andre doesn't trust them?"

My face burns and I bristle at her angry words, which are clearly directed towards me. "I don't know. I don't make the choices. My father does. Peter and Jennings can't be trusted. Not yet. Peter goes missing for almost two years. He cut all ties to us, and then Evan set fire to our home like the careless dictator he's become. And Jennings is a stranger." I pause and look directly into her eyes. "Besides that, it doesn't seem like *you* trust Peter much. You'd never turn down a chance to talk to him, and you've barely looked at him since we got them back here."

Tears well in her eyes and then spill over. "Because… because I know he's hiding something."

She speaks so softly that I almost wonder if I've heard

anything at all. But then she adds, "I tried talking to him when I saw them in the woods. I asked them how they got away from the base. I'm not a fool. I know deserting is nearly impossible, just as infiltrating any of the bases is impossible. Their escape should've ended in death. No one succeeds. So, I wanted to know how they got out. Jennings was about to say something to me, but then Peter interrupted and gave me some excuse about luck. He lied to my face, and I know it." She looks at me miserably. "But telling you that will only make you more suspicious of him. I don't want him to face more trouble. I want to trust him. I want him to be…"

"You want him to be the same as he was two years ago," I say calmly.

She's sobbing now, sliding down to the floor of the tunnel. "Yes. Of course, I want him to be the same. We were apart for six years when he moved to California. Nothing changed then. So how does two years make such a difference? He couldn't hide his involvement with the resistance before. But now he can lie to my face about his escape from the military base?"

She pushes her face into her knees, her sobs shaking her body. I kneel down, resting my hand on her shoulder. "Don't give up believing the best in him."

Raegan looks up at me, wiping her eyes with her

hand. "You don't trust him. Why are you telling me to?"

"I'm not telling you to trust him. I'm saying you have put a lot of hope in his heart. You love him. So don't give up on him. Whatever he's hiding from you, it won't be for long. I saw the way he looked at you… like you're the only girl on earth. I may doubt him. It's my job to be suspicious. It's yours to not be. Just… breathe. You can be cautious. But don't give up on him, because at the end of the day, the love between you is strong."

She sniffles, rising from the ground with my help. "You're right," she exhales. "You're right. I'm sorry I lost it."

"It's okay. You needed to. Go get some sleep. Tomorrow, we'll have more answers and then maybe all of this will make more sense."

Raegan sighs. "I hope so."

Then she's gone, down the tunnels towards the sleeping quarters. I turn and head back above ground. No one lingers now; everyone has long since retired to bed, even those that tend to stay up late to finish their work. My father likely returned to his office and will fall asleep at his desk.

Spencer and Jackson probably returned to their room.

I march towards the cabin Peter and Jennings are in. I knock on the door before unlocking it. Neither of them is in bed. Jennings is leaning against the back wall. Peter sits at the end of his bed, head in his hands as his elbows rest on his knees. He looks up as I enter their room.

Raegan is right. It's already hot in here.

"Carissa?" Peter asks. "Is everything okay?"

"Yes. It's just uncomfortable in here. I thought I should tell you to open the windows to get some air flow. But don't tell anyone I came by."

Jennings leans back to stretch, his hands behind his head. "Couldn't get enough of me, could you?"

I roll my eyes. "I'm happily taken by Jackson. You'd do well not to flirt with me. He won't hurt you. But I will."

I leave him with that threat hanging in the air. Peter knows what I'm capable of. He'll relay that to Jennings.

I'm not really bothered by the mindless flirting. I don't care for this man much at all, but his words are nothing to me. I love Jackson so fully that it scares me how comfortable I am with him.

How myself I am with him.

I often wonder if this is safe. If I should be this open, this free, this *happy* when I'm with him. When the world is falling apart or when everything feels wrong, is it okay for this to feel right?

I shake my head and march to the tunnels. I want to sleep for what few hours are left in the night. I want the morning to come so I can interrogate our guests. I want to move, to feel my fist connect with the punching dummy. I want my emotions to be zapped from my body so I can go back to rational thinking.

I want.

I want.

I want.

Am I so selfish? Is it all about me?

I make it to my room, where Linley now lies asleep. I kick off my boots and climb into bed, the pistol still burning against my back. I pull it from my pocket and put the safety on, then throw it in the drawer of my bedside table and shut it.

Rolling over, I close my eyes, shutting the world out. Quieting the voices in my head telling me lies.

I can be rational.

I can be clear.

When the morning light comes, I'll be fair to Peter and Jennings. I'll smack the latter if he keeps flirting. Or maybe Jackson will do that for me.

I'll figure out whether Peter is telling the truth.

But for now… I'll rest.

Raegan

I LIE ON TOP OF MY COVERS, LOOKING UP AT THE ceiling. Nicole's soft breathing is the only sound in the room. My face is still wet with tears, but they've finally stopped falling from my eyes. The cool air blowing on me feels wrong. Peter and Jennings are probably burning up in the hot cabin while I get to lie here with air conditioning and running water.

Peter's hurt expression haunts my mind. I should've talked to him for the minute he asked for. Now I wonder what he had to say to me. I shiver against the cold, but I don't move to go under my covers. Not yet. The cold soothes me still; I welcome it like an old friend.

I want to believe in his innocence. I know Peter is good. And Jennings doesn't seem like much of a threat. But there's still an ache inside of me. I know Peter is hiding something. I feel the secrets forming a wall between us. A wall I don't know how to tear down.

How can six years mean nothing, but two mean everything?

Something inside of me is scared of the secrets. Not because of the damage they're causing, but of what weight they hold. Peter's never been able to lie to me before, so whatever this is, it's big. And that's terrifying.

I shut my eyes, trying to block out the thoughts that circle my mind. I just want to sleep, if only for a few hours. I get my wish, because what seems like just moments later, I'm waking up to Carissa calling for me from the doorway of my room. Nicole's bed is made, meaning she's long gone.

Carissa leans in the doorway and says, "The interrogation is happening in ten minutes. I thought you might want to be there. To support him."

I run a hand through my unruly brown hair. "Yeah, I do. But…"

"I'm going to be fair and balanced. I thought about what you said last night—er, a few hours ago. And you're right: I have let my father influence a lot of my opinions. This business isn't easy. But I'm willing to let them talk. I want to hear their side of the story."

Carissa leaves as I hop out of bed. I quickly throw on a t-shirt and shorts, pulling my hair back into a braid and slipping on my boots. I'm out the door in seven minutes, rushing through the halls for the final three. I make it to the interrogation room just in time. Andre glances up at me, but doesn't have time to say anything as the four other resistance leaders who make up our council file in.

First is Ryker, a tall man with a bald head and dark facial hair. His dark eyes match the tone of his skin, and he's always on high alert. He'll be the hardest one to convince.

Then there's Callahan, the very opposite of Ryker. His blond hair is long enough to be pulled into a ponytail at the base of his neck. Though he's taller than me, he's not that tall compared to Ryker. And where Ryker is dark and brooding, Callahan has a fair complexion and is friendlier.

Zaire, the youngest on the council at only thirty-two, is often the quietest of the men. His bronze skin often seems to shine gold in the sun and his green eyes never miss anything. But he hardly speaks, so when he does, we know it's important and well thought out.

And finally, there's Radcliffe. Many of us joke that he must be a vampire. The man is pale, always taking shelter from the sun. Always dressed in black. His hair is dark and his eyes a paler blue than mine. He's tall, lanky, and is not seen often outside of council meetings. No one really knows what he does or where he goes when meetings aren't in session.

Despite their differences, the council often works

well together. But all are tough to impress. And if Peter and Jennings can't convince them of their innocence, I don't know what will happen.

Spencer brings Peter in first. He looks over at me, still wearing a hurt expression on his face. Hurt that I caused. My heart aches, but I can't reach out or say anything now. Not with a room full of Andre's council and everyone we know watching.

Peter's mom and my parents sit close to the window. Spencer comes back out into the small lobby with the rest of us, taking a seat by me near the back. The only person missing is Linley, but she was sent to her next mission yesterday.

Peter's taken into the next room, separated from us only by a one-way window. We can see in, but they can't see out. Carissa enters the room with Jackson.

The door separating us closes. I count every beat of my pulse as it throbs in my ear. My palms become sweaty and I try to hope that this will all be figured out soon enough. That the council will be as open-minded as Carissa seems willing to be.

Carissa clears her throat, pacing in front of Peter. He's seated behind the small, rectangular table in the room. He keeps his hands clasped on top of it, his head down. He's avoiding eye contact, which seems unlike him. But there's exhaustion written on his features.

"Tell me how you escaped the base," Carissa begins.

"It's well known that this should be impossible. So how did two soldiers do it without getting caught?"

Peter shrugs, finally looking up to meet Carissa's eyes. "The guard change at night is a five-minute gap of time in which the north gates go unguarded. It's also common for the night patrol to forget to lock the gates when they leave at night. It's a crapshoot, but we made the shot and somehow got out."

Carissa's hands come to rest on the back of the empty chair in front of her. Jackson stands near the door, presumably to protect Carissa in case Peter were to attack. Though I doubt that's the issue we'll have today.

Carissa says, "Okay. And how did you end up in the exact woods that we're located in? And don't say you got lucky."

"I don't believe in luck," Peter says, and sighs. "The government knows more than I wish it did. They've long suspected the rebellion was hiding in these woods. And we were told that the patrols we were put on were for the census. But it wasn't just that... We were told to make note of anyone who seemed to be missing. And I didn't realize it at first, but that told us—then—who the resistance had removed from society."

I look towards the council members, trying to gauge their reactions. Everyone seems surprised.

"And what exactly do you know about the day you cut off contact?"

Peter's head lowers slightly. "I didn't know Evan's plans. Not right away. My cutting off contact was unrelated to what he did. I know it looks bad. But if I had known what was happening, I would've figured out a way to warn everyone here. I didn't find out until I had already destroyed my burner phone and Evan had already acted. He used it to hold over my head that he could destroy everyone I love with a snap of his fingers. He made sure I knew he was in control of the situation at all times to keep me obedient."

Peter looks spent, beaten down and weary.

But suddenly my heart feels as light as air. It's clear to me now that he wasn't trying to hide anything from me. At least, nothing he hasn't aired out here right now. I misjudged him.

Carissa turns towards Jackson. "I think we've heard everything from him. Bring Jennings and take Peter back to the cabin."

Jackson leads Peter out through the lobby. This time, Peter doesn't look towards me. Instead, his eyes stay down. I'll talk to him after all of this. I want to chase after him now, but I need to hear what Jennings has to say. I need to know his story is the same.

Not five minutes later, Jennings is brought in and the interrogation begins in much the same way. Though unlike

Peter, who looked both calm and weary, Jennings seems bored. He fidgets with a smooth rubber ball that he's brought in with him. I'm not entirely sure where he got it, but it clearly wasn't deemed a threat when he was searched for weapons.

"So, Seth Jennings," Carissa begins. "Tell me how you escaped the base. It's well known that it should be impossible."

"Simple. Guard change leaves a five-minute gap where the north gates aren't watched. Night patrol for that night left the gates unlocked, because they're lazy asses who forget. We slipped out easily. It was definitely a risk, but we made it out."

The stories match.

And I can tell from the looks on the council members' faces that they're taking note of that.

Carissa asks Jennings questions similar to those she asked Peter, to which she gets answers pretty similar to what Peter said before. Once all is said and done, Jennings is taken out of the room, and the council departs to meet at Andre's office and decide what the right course of action will be.

I walk back to the cabin with Spencer. He opens the door and we see Peter waiting, sitting on the end of his bed. Moments later, Jennings walks in and collapses on the other bed. Peter sees me and stands up.

"Can we talk?" I ask softly, almost afraid.

"Yeah," he says, glancing over at Spencer, silently asking permission.

Spencer nods his head towards me. Peter steps forward, but Spencer stops him at the door, glances between us and says, "You have five minutes."

The morning air is still fresh, but the sun is already burning high. I lead Peter just out of earshot of Spencer, under a shady tree. Peter leans against the trunk, crossing his arms and not making eye contact. "What did you want to talk about?" he murmurs.

"Us. Everything."

"Five minutes isn't a lot of time for everything."

A mourning dove begins to sing in the branches above our heads. I glance up, blinking away the tears already threatening to spill over. "I messed up," I say. "I let doubt take over and I pushed you away. When you didn't seem to want to answer my question last night… I thought it seemed strange. This morning, you talked to Carissa and told her everything. And Jennings gave the same story. I just wanted to say… I'm sorry."

Sweat pricks at the back of my neck. Peter looks at me—really looks this time. "I'm sorry, too," he says. But there's something hidden in his tone. A deeper meaning. When I look into his eyes, I know he's holding back.

But I can't push him away this time.

"It's been two years," I say. "We've fallen out of place

a bit. We can find it again."

"Yeah," he says, relenting a bit. "We'll find us."

Neither of us says a word for a long moment. Finally, Spencer calls over to us, pointing at the watch on his wrist.

Time's up.

Peter leaves without another word and walks back to the cabin. I had hoped that talking to him would give me a sense of peace. Instead, I'm left even more unsettled. He didn't try to talk things out. Not really. Almost like he didn't want to. I shake my head, knowing that all this overthinking is what led us over here in the first place. I need to get a grip.

But what am I supposed to hold on to?

BY AFTERNOON, THE COUNCIL has decided we have no evidence that either Peter or Jennings is lying. Their belongings have been searched again, more thoroughly this time. They've been questioned a few times now. There's nothing to indicate anything other than sheer luck and determination to escape the government led them here.

Nothing except the gnawing feeling in my gut that tells me something else is up.

As night begins to fall, the busyness of the camp starts to dwindle down. Night patrol is coming. Though I've barely gotten any sleep today, I'll be sent out tonight.

I pull on my shorts, my navy-colored athletic top, my vest, and my boots. When I walk through the tunnels, I find Andre leading Peter and Jennings towards the boys' living quarters. Despite the tension between us, there's no denying the pull we have, like magnets attracting one another. Peter stops only for a moment, reaching out his hand to me.

I intertwine my fingers with his in this dim tunnel, and he pulls me into a hug. Andre has continued on down the tunnels with Jennings. Peter looks down at me and says softly, "I'm staying awake until you get back. I want to see you. I was cold earlier."

"I deserved it."

"No. You wanted to talk and I should've talked. Everything is…"

"Crazy?" I offer.

He smiles. "Yeah. But I want to see you when you get back."

"Okay," I say, unable to keep my smile away.

He lets me go, and my heart is lighter now. I make my way through the tunnels and above ground to meet up with the rest of my team.

Maybe there is hope for us after all.

CHAPTER THIRTY-TWO

Evan

TUESDAY, AUGUST 19TH, 2025

THREE DAYS.

For three days, I have waited. Watching the unmoving dot as it blinks back at me on my hologram screen. The burner phone has not moved. But Peter has.

I suspected as much. Good thing it was never my plan to wait for a message from him; I know now—have always known—that it will never come.

He's a fool to believe the burner phone is the only thing being tracked.

His blip moves around, though not much. I figure I'll watch it for a few days, then I will fly back out to Texas to find his coordinates. If the blip doesn't move much at all, then that must be where the resistance is.

It's almost too easy.

Getting a call that another soldier deserted on the same night did not help matters. Whether Peter grabbed an accomplice or not makes no real difference to me. I can see both of their dots on my holographic map. Seth Jennings presumably has his own motives. For now, I don't really care. He's not a pawn in the game I'm playing.

I push away from my desk, my chair rolling back ever so slightly, and get to my feet. I know I shouldn't, yet I find myself entering the secret passage anyway, all conviction to stay away vanishing the moment the bookcase seals me inside.

My footfalls echo off the stone walls of the passage. After I leave to hunt down the resistance, I don't know when I'll be back—assuming I make it back. I want to make one final plea to Sam, or maybe to myself, to convince my heart not to love her anymore. I tell myself I don't need her, that she was always destined to betray me. But I know it's a lie because every time someone refers to her as my prisoner, or says her name, my heart kickstarts again like it's found a new reason to beat.

It's stupid of me to think she'd ever love me.

She said as much from the beginning.

Yet I let her fool me. But now I need answers. I need to hear the harsh words from her lips. For her to say she never loves me. A final goodbye in the list of ones I've made by choosing this life.

I shudder against the chill. It's always cold here. My hand rests on the door. I contemplate turning back. She never says anything to me besides what I already know.

Why would today be different?

Still, I push the door open and I enter the shadows of the prison.

She looks up immediately when I stop outside her cell. I didn't bother to be quiet this time. This is the last time I'll try to figure any of this out. There isn't time for pleasantries.

"What brings you back to the dark side?" she asks, almost taunting me.

"Tell me why you did it. You never gave me the truth. And I want to know why you went through the charade of playing with my heart if your plan was to betray me in the first place."

"Why do you care so much?"

"Things are about to change. This is the last chance I'll have to learn anything from you. And I want to hear you say you wanted me to suffer. I want to know that everything I believed you to be was a lie."

She looks directly at me now, sitting cross-legged on her cot. Her hair is pulled back, her face bare of any makeup. The light is dim but it reflects in her hazel eyes. She studies me for a moment, searching for any indication that this is a trap. When she finds none, she sighs.

"I did it because I don't trust anyone. I have to watch out for myself. The emperor killed my first love and he killed my family in his rise to power. I don't plan on making the same mistakes. I betrayed you because I knew you'd talk your way out of it. But getting involved with me is a death sentence. I needed you to leave. I needed you to break our ties."

"That's a steaming heap of—"

"I know," she says roughly, rising from her bed. "I wouldn't believe it, either. You made me feel something, Evan Williams. That kiss wasn't a lie. I was frightened of myself because, just for a moment, I could actually see myself married to you. Maybe that's crazy. We hadn't known each other that long. But you made me feel safe. Unfortunately, you're also collateral damage. I have to fight for my freedom. I can't be kept here any longer."

"So you betray me and my heart for your idea of freedom?" I laugh, but I'm not amused. "How'd that work out for you?"

She looks up, clearly hurt by my words. "Obviously you've lost whatever sympathy you had for me, so let's stop playing these games. You've kept me alive in here. I know the emperor would've killed me by now."

"And I'm leaving, which means he could very well kill you while I'm gone. So, speak now or forever hold your peace."

She looks at me coldly for a moment. "I don't love you, Evan Williams. I loved the safety you brought when you held me in your arms. I loved the idea of fixing you. But I've been in here long enough to know I can't fix you.

You've lost yourself in the mind games the emperor has played. Wherever you're going, get out before you're entirely lost. Otherwise, he's already won the war."

I don't begin to know what that means, but there's no time to ask her to explain. I can hear the guards approaching now, their footsteps scuffing against the stone floor. I leave without another word or sound. Whatever mind games she's trying to play on me won't work.

I don't believe she did it for me or for herself. She doesn't know a thing about me, either. She was a dream, an idea I had, but not real. I arrive back at my office, sealing the bookcase behind me one final time. I won't go see her again. I won't have time when all is said and done. She's on her own.

And so am I.

CONVINCING THE EMPEROR TO let me return to Texas to investigate how two soldiers escaped the base wasn't hard. He was enthusiastic that I was showing such dedication in looking into matters like these.

If only he knew the truth.

I visit the base as promised, making a show of looking concerned and determined to find the two missing soldiers. The generals seem pleased by my efforts.

"I'll need a small group of ten soldiers to accompany me into the woods," I tell them.

One of them, a General Caxton, says, "Only ten? If you're looking for the hornet's nest, you have to expect them to sting."

I laugh, feigning amusement. "I know. But I don't plan to strike. I'm looking for the two soldiers, and I plan to catch them before they find the rebels. If I'm lucky, I'll learn the location of the base. Then we can kill two birds with one stone—literally. But for now, this is simply recon."

"Of course, Your Highness. But should you even be out there in the line of fire with them? We can trust the best men here to do the job."

"I trust your soldiers, general. This is personal."

The concept of personal revenge is something they understand in this place. Ten soldiers are called to the gates. I pretend to inspect the area, though I know perfectly well how Peter and Jennings would've escaped. I set up everything myself.

Once I've made a show of checking the gates, we leave and drive through the streets of Cyrus. The soldiers in my vehicle remain quiet, likely too fearful to speak around me. I know I'm not well liked among the army personnel, but I simply don't care enough.

We arrive at the edge of the woods and we all step out of our vehicles. I pull out my hologram map. The two dots blink a few miles north of here. But the tracker on the burner phone blinks not far from where we enter the forest.

"Your Highness, what are we looking for?" one of the men asks me uneasily.

"Evidence that they were here."

I start off towards the river on my map. The soldiers follow, though I think they're surprised that they aren't leading the way. Most of them likely don't know my past. I'm stronger than I look. I could fight any of them. I'm a soldier. At least I used to be. But not for their cause.

I used to fight for something good.

We walk for a while before we come to a river, where I notice something. I kneel down on the soft earth at its edge and find the phone buried in a shallow grave. It's not damaged, but it's close enough to the water that it might have been washed away if the river ever flooded. I suppose that's exactly what Peter hoped would happen.

I put the phone in my backpack, though it's useless to me now.

"We have a few miles to go," I say to the soldiers, taking the lead. We set off again. The miles seem to go on forever. But soon, I see it. Hidden in plain sight. A large base, walls surrounding every side.

Many of the soldiers gasp when they see it.

Something so organized, so massive—and yet so elusive. They've probably spent a lot of time trying to find this place. The base has been under our nose the whole time.

I laugh, despite myself. My father thinks he knows best, but this is by far his worst plan.

I turn to the lead soldier, Jose, and say, "Let's head back to the base. We're not taking action yet. I have to report to the emperor what I've found."

It's a lie, of course. I already know what I'm planning to do. But we can't do it yet. Not without the weapons we need.

I'm going to put an end to this war. I'm going to stop my family from continuing to put themselves at risk. And hopefully, without their interference, I can finally end the emperor's reign, his stranglehold on the country, and take over.

I've never craved power, but now that the corruption is so deep, I don't trust anyone but myself to fix everything that's broken about the system. Everything about the government needs to be rebuilt from the ground up. Once it's fixed, perhaps America can return to the freedom of democracy and elections.

That system used to be broken, too. Which is why it was easy to mess up and get someone like the emperor in power. But it doesn't matter. I can fix the broken things about this country. I can save it and redeem myself. I'll show my parents that I'm not the failure they think I am. I didn't do this to hurt them.

I don't care what steps I have to take to protect them from getting hurt. I'll do whatever I have to.

When we arrive back at camp, I pull the soldiers aside and say, "Do not speak a word to anyone about what we saw today. I know you are the ones who helped me find the base, and that's something you will be rewarded for in due time. But I was told to tell the emperor about this first, before we tell the generals and officers."

They all dutifully speak their agreement and then part ways with me, leaving me alone in the base.

I find my driver and my guard, and we set off back to my hotel. Once I'm settled in there, I'll put together everything I've learned and begin to plan the end of the resistance. The soldiers will help me.

And then this war will be over.

CHAPTER THIRTY-THREE

Jackson

"WHAT HAVE THEY GIVEN US TO TRUST?" RYKER directs the question to Andre, his Russian accent growing thick with his anger.

The council is all together, plus me, Carissa, and Spencer. Andre pinches the bridge of his nose. "They've given us nothing to doubt. Their stories add up. We agreed that they could roam free. I don't understand what reservations you have now."

"I always had reservations, Andre. No one listens to me. The rest of you voted against keeping them prisoners."

Carissa shoots up her seat, hands on her hips. "Yes, because we can't keep people locked up when there is no evidence against them. We're fighting for that right. How do we justify ourselves by going against what we fight for? You want the old America back. This camp is supposed to embody old America, isn't it?"

Callahan nods once. "Indeed, we are. But perhaps

Ryker would care to explain his sudden reservations about letting them be?"

Ryker turns away from the rest of us. "What does it matter? You have made your decision."

"Ryker." Andre rises from his seat, leaning slightly over his desk. "Your opinion is valid. I'm listening to you."

Ryker makes no move to look at Andre, but he says, "I know that other soldier. I know his sister. I don't trust either one of them farther than I can throw them."

Zaire clears his throat. "Ryker, you could probably throw them pretty far. You're quite large and…built."

Ryker shakes his head. "It's an expression. Seth Jennings is bad news."

"They'll be watched closely, Ryker," Andre says assuringly.

Ryker says nothing. He gets abruptly to his feet, strides to the door, pushes it open and walks out into the rain. Carissa shakes her head.

"He's getting more and more unruly, Dad. Every time a decision is made, he makes it a battle."

"He's part of the council."

"He's causing everyone to fight constantly. We have to be a unified team."

Radcliffe rises from his seat. He's so quiet, I almost

forgot he was here. Like Ryker, he doesn't speak a word and simply leaves. Clearly, he's not a vampire, like everyone suspects. The rain would make him melt.

Or maybe that's witches.

Zaire and Callahan leave, too, recognizing that Carissa and Andre's conversation is a private one. Spencer glances at me, seeming uncomfortable with the sudden tension in the room. I motion to the door. He nods. We both stand up and are carefully walking to the door when Carissa says, "Oh no, you don't. Both of you need to help me out here."

"So close," Spencer mutters.

"I know." I sigh.

Spencer turns on his heel. "There's nothing to talk about. Ryker has gotten antsy lately. There's been no real action happening. He's always one for action."

"I'm doing the best I can," Andre says. "Ryker is a man of impulse and war. I've always tried to avoid war. But I know it's on the horizon. We can't just pretend like we're ready to march into battle. I'm not blindly trusting two soldiers who simply appeared out of nowhere, even if their stories match. I'm watching them closely."

"It's not about that," Carissa grumbles. "It's the disrespect. It's the way we're not all a unified team. Every time Ryker is opposed to something, he runs to the people from his own resistance and gets them on his side. How much longer can we tolerate that?"

"Rissa," I start. "We can't—"

"Can't what?" She turns on me.

"We can't just cut Ryker or his team out," Andre finishes. "They're an asset. Physically, they're the strongest team that joined with us. They've brought a lot of fighting techniques that we've added to our own training. Ryker is suspicious of two boy soldiers who claim to have escaped the base. You were skeptical, too."

"I'm still skeptical," Carissa relents. "I don't trust them yet. But this kind of discourse will only tear the resistance apart. We don't need it."

"I know. I'll take care of it."

Andre walks over to his office door and opens it. The meeting is over, whether Carissa wants it to be or not.

Outside, the air is surprisingly comfortable. A gentle breeze blows through the camp. Spencer walks on my left side, Carissa on my right.

"That went well," Spencer says. "Next time, maybe we can start a civil war and then the soldiers won't have to work hard to take us out."

Carissa rolls her eyes. "Don't you have work to do?"

"As a matter of fact, I do. I'm always working. You know that."

"I'm going to go check on our new recruits," I say, excusing myself. Really, I want to get away from

Spencer and Carissa before their fight turns into a heated battle. I don't want any part of it.

I don't find Jennings in the room. But Peter sits at the edge of his bed, his elbows resting on his knees. He looks up as I walk by.

"I'm surprised," I say. "I thought you'd be with Raegan."

"She's on a mission or something. I don't really know. My mom is busy with work. And my soon-to-be step-sister has basically claimed my dog as her own. Everyone is too busy to see me," he says dejectedly.

"Ah."

"What do you want?"

I shrug, leaning my shoulder against the doorframe. "Nothing really. I thought I'd check up on you. See how you were adjusting to life here."

"They don't trust me," he says, shaking his head. "None of them do. I stay down here because when I walk around, everyone looks at me like I shouldn't be here. I'm starting to wonder if I should've…"

"Should've what?"

"Even looked for this place," he finishes, running his hands over his face. "Everything has changed. And I know it's been two years. But… I guess I expected…"

"You expected to come back and have everything be how you left it."

He sighs. "Yeah. Everyone's changed. And this camp

is something else."

I push off from the doorframe, but I don't enter the room. "It's hard to lose all that time being away from everything you've ever known. I get that, Peter. But if you want to prove your good intentions to everyone, you don't do it by sulking in your room. You do it by working your ass off and proving it to them."

I leave him with my words, nothing else. I need to find Carissa and check on her after everything that just happened. I'm sure she's in the training arena, punching the training dummy and getting angrier with every hit.

I FIND CARISSA EXACTLY where I expect to. She's kicking at the punching dummy and as I watch, she knocks it to the ground and then jumps on it, landing blows to its face. She doesn't acknowledge my presence. She doesn't need to.

She rises, leaving the training dummy lying beaten on the ground. Carissa wipes the sweat from her face with the back of her arm.

"Rough day?" I ask.

She doesn't look at me as she grabs her water

bottle, gulping some down. She wipes her mouth and says, "You could say that again."

"The training dummy probably deserved it."

"Perhaps."

"You want to talk about it?"

She shakes her head, her eyes finally meeting mine. I sigh. "I talked to Peter."

"About what?"

"He's been hiding out. I figured he needed a little pep talk."

Carissa laughs. I tilt my head. "What?"

"You gave Peter a pep talk?"

"I can be very peppy, thank you very much."

She laughs again, and I smile. Because if I can cause her worries to fall away for only a moment, that means everything. The glow returns to her eyes. And for a moment, there is no war looming in the distance. There's no rebellion built up around us, fighting for power.

It's me and Carissa.

And maybe, if we're lucky, when the war is over… that's how it will be.

CHAPTER THIRTY-FOUR

Peter
WEDNESDAY, AUGUST 20TH, 2025

JACKSON'S WORDS ECHO IN MY HEAD, A MANTRA of sorts, driving my feet forward, one after the other, and moving me through the tunnels. I belong here. I used to be someone everyone trusted and cared about. I can't let that fall away because of choices I made. I'll prove myself.

I'm clutching a note I found on my pillow when I woke up. I don't know how it got there, but I know who it's from.

I find Raegan in the first place I look.

Among the trees.

"Someday, when all of this is over, we're going back to our spot in Bent Ridge," I say.

"You think all of this will be over?" She sighs, leaning against the tree.

"I hope so. What did you want to talk to me about?"

At first, she's hesitant, but then she says, "I know

you're hiding the truth about your escape. I saw the look on your face when Jennings nearly said what happened. I always know when you're hiding something. I know you, Peter Daniels. Don't hide from me."

The truth.

It's a scary thing. If she knew how I really escaped, how I begged Jennings to lie with me at interrogation in exchange for covering his ass if we got caught, she'd lose all trust in me.

I don't know why I didn't tell her from the start. Maybe because it seemed like our escape was too easy, that Evan wouldn't really have let all of this happen. I know that the first time I met Raegan in the woods was no coincidence.

He planned this. Somehow, he knew every one of our moves in advance.

And if she knows that Evan had a part to play in getting me out of the base, then she'll know that something isn't right. Evan is up to something sinister.

"I'm not hiding anything. I'm sorry if I seem off. I'm still... trying to adjust. It's been a hard couple of years."

"Don't give me that. I know you. Please... You've always told me everything. We never keep secrets," she says, her words growing softer and more pained.

I hate that I'm lying right to her face. But the truth will only get her in trouble. She'll keep my secrets if I ask. I don't want the burden on her shoulders. I did this once and almost lost her.

I won't do it again.

"If you won't tell me… then I don't want to talk to you until you can tell me the truth."

Raegan marches past me. I follow. "No. Please listen to me. I'm not hiding anything."

"Lying more won't help you. You can come to me when you're ready to tell me the truth."

I hear the tears in her voice, the way they clutch her throat and make her words come out choked. I take her arm and turn her gently towards me. I wipe the tears from her face with my fingers.

"Raegan, I love you. I don't want to lose you again. Please… trust me."

"How can I trust you when you're hiding things behind my back?" Her tears are steady now as the sobs shake her body.

I kiss her lips, instinctively comforting her. I expect her to shove me back, to yell at me like she seemed to want to moments before. But her arms wind around my neck, pulling me closer.

The tears fall, and I realize I'm crying as well, my cheek against hers. The built-up emotion of two years' worth of distance and pain, mingling now between us.

When she pulls away, I feel the warmth leave me. Everything is cold. She wipes her tears with her hand and says, "I can't trust you, Peter. I love you. I'm dying from the idea of stepping away from you. But if you can't tell me what's going on, I can't pretend like it isn't there."

"I'm not asking you to pretend."

"You're not even denying things now. Which only confirms you were lying before."

"I was." I sigh, not meeting her sky-blue eyes. "I did lie. And I'm sorry. I hate lying to you. You know that. I want to protect you. And I know if I tell you the truth right now, it will be a lot to take in. I only ever want to keep you safe."

She bites her flushed lip, her cheeks red from crying and from kissing me. I can tell there's a moment where she wants to give in, but she shakes her head. "I've been fighting to protect myself for a while now. I'm happy you want to be my knight in shining armor. But what are we without trust? Find me when you're ready to tell me."

With that, she walks off.

This time I let her go.

I let her leave me there among the trees. I feel the wetness of her tears mixed with my own still on my face. I wipe at them with my hand, trying to erase any trace of this moment.

My heart sinks further and further into my stomach over the course of the day as I realize she means it. She doesn't talk to me at lunch. She won't meet my eyes when we're in the training arena. She hardly looks at me when we pass one another in corridors or on the grounds of the camp.

Even Nicole seems to ignore me now, though I take that slightly less hard. Jackson and Spencer don't ask questions whenever they're with me, but I know they've heard something.

Raegan's version of the story.

The only version that can safely be told. I can't defend myself or my actions without telling them. And giving them the answers to their silent questions would be tragic.

I try to go about my day as if I'm not weighed down, but it's nearly impossible. Between Raegan ignoring me and everyone else looking at me like I'm some kind of traitor, I'm starting to crack again. Jackson's words were inspiring. But I can only handle so much. When I return to my room for the night, I find Jennings already lounging on his bed, reading a book.

"I didn't take you for the reading type."

"It's pretty boring around here when they don't want you to participate in anything. They don't trust me enough."

"Yeah, well, that makes two of us."

He closes the book, tossing it aside. "I heard what happened. Have you considered telling her the truth?"

I shake my head. "I lost her once when I chose not to keep secrets from her. I'm not making that mistake again."

"Haven't you heard the rumors? Soldiers have

been spotted closer to the camp now. You know he's hunting you down like prey."

"What?"

Jennings sighs. "I suppose I'm the only one around here who likes to eavesdrop. It's all I can do. No one talks to me."

I've been so focused on my own problems I didn't think to see if Jennings was faring better than me. "I'm sorry," I say. "I should've seen how this was going for you."

"I'm not worried. They can think what they want. This place is a thousand times better than the base. No annoying bunkmates. I do have one annoying roommate who's broody and angsty all the time, but I can handle him."

I chuckle. "Fair enough." Then I grow serious again. "I'm tired of people who used to treat me like family treating me like some kind of... kind of..."

"Trash?"

I nod.

"Yeah," he says. "It's part of the job. Anyway, your girlfriend is mad at you. You should tell her the truth."

"I can't."

"Why?"

"You said it yourself. Soldiers are closing in. The less she knows, the better."

"The less she knows, the more she pulls away from you."

Every beat of my heart seems to throb against my chest.

"I know. But if her hating me is what it takes to protect her, then I'll do it. I'm willing to throw myself to the wolves to keep her safe. And I will do exactly that. But I'm not letting Evan get to her again."

Jennings rises from his bed, stretching his arms above his head. "Our lives are at stake. You don't know what will happen when war breaks loose. How do you want this to end?"

"The war?"

"No. Your relationship."

"I…" He's right. And he knows it.

"So talk to her," he says. "Don't let time slip away. You don't want to lose her again, but you will if you let things go on like this. Fight for her by showing her you trust her enough with the truth. She'll hold your secrets. I'm sure of it."

I don't like how right he is about that. Or how wrong I feel. But I relent. "Okay. I'll talk to her in the morning. It's late now and I'm sure she's asleep or out on patrol."

Jennings pats my shoulder. "Good. I'm gonna shower."

"Didn't you shower this morning?"

"Yes, but it's been a long time since I've had a private shower and I'm not going to let such luxury pass me by without using it as much as I possibly can."

I shake my head, but say nothing else. My mind is on Raegan. Tomorrow, I'll tell her the truth. And everything will be okay.

CHAPTER THIRTY-FIVE

Raegan
THURSDAY, AUGUST 21ST, 2025

FOR ALL OF YESTERDAY, I MANAGED TO AVOID saying anything to Peter. I've not let my eyes meet his when he's looking at me, but to say I haven't searched for him in the crowds would be a lie. I've looked. I've wanted to run back.

But trust is important and if I can't have that, I don't know if I have anything.

I sit in my room during my free hour. Usually, I walk around, but I don't want to run into him out there. Not now. Not when I'm too weak to resist.

"You look like you're falling apart," Nicole says as she enters, shrugging off her utility vest.

"I am. I miss him. What am I doing wrong?"

"You're not doing anything wrong."

"Then why does it feel wrong?" I throw myself backwards onto my bed with a groan.

Nicole sighs. "Sometimes the right thing is the

hardest thing to do. You just have to stay firm. If you can't trust him to tell you the truth, then you should be careful. I'm surprised he hasn't cracked already."

I sit up again, looking at her. "What do you think he's hiding?"

She shrugs, taking a seat on the edge of her bed. "Who knows? Peter has never struck me as a guy to keep secrets—especially from you."

He never was that kind of guy. But maybe two years away in a place that isn't safe changed that. Maybe I am being too harsh.

Yet… I can't bring myself to reach out. Not yet. The wounds on my heart are growing deeper and I don't see how to fix any of this.

Peter has my heart, no matter what is between us. This is only a moment in time. I have to remind myself that.

When I wander out for dinner, I feel the soft touch of his hand on my arm. I inhale sharply, then turn.

"Sorry," he says, looking entirely ashamed. "I didn't mean to scare you."

"It's okay," I say, because it is.

"Can we please talk? This has been torture."

I follow him over to the picnic tables and take a seat across from him. His eyes hold something besides the softness they've always had for me. They hold misery, pain, and trauma. I don't know all of what he's gone through in our time apart. Maybe I have been too hard on him.

Peter takes my hand and says, "I hate keeping secrets from you. And if I could tell you, I would. But telling you would mean putting you in danger. I didn't know how to say it because I know you'll only want to know more. But the last time I told you something that was meant to be a secret, I—"

His voice cracks and tears fill his eyes. Peter isn't the kind of guy to cry much at all. No matter the pain he's gone through, he's always been too tough to cry. But this is the second time in a few days he's been like this. I can still feel our tears as they mixed on our faces yesterday, before I walked away.

He clears his throat. "I lost you. You were gone and everyone thought you were dead and I don't ever want to lose you again."

"Peter," I say, hating myself for putting him through this pain. "Whatever's going on, you know I'm here with you. I'm not leaving. We're safe here."

He sighs. "You're right. I guess I should start with the fact that escaping the base would've been impossible without inside help. And I know you're going to think I'm insane for this."

He pauses, seeming to collect the right words. My heart begins to race as I tighten my grip on his hand. Despite everything inside of me saying no, I need to comfort him. I need him to feel safe telling me everything.

"What's holding you back?" I ask, nearly whispering.

"I'm scared you'll resent me if I tell you what happened."

His words are honest, raw. I shake my head slightly. "I won't. I just want the truth. I want… I want to trust you again, Peter. You mean everything to me. Do you trust me to believe in you?"

He searches my eyes and I can see he's scared. But his mouth sets in a grim line and he takes my other hand in his. "I trust you."

Then he tells me the truth of his escape—the truth that involves Evan and Peter's plan to double cross him.

The truth about Jennings finding him a little later, and about burying the burner phone.

He tells me everything that happened during his time at the base and after they escaped. "I didn't know I'd really find you out here, at least not this quickly. I know this had to be Evan's plan. Which is why I worried. Jennings kept telling me to give you the truth but I didn't know how to explain all of this. And I thought you'd resent me for going along with a plan made by Evan. But I saw this as my chance to escape."

"They used the explosion at the base … to keep you in line?" I say, words blurring together and my heart sagging in my chest.

"Yeah. I was their super-soldier. I did some things I'm not entirely proud of. Things I'm not ready to say out loud.

But I will tell you everything. Eventually. I promise you that you'll know everything about my past."

"I know," I say, feeling lighter than I have in a while. "I trust you, Peter. I shouldn't have ever doubted you."

"I would've doubted me, too. I should've been honest from the start. I want you to be safe. I can't live without you, Raegan. Not again."

My heart begins to race as my pulse picks up. Butterflies dance in my stomach. Whoever said romance is dead lied. Romance doesn't have to mean sweeping a girl off her feet. It's simpler than that. Sometimes it's words affirming what someone means to you. Sometimes it's simple acts. For me, it's when he looks in my eyes and tells me I matter to him.

"You have me. I'm not leaving you."

"Well, well, well. What do we have here. Canoodling during mealtime hours. And in public, too?"

Jackson slaps his hands down on the table, breaking us apart. Peter glares at him, but Jackson doesn't seem to care.

"Why are you like this?" Peter asks.

Jackson smirks. "I'm not always like this. Sometimes, I'm actually charming and nice. But so many people miss my sparkling personality. It's really a shame."

Peter runs a hand over his face. "What do you want, Jacks?"

"I want to know the whereabouts of your roommate," he asks, seeming slightly miffed.

Peter shrugs. "I don't know. Last I saw him was this morning. He's probably in the dining hall… where you should be."

"Don't tell me what to do, mister. I am your superior."

Peter rolls his eyes.

Jackson takes a couple of steps back. "Well, if you see him, let me know. There's been some suspicion around the camp that he's accessing information he's not really supposed to have."

Peter seems more alert at this, but doesn't say anything. Jackson leaves, finally.

I take Peter's hand in mine again. "We need to tell them about Evan's plan. If he was willing to use you, he'd be even more willing to send in a soldier entirely loyal to him to corrupt the resistance."

Peter tenses. "If I tell them that, they'll trust me even less than they already do. It's bad enough that everyone looks at me like I don't belong, like I didn't fight alongside them before."

That cuts him deeply. I see it in his eyes.

"Telling the truth is the only thing that will get them to trust you more," I tell him. "We have to talk to Andre before it's too late."

I can tell he's not convinced. But letting this go unspoken is dangerous. I open my mouth to tell him this when a deafening cracking noise fills the air. *An explosion.* My heart thumps wildly in my chest as I look around. "What was that?" I whisper.

"I—" Peter begins. But another explosion shakes the ground. The vibration nearly knocks me off the bench. My eyes meet Peter's. All I see is fear.

I jump up at the same time he does.

Plumes of smoke rise steadily from the wall on the far side of camp.

"*No,*" Peter whispers near my ear as the walls start to crumble and burn.

Rebels have begun to pour out of the buildings and tunnels. But soldiers are entering through the smoke, dodging the flames with ease. They climb over the rubble, swarming into the camp.

The remaining walls catch fire, and smoke blackens the air.

I start to choke on the fumes, coughing into my sleeve. Carissa comes rushing out of the training arena with Jackson and Linley.

Andre's office is the first building to catch fire. Carissa starts running towards it, but another explosion shakes the ground, throwing us all to our hands and knees. I grip the grass, dirt catching under my fingernails. Some of the soldiers have also fallen to the ground, but there's no time to take advantage.

There are simply too many of them.

Peter is on his feet first, pulling me up. The others have already risen and resumed running. I'm panting, shaking. Every part of me is frozen in this spot. How could we have been found so easily? It dawns on me a split second later: they've known for a while. They've had to. An attack like this takes planning.

Peter grabs my hand, catching my attention. "We have to go," he says urgently.

He leads as we run through the camp, towards the tunnels. I don't know where we'll go beyond that, but for now, escaping the soldiers is what's important. The thick smoke will cloak us enough that they won't see us leaving.

Spencer is standing by the tunnel entrance, ushering everyone inside. "The emergency exit is open," he yells out as we run by. Peter helps me in first, then follows me down the ladder. More rebels crowd in around us. I don't know if the soldiers are chasing us, but that doesn't matter: we run for our lives. Vibrations shake the tunnels. More explosions, most likely. But we keep running.

It's dark down here. None of the lights flicker on.

"They must've cut the power," Spencer grumbles near my right. Everyone has slowed down to a steady walk. Footsteps echo off the walls from all directions. When there's a glimpse of light, I know we've almost made it to the exit.

Peter and Spencer help guide people up the ladders. I'm caught in the flow of bodies. I find my parents and Peter's mom, and we embrace tightly. Nicole finds me in the crowd as well and clings to me. Her arm is burned, blistering from whatever touched her.

Once everyone is out, Spencer seals the hatch. "I don't think anyone followed us out," he says, out of breath as he and Peter both double over. "But we need to keep moving."

"Where are my parents?" Carissa nearly yells.

Spencer looks pained. "I didn't see them. They weren't with the crowd."

"NO!" Carissa screams. "We have to go back for them!"

Jackson grabs her before she can run to the hatch. "Hey, hey. Shh, baby. We'll give them time to get here. Spencer, open the hatch and see if they're coming."

Spencer frowns. "If the soldiers—"

"If the soldiers try to come up here, we close it on them and scatter."

Spencer obviously is not thrilled with that plan, but he does as Jackson says. No one is in the tunnels. Not soldiers. Not Andre or Maya. It's empty. I look around me. Quite a few people are injured. Some are hurt worse than others. Jennings claps his hands, gathering attention to himself.

"The river isn't far from here," he says loudly. "If we can get to it, we can gather supplies and food from the underground garage that's nearby. Keep an eye out for aloe plants on the way. It will help with the burns. They grow better in dry soil, though."

"Who put you in charge?" someone demands. "You're a government soldier spying on us. For all we know, you brought those people here."

Jennings tenses. Peter steps up next to him and says, "He has nothing to do with this."

"How do we know we can trust you?"

Anger boils beneath my skin, but Peter shoots me a look that says *Don't you dare.*

I sigh, keeping my cool… for now.

Carissa still fights against Jackson's hold on her. All eyes turn to Spencer.

"Oh no," he says. "You're not putting me in charge. Carissa is next in line."

But Carissa pays no attention to him. "How do we know?" she whispers, falling against Jackson. "How do we know they didn't make it?"

One of the council members, Zaire, touches her shoulder. "We saw his building explode. He had just gone in there with Maya."

She sobs against Jackson's chest. Tears well up in my own eyes as my parents embrace me more tightly. I could've lost them, too. We all stand clustered together, dirty and disheveled. Some stand mute and shocked; others cry quietly, alone, or in groups. Everyone is badly shaken up.

Andre and Maya are dead at the hands of their own son.

CHAPTER THIRTY-SIX

*A CRACK ECHOES THROUGH THE AIR. I'M MID-*punch, my fist stopping short of the punch dummy as I glance at my students. I straighten my posture and look over at Jackson, who looks equally concerned.

Linley is the first to push away from the wall and check outside. When she screams, I know something's wrong. Jackson and I both break into a run. Linley's already slid her boots on and is running to the chaos.

The wall on the other side of camp is up in flames.

Smoke billows into the air, rising higher and higher.

The fire begins to spread to the two adjacent walls.

My stomach clenches and my breakfast threatens to spill at my feet.

We've been found.

Screaming fills the air as people from the canteen and other buildings on the far side of camp come running. I start running against the crowd, not seeing my parents in the frenzy.

My dad's office is in flames, smoke pouring out of it. The fire eats it so fast. The movies lie when they show things like this happening in slow motion. Jackson pulls me back and it all seems to happen too fast.

I'm being rushed towards the tunnels. When I look back, the ground is shaking as another explosion rocks the camp. My dad's office collapses.

"My parents." The words come out choked.

Jackson grimaces. "I didn't see them, but they may be in the tunnels. Come on. Let's not think the worst yet."

I'm numb. Everything we know is crumbling around us.

Jackson urges me into the tunnels. More people push in behind us. When the last one is in, we seal ourselves off and run towards the exit, the one that leads further into the woods. I don't know if that's entirely smart, but I can't think straight right now.

And maybe I don't care at this point.

Jackson keeps his arm around my waist, holding me steady as we push through the tunnels. I don't know if the soldiers are following us or not. If this was Evan, he's all about the dramatics and showmanship. He wanted to make a statement and clearly has no intention of capturing us yet. He'd rather hunt us down for the thrill of it.

We reach the outside; the day has already gotten warmer. Spencer and Jackson perform a headcount. A few people fall to the ground as the adrenaline wears off. Some are injured. A headache begins to grip at my temples, but I ignore it.

No pain can be worse than the one in my heart.

I know for sure that my parents aren't here when Jackson and Spencer whisper to each other out of my earshot. I know they're gone when Jackson takes me into his arms and Spencer, who never shows his emotions, looks like he might cry, too. I know they're gone when the men of the council hang their heads, looking weary and lost without my father to tell them what to do.

They're gone.

They're gone.

They.

Are.

Gone.

I succumb to the shaking inside of me, to the sobs that wrack my body. I'd fall to my knees if Jackson didn't hold me to his chest. He runs his hands over my head and down my back repeatedly, trying to soothe me.

I watch as, across the clearing, Raegan's parents take her in their arms, all of them crying.

Peter hugs his mom, who's sobbing. This is the first time I've seen her embrace her son since his return.

Nicole sits on the ground, Linley tending to her wounds. She has burns going up her arms.

Ryker crosses his arms, stepping forward. Jackson tenses. No one is at ease when Ryker is about to speak. He glances around, finds Peter, and says, "The soldiers you let in probably led them here."

Raegan looks ready to strangle him, but calms when Peter glances at her. He then says, "Mr. Ryker, with all due respect, this resistance is one I've lived and almost died for countless times. Andre is—was like a father to me when mine wasn't present. I would never lead Evan here."

"Okay, but what about the other one you dragged in with you? We don't know him. He could've led Evan and his army right to us."

A few people murmur their agreement. Everyone knows Peter. No one knows Jennings. Jennings looks around uneasily as people's voices grow louder. I don't have the strength to be calm or be rational, to take charge and counter them. But someone should: people are already out of control without my father to tell them what to do.

And maybe that's the problem.

I pull away from Jackson, drying my face with the back of my hands. "Look," I say as loudly as I can. "Peter and Seth didn't do anything wrong. They came here because they deserted. If they could find us in these woods, soldiers could, too. It doesn't matter how we were found. What matters is that we have to figure out where to go from here."

A few people mutter, but no one rejects this. Some of them look at me hopefully, but I'm too weak and broken to lead anyone. I can't take over. My father knew everything. I know nothing.

The council starts herding everyone deeper into the woods.

"We need to get to the river," Callahan says. "It should be cool enough to at least soothe the burns of our injured right now. And we'll need the water to drink, too."

Everyone slowly gets up, or is helped up, and we move. My legs feel shaky; my whole world feels upside down. My thoughts churn as I stumble along.

I don't want to give Evan this victory. He's waging war against us, a war we're not in any shape to fight. I should be angry. I should be plotting every possible way to counterattack. But instead, I'm numb. My parents are dead, killed by the actions of my brother. The resistance is looking to me, but I'm falling apart.

Whatever they think they'll get from me is an illusion.

I'm not my father.

We reach the river and Jackson eases me down near a tree. "Just rest. I'll get you some water. Jennings has a filter. He said I could use it."

I nod absently. I should give a better response. But I

don't have it in me. I drink the water he gives me and I idly chew some dried meat someone grabbed from the canteen. I watch as everyone else begins to rest, some falling asleep and others just sitting with their eyes open, numb, as we settle in to our makeshift camp of blankets and pillows.

An ache takes over my heart, spreading through my body. I don't have it in me to lead these people.

My parents are gone.

And that thought consumes me completely.

CHAPTER THIRTY-SEVEN

Evan
THURSDAY, AUGUST 21ST, 2025

"THE WALLS ARE DOWN, SIR. WHAT NOW?"

Smoke fills the air. I smell the fire, even from a safe distance.

"Now we wait," I say. "We go back to base and wait for the resistance to come out like ants fleeing their anthill."

All the soldiers don't seem convinced, but I don't particularly care whether or not they believe it. I need obedience, nothing else. They can believe whatever they want. Unlike the emperor, I don't care about people's private thoughts. I care only about what they do.

The actions of the men with me show they will do what needs to be done. And that's all I need.

I'm calm throughout the drive. The resistance hasn't shown signs of activity. I watch the feeds from the cameras we set up around the perimeter before attacking. No one runs out. It's almost like it was already abandoned. But knowing my father, there are two parts to this camp.

Whatever's below ground will be where they retreated. They'll have to come out at some point to assess the damage.

I never wanted it to come to this point. I never thought I'd be the one to fire the first shot in this war. But my family has maintained a steady hold on all things *rebellion*. And while I want to keep them safe, I have to play my part, too.

Acting now will protect them from the emperor's wrath. If I take care of it my way, they may have a chance to get out of this war alive.

My driver delivers me to my hotel, where I quickly escape to my room, avoiding the news reporters with cameras. They question why I'm here, in Texas. I never answer the press, something I've learned by watching celebrities get hurt by what they say, even if it's innocent.

I begin pacing my room, my eyes glued to the hologram screen. No one moves out of the resistance camp. There's nothing. I rewind the footage, trying to see where they go during the attack, but the cameras are shrouded in smoke.

I sigh, tossing my hologram pod onto my bed. They have to come out of the woodwork at some point.

Unless... they escaped through something underground.

I don't know how safe it would be for me to visit

the camp, in case they truly are just waiting for some sort of ambush. But maybe there's something more that I'm missing. It couldn't be a decoy base they set up to lead me astray. I heard the screams and saw people running as the walls caught fire.

But something seems strange.

I collapse onto my bed, exhausted. The day has not yet come to an end, but every bone in my body is aching. I must fall asleep because it's dark when I open my eyes. The sun is lower in the sky now, no longer pouring into the room. I draw the curtains shut and go over to my hologram pod, setting it up again.

I watch all the footage it recorded while I was asleep. Then I go back to the live feed.

Nothing.

They must be on the run. I misjudged everything.

It doesn't matter. I'll find them in the woods again. I know that much. For now, I'll let them have their run. Their base is gone. They have nowhere to operate from.

I know the emperor will want me back in DC as soon as possible, so I'll go back there. Meanwhile, I'll let the resistance figure out their next move.

Then I'll strike before they can. I can't let them win if I want my family to live.

CHAPTER THIRTY-EIGHT

IT'S DARK OUT, BUT I'M WIDE AWAKE. IT'S ONLY been a few hours. Everyone's spread out in this clearing by the river. Some sleep. Some are only resting. It's hard to do either when soldiers could be on us at any second.

I sit away from everyone else, needing a moment to think. To breathe.

"Mind if I join you?"

I glance over to see Peter, whose hands are tucked in his pockets.

"I never mind you," I say.

He sits next to me and I rest my head on his shoulder. "Are you okay?" I ask.

"Shouldn't I be asking you that?"

In the chaos, Gunner was left behind. Michelle cried for a long time, full of both guilt and grief.

Andre and Maya are gone.

Many of us are injured.

And Gunner either ran out into the chaos or is gone, too. The knowledge of that weighs heavily on me. I know it's weighing on Peter, too. But he's trying to be strong about it. Probably for my sake and maybe a little for his own.

His arm pulls softly around my waist, and his head rests on mine. It would be the perfect moment if this were any other time and any other place.

"I wish I could bottle up the good times and pour out the moment when the bad times come," I say softly.

"That's strangely poetic."

I almost smile, but my heart is still too heavy to allow any happy expression. "I sometimes made up poems in my mind to help me fall asleep at night when I was overwhelmed with missing you. I used to read poetry books, but I didn't bring any with me when we came to the camp. I tried to remember the words, but ended up making my own."

He presses a kiss to the top of my head. "Maybe when this is all over, you can write a poetry book. Get rich and famous and never worry again about what you'll do."

The thought is mildly comforting. But I don't ponder it for long. "I've never considered what comes after this."

"Neither have I."

What would we do? If the war ends and the world gets better? Or if we're defeated and everything falls apart?

The camp is quiet and so are we. Words don't seem to

be the right thing to fill the space. Silence seems to be the best option. A shuffling noise behind us alerts me to movement. I jump slightly, and Peter and I both look back. Nicole rises from her sleeping mat on the ground. Jennings, who isn't sleeping either, says something to her quietly. She motions to the burns on her arms. He takes her down to the river, away from the sleeping forms on the ground, and pulls something out of his bag. They're talking, but their words don't carry far enough for me to hear anything.

"I feel bad for Nicole," I murmur.

"I do, too. But Jennings is a survivalist. He knows what to do. He's helped everyone be able to at least sleep comfortably."

Nicole's burns were the worst of anyone's, since she was near the wall on her morning run when it caught fire. Jennings carefully puts the ointment on her arms, just like he's done for the other burn victims. I notice Spencer approaching them quietly. I turn away, looking back out to the water.

Peter smirks. "Jennings is single, you know."

"Nicole isn't. I guess Spencer never told you, but they've been dating for a year. It's been pretty low-key, but they're happy."

Peter turns to look over at them again. I do the same. Jennings has returned to sit under a tree. Spencer holds Nicole gently in his arms; her body is shaking slightly.

"They seem like they would be a good match. Spencer can keep Nicole grounded and Nicole can bring Spencer out of his shell."

"Yeah," I say, smiling softly.

The night burns on. Eventually, my eyes begin to droop. Peter yawns.

"Maybe we should sleep," I suggest.

"Probably."

I move to get up, but Peter pulls me closer and lies down on the grass. "This is perfect," he mumbles against my hair, his breathing softening.

I close my eyes and drift off to sleep, for once at peace.

CHAPTER THIRTY-NINE

Jackson

DAWN BEGINS TO LIGHT UP THE SKY. IT'S STRANGE seeing it happen before I'm fully awake. The underground was pitch-dark as we slept, and even the courtyard of camp held only broken, muted light.

Carissa shivers, despite the hot air. "I could've saved them. If I was faster. Or—"

"Stop saying that. You did everything you could do. Now you have to lead."

"I can't lead, Jackson. I can barely breathe."

I sigh.

Suddenly, Carissa is on her feet. "We should check the garage. If the cars are safe, we can migrate somewhere. The vans would be good to transport the injured. Callahan talked about his base somewhere north of here. We could at least take shelter."

"You make a fair point. It's not like we're sleeping anyway. Let's go."

I take her hand and we make our way out of the makeshift camp. No one seems to notice us. I let Carissa take the lead once we're farther away. We take to the tunnels, cautiously. I'm expecting some of Evan's men to be stationed somewhere inside.

But it's empty.

Cold.

No one waits for us. Still, I keep my hand on the grip of my pistol in my back pocket. We make it to the tunnel that leads to the garage. Once inside, I see nothing here has been touched.

Carissa hesitates at the threshold. "I want to go see the camp."

"I don't know… They could be there."

"I know. But I need to know. I need to know if everything's really gone."

I follow her, knowing I wouldn't win this argument anyway. We arrive at the hatch and I go up first. I'm greeted by the sight of nearly everything turned to ash. It's clear the fire was put out before it could spread too far.

But the message is clear.

Carissa follows me out. She gasps, and I see a few tears escape her eyes. Her spine straightens. One look at Andre's office makes it clear. It's a pile of rubble and soot.

We turn to leave before we can get caught up in anything else. A soft whimper reaches my ears.

I know instantly it has to be Peter's dog.

"Gunner?" I call out.

A short bark greets me as the dog limps out of the shadows.

His fur is dirty, but he seems all right otherwise.

Carissa smiles, despite everything. "Hey buddy." She kneels down and runs her hands over his fur. "I know of three people who will be happy to see you."

"You mean to tell me I have to carry him down this ladder?"

Carissa stands up and gives me a look. "I can carry him if you feel like you're not strong enough."

I glare, taking the dog up over my shoulders without a second thought. "Very funny. Get down there so you can get him off my back when I get to the bottom."

Carissa smirks and descends the ladder. Gunner whimpers and licks my ear. "Yeah, yeah, yeah, I'm happy to see you too. Keep that tongue to yourself."

I make my way slowly back down the ladder, the extra forty pounds not making it easy. At the bottom, Carissa lifts him off my back and sets him on the ground. Gunner sticks close to us as we walk back to the camp.

"Hopefully we can get back through the tunnels," Carissa says, thinking out loud. "At least those of us who are uninjured. Then we can drive to the injured with the off-road vehicles, collect them, and get to the rest."

"Where will we go?"

She shrugs. "I don't know yet. But anywhere other than here would probably be safer."

"Hiding isn't going to keep us safe for long. You know that, right?"

"I know. But I don't know where Evan is—whether he's around here, or if he's already skipped town. I'll talk with the council and we'll figure out our next moves."

We reach the end of the tunnel. I'm grateful this one opens up into a ditch so I don't have to carry Gunner again. I glance at him. He'll need a bath in the river, but the idea of drinking river water that he bathes in is less than enticing, even with Jennings' filters.

As we approach camp, the sun is burning higher in the sky. Gunner immediately runs up to a startled Raegan, who collapses onto her knees and holds him close.

Peter runs over to them once he sees what's going on, and Michelle begins sobbing again.

Spencer rushes up to us. "I'm glad you're back. The council has been asking me so many questions. I really do not want to run this show. They'll want you, Rissa."

Carissa gnaws her bottom lip and crosses her arms across her chest. "Maybe I don't want it, either. They're all a bunch of rebel leaders. Why do they need me?"

"Because," Zaire says, approaching with the others, "Andre knew what he was doing. And we see that same fire in you. You're wise beyond your years. You have the same passion and fury that Andre possessed. It got in his way sometimes, but it kept him alive. It kept us all alive."

Carissa's eyes brim with tears. I wrap my arm around her. "You know I'll be here every step of the way to help you, right?"

She nods. To the council, she says, "We checked up on the camp and the garage. The vehicles are all untouched and no one seems to be in the tunnels. I think we could safely take most of the vehicles and go somewhere safer."

Zaire glances at Ryker and Callahan. Callahan runs a hand over his shaved head. "I don't know if that's the wisest move. Likely they'll be patrolling the area heavily, waiting for us to make it out of here. If the underground seems safe, maybe we can still use the sleeping quarters for now."

Carissa tenses at my side. "The issue with that is..."

The council waits. I speak up so Carissa doesn't have to keep talking about what happened. "The issue is Andre's office was burned down with him and Maya in it. There's still a chance they're... in there. It would be a bit wrong to expect any of us to live there at this point. There's nothing there for us and the underground is not really where we want to be."

Ryker strokes his goatee. "The garage is near the

tunnel that led us here. We could use the garage as shelter for now, especially so the burn victims aren't in the direct sun. We could send a team to go bury the casualties and search for anything of use."

Carissa nods. "I want Jennings in charge of the medical unit. He seems to know how to care for the injured."

"Fair enough," Zaire says. His distaste for Jennings seems to have lessened. "His survivalist background may come in handy after all."

"Whoever is sent to search for my parents' bodies needs to… bury them within the camp."

Zaire's features soften. "Of course."

Callahan claps his hands. "I'll gather a team of hunters. We need to get some food."

"We might be able to send some people into the city," I offer. "Not everyone there is known to be a rebel. We can get simple food like canned soups and items that can last a long time."

The council seems to agree to this.

"Now," Ryker says. "All we need to figure out is our counterattack. We can't take this lying down any longer."

"I know," Carissa says. "But first things first. We need to find out where Evan is hiding. Confronting his soldiers or anyone else will lead to nothing. We have to start with him."

I can tell the words are hard for Carissa to say. Even now, I know she misses her brother. At least the one she knew.

Something's snapped in Evan. I don't know if he intended to kill his parents—or anyone at all. The Evan I knew, even though he was working for the emperor, couldn't make a kill shot.

I don't say that here, knowing that the council doesn't care.

Andre and Maya are dead.

And that means war has been declared.

CHAPTER FORTY

Peter

FRIDAY, AUGUST 22ND, 2025

GUNNER WALKS ALONGSIDE ME AS I CARRY MORE supplies into the garage. Some of the vans have been opened, turned into makeshift care units for the injured. Thankfully, not too many people were close enough to the blast to be injured, but there are still enough of them that Jennings has his hands full. Linley helps him when she's not sent out on patrol.

Spencer sits in the passenger seat of his jeep, his laptop resting on his knees. He doesn't wear his headphones. But he's focused.

I walk over, leaning against the hood of the vehicle. "So," I say. "I haven't been able to really talk to you since… everything. But I wanted to say I'm really sorry for—"

"Don't say you're sorry for my loss," Spencer interrupts. "I don't want pity or condolences or anything. That's all I got after my aunt and uncle took me in. I hate it."

I turn my head to look at him. Spencer, the most logical and emotionless man I've ever met, has tears running down his face. His voice strong, he says, "They were like the parents I never had. I didn't appreciate them enough. I didn't make my uncle proud. It me took this long to earn his trust again."

"I'm sorry. I know that's my fault."

"I regret nothing. We saved Raegan. I work by my morals, not by what people tell me to do. But my uncle… I wanted his approval. I looked up to him. I was sixteen when they took me in. The home my mom and I lived in was turned to ash because my abusive father wanted us dead. Half of his wish came true. And I knew I wasn't wanted by the parent that was still alive. In my brief time in foster care, I knew I wasn't wanted because in two years I'd be an adult and moving on with my life. My aunt and uncle learned of my situation and adopted me. Do you know the first thing he said to me when they took me in? The moment we pulled up outside the ranch. He said, 'Spencer, you've been handed a heavy load in your young life. And I know it will probably be hard to adjust. But just know that we want you here. We want you with us for as long as that is. Whether you live here just for the next two years, or whether you're here longer than that, we want you in our lives regardless. You're capable of great things, Spencer.' That's what he said to me."

Spencer wipes his face with his hands. The ache in my chest grows. He recovers quickly, or at least pretends to. His fingers go back to his keyboard, typing furiously.

"What are you looking for?"

"I'm hacking the cameras they managed to put around the camp. When I opened my laptop a while ago, it was still syncing to something in the camp. I couldn't figure out how or what it was. Turns out, my dear cousin had cameras mounted all around to watch us after the explosions. Probably thought we'd all come running out or something."

Anger surges hot through my veins. "Isn't it enough to destroy everything else?"

"Apparently not. But that's not all. I've been messing around with my holographic map. It has a GPS. And I've been picking up signals nearby. They were there even when we were in the camp—coming *from* the camp. I thought it was an abnormality, or something conflicting with all the technology my uncle installed in camp. But I think… I think there are trackers inside you and Jennings."

Time freezes and the hot anger goes ice cold.

"What?"

Spencer looks up at me. "Don't start doing that blaming yourself thing that you do. If there are trackers on you, I doubt you volunteered for them. But I don't want to tell the council. They'll think you brought this on purpose and I know that's not true. But we have to figure out how to get the trackers out of your body."

Trackers are implanted somewhere in my body. In me. But how? "There was never… we never went through a procedure to implant anything."

"I'm thinking it was done without you being entirely aware. Disguised as something else. Did you ever undergo any medical examinations?"

My heart drops to my stomach. "Yeah. I think I know how they did it."

Spencer looks up from his computer to me, waiting. I swallow the bile rising up my throat. "When we arrived, everyone was taken for a medical examination. It was simple. Just a check-up to make sure no one was sick or unfit for training. Everyone got a shot. We were told it was an immunity boost."

"Where exactly did they give you the shot?"

I turn, showing him my right bicep. He looks closely, then says, "I'll have to have Hannah do a quick examination on you and Jennings."

"Hannah as in your ex-girlfriend Hannah?"

"Yes. It's as awkward and horrible as it sounds. But she's the medical expert. I know she's been helping Jennings a lot. You both need to have her inspect your arms. If that's where the trackers are, it's only a matter of time before they find us again. We can't take another hit."

Grim reality sets in. Time is really of the essence.

Spencer closes his laptop and gets to his feet, carrying the machine with him as we approach the van Jennings and Hannah are operating out of. If Hannah notices Spencer, she doesn't say anything. Jennings looks at me and instantly knows something is wrong.

"What's up?"

Spencer says, "I think I know how they found us. But… Hannah, you need to check their right arms."

Hannah tilts her head. "Why?"

"Because," I begin, "when we were taken to be soldiers, we were each given a shot. It was called an immunity booster. But most likely, it was a tracking device."

Jennings' eyes widen. "What the hell?"

Spencer turns to me. "I'm going to get Carissa and Jackson. They're going to have to decide what to do if it's true."

Hannah motions into the back of the van. "Take a seat. You too, Jennings. I'll inspect your arms."

I sit across from Jennings, my breathing shallow and harsh. This could be all my fault. Hannah walks to the front of the van and comes back with a scanner of sorts. It's strange tech I don't begin to know how to describe. She waves it over Jennings' arm, then mine. It beeps once for each of us.

"There is definitely something implanted in your

arms. Strange thing is that I don't think it's deep."

She leans down, feeling my bicep. Her fingers stop halfway. When she presses, I feel it. Something hard, but small. She turns to Jennings and presses his bicep, her fingers stopping about the same place on his arm. He inhales sharply.

"What's going on?" Carissa asks outside the van.

"They have trackers in their arms," Hannah says. "Implanted unknowingly. But clearly, we have to get them out."

"Trackers?" Jackson glances at Carissa, then at me and Jennings. "How did you get trackers?"

"We were lied to," Jennings remarks bitterly. "No shocker there. But we did this. We caused all of this."

Carissa shakes her head. "No. You didn't do this on purpose. Even with the trackers, my brother made his choice. Hannah, is there a way to get them out?"

"I'll have to make an initial cut in each one of them to see if it's deep. If I can get the devices out safely, I can stich their arms back up and we can destroy the tracking devices. But if they aren't just below the surface like I'm hoping… we're stuck being tracked as long as Jennings and Peter are here."

"We'll leave," Jennings says firmly. "If you can't get it out of our arms, we will be gone. We'll lead Evan away."

The thought of leaving again breaks me. It's only

been a few days, but I've already grown used to being here.

Being home.

But I won't stay if it endangers everyone I love. Jennings is right. We'd have to leave.

Carissa bites her lip, her nervous energy buzzing through the air around us all. "See what you can do," she says, relenting.

Hannah nods. Then she looks between me and Jennings. "Who wants to go first?"

"Me," Jennings says before I can speak. "I'll do it."

Hannah nods grimly, then motions for me to step out. She reaches for the back doors of the van and starts to pull them shut. Right before they close, she says, "This is probably going to hurt a lot. If there's screaming or yelping…"

"You're doing your best," Carissa offers a sad smile. "We trust you."

Hannah doesn't say anything, closing the doors. I run a hand through my hair. "I need to find Raegan."

"Last I saw, she was out by the river." Jackson sighs.

I don't waste any time. I march through the woods, taking it all in as I go. The wildflowers growing in patches, the fallen branches of trees. I find Raegan where Jackson said I would, sitting by the river. Her knees are curled to her chest and her hair flutters slightly in the warm breeze.

"Hey," I say softly so as not to startle her.

She glances up at me. "Hello."

"We need to talk."

"Those words are never good."

I take a seat next to her on the riverbank. "We found out how they found us."

She looks at me now, pale blue eyes searching mine. "How?"

"Jennings and I each have a tracker in our arms. We didn't know about it until Spencer was doing his research and came across a strange signal coming from our camp. Hannah is working to see if she can remove the trackers. Jennings volunteered to be first... but if they can't be removed..."

Suddenly, I'm too weary to finish the sentence. As often happens with Raegan, there's no need. She's read my mind.

"Where will you go?" she asks softly.

"I don't know. Haven't gotten that far in the plan yet."

We both stare out at the river for a while, watching the way it moves with the curve of the land. The trickle of water is soothing, yet all I can manage to think about is the feeling of impending doom that's like a heavy hand on the back of my neck. And yet here I sit, with Raegan, my best friend and someone I don't want to be without. I've caused the rift between us, the lack of trust and communication. I'm breaking down and there's only one thing I can do to make this right.

"Evan helped me escape," I say before I can stop myself.

Raegan stills beside me. "What?"

"I didn't want to tell you because I knew it would look bad. I know it looks bad now that I've said there's a tracker in my arm. But I promise you I didn't know about the tracker and I also promise I never intended to do what Evan wanted. He told me all he wanted was to protect his family. I didn't believe him. When he asked me to desert my post, at first I thought it was a trick. But then I thought maybe I could use it to my benefit. He gave me a burner phone, but I figured it had a tracker in it, so I abandoned it." I give a harsh little laugh. "Never thought there'd be a tracker in my own arm. As for Jennings, he followed me out that night, but I didn't know he was going to. That wasn't planned. My only plan was to find my way back here… to you. And I'll understand if you hate me for everything I've caused now."

Silence first, then she shifts beside me and places her hand gently against my cheek. Tears well in her eyes. No words pass between us. They don't have to. My lips find hers, her tears falling as I pull her closer. It's goodbye, even though it isn't. My hands go to her waist; her arms wrap around my neck.

When we break apart, she's crying harder. "I don't want you to go."

"I don't want to go, but if the trackers aren't

removable, I'm not putting you or anyone else in any more danger. People have died because of me."

Raegan shakes her head. I reach up, brushing away her tears. She leans into my hands. "It's not your fault. You didn't do this on purpose."

"I know. Carissa and Jackson basically said the same thing. But it doesn't change the fact that we were attacked. Andre and Maya…"

My own emotions rise up to my throat now.

Andre and Maya are dead. All because of Evan. And because I helped lead him here.

Raegan rests her head on my shoulder; our hands are still twined together. "I'm sorry," I say. "I should've told you from the start."

"It's okay. I'm glad that we can feel normal again. It's all I wanted."

"Peter, are you—am I interrupting?"

We both turn at the sound of Jackson's voice.

Jackson steps out onto the riverbank, shaking his head at us, with Spencer following close behind.

"Hannah was able to get the tracker out of Jennings' arm," Spencer says. He looks mildly sick.

"What happened?"

"Well…" Jackson says, "Hannah needed some help and Spencer was the only one nearby at the time. Turns out the sight of blood and gore makes our dear friend Spencer sick to his stomach. He's almost fainted twice on the way here."

Raegan and I rise up from the ground. "So I'm next?" I ask.

"Yeah, but it won't be a picnic," he says, clearly enjoying himself. "Jennings is unconscious. He was in a lot of pain. Hannah ended up giving him a high dose of calming tea and she put some numbing cream on his arm. He's resting now. The tracker is out of his arm. She checked with her scanner to make sure. Once we get yours, Carissa and I will dispose of them while you and Jennings rest."

Raegan takes my hand, squeezing it softly.

"I'm ready," I say firmly, squeezing back.

Raegan walks with me to the van. Hannah's wiping down her tools with alcohol when we arrive.

"Take a seat," she says.

I turn to Raegan, caressing her face. "She'll get it out," I say. "And I'll be okay."

"Actually, Raegan," Hannah begins, "If you don't mind, I could use some help."

Raegan nods. "Of course."

Hannah closes the doors. It's dimly lit in here, with just a lantern hanging above us. Hannah moves it closer, adjusting it so that it's close to my arm. She turns away again and I hear liquid being poured. Turning back to me, she hands me a mug and says, "Drink this tea. It will make you drowsy."

I take the steaming mug, chugging the tea in a matter

of four gulps. She takes the empty mug from me and puts it aside, and then says, "Lie on your left side. I'll put numbing cream on your arm, but understand that it's not going to prevent you from being in pain. It's only going to help it be less intense."

"Okay."

She applies the numbing cream all over my bicep, then uses her scanner to detect where the chip is. I feel the cool tip of a marker drawing a line on my arm.

"Okay, Peter. Try not to move too much."

I brace myself for the cut of her knife. Hot pain shoots through my entire body and the world goes black.

CHAPTER FORTY-ONE

Carissa
SATURDAY, AUGUST 23RD, 2025

"THE TRACKERS ARE DISPOSED OF, BUT WHAT DO we do now?" one of the men asks me. "Evan's proven he will stop at nothing to destroy us. He's clearly willing to blow up our entire base camp. This is no longer a game of tag or hide and seek."

I don't allow the tremor in my body to show as I face them. My parents are dead at the hands of my brother. I've made no peace with this. I cry myself to sleep every night because of it. But the men before me are ready for war, not weakness. And for some reason, they've decided I am their new leader.

My father was made for these decisions. I wasn't. I'm not ready.

But as Zaire, Callahan, and Ryker stare at me, waiting, I know we can't sit here doing nothing.

"I know we can't hide forever," I say, glancing over at Jackson. He nods his encouragement. I sigh. "But we lost my father, my mother, Radcliffe, and a few others. We're weaker because of it. I want to fight. But how do you suggest we do this?"

Ryker crosses his arms. "We'd march on the capital."

Jackson laughs humorlessly. "And get killed immediately. You don't just march on the capitol. You have to be more clever, more strategic. Boldness gets you nowhere except dead."

Ryker doesn't seem to agree, but he doesn't argue. Jackson knows better than the rest of us what it would take to get into the White House. Cold creeps up my spine.

"Any other suggestions?" I look around the room at the council. No one speaks up. No one has a clue about what to do.

Jackson sighs, standing. "All right. If we're going to attack, it can't be big or bold or loud. We need a small group of agents. And we can't go for the kill or the big win. This is war. Battles will need to be fought. We'd need to take Evan down first if we plan to get any further."

Zaire perks up slightly. "What do you have in mind?"

Jacksons smirks. "A small team goes to DC. We get in through the tunnels. I'll lead the team, since I know about the tunnels and where they go. We'll find

Evan's room in the White House. I don't know what room he's in, exactly, but I know Spencer can do some digging for that. Then we capture him and take him prisoner. We don't have to bring him back here, but we do need to take him somewhere he has no power. We can interrogate him, though I doubt he'll give us any information. Once we have him, however, we have leverage."

It's all too real.

My parents are dead.

My brother is an enemy to our cause.

The government is only going to get worse.

We have to win a war. We can't afford to lose.

The council members look around the room at each other.

"Let's take it to vote," I say uneasily. "All in favor of this plan, raise two fingers."

Jackson raises two fingers, waiting to see who will join him.

Zaire is next.

Then Callahan.

Then Ryker.

All that's left is me, though it's decided already. Majority rules. Still, I raise my arm dutifully, bringing two fingers up.

"Now then," Ryker smirks. "Who's on this team?"

CHAPTER FORTY-TWO

Raegan
TUESDAY, AUGUST 26TH, 2025

EVERY BEAT OF MY PULSE REVERBERATES IN MY ears. This is war. I'm fighting in a real war. Most of the resistance has already loaded up to fight. Some stayed behind to defend the injured in case we're found.

Some people I don't know, along with a few familiar faces, sit in the same van as I do. Peter sits beside me, squeezing my hand, whispering comforting words in my ear.

The plan is to get to DC. We'll be staying at a rebel base there run by some people Zaire knows well. They have rooms for us to stay in and a place for us to plot our entire attack. Carissa says they know what they want to do, but it's best to review the plan when we're closer to the target.

We don't want any unnecessary deaths due to poor planning.

Every time I'm anxious, I squeeze Peter's hand

slightly. Each time, he murmurs something in my ear, leaving a lingering kiss there. I don't know if that does anything to slow my heart rate, but it distracts me enough from the anxiety.

We've been driving for the past day and a half. Last night, we pulled off near a wooded area to try and get some rest. But no one really slept. Not for long. We're always on alert.

I'll be happy when we reach the rebel base and can sleep on real beds for at least a little while.

Peter's head rests against mine in the van. His soft breathing signals that he's dozing. We stay like this until we reach the base. I wake him gently and he smiles when he sees me there next to him.

Rubbing the sleep from his eyes, he hops out of the van, then helps me.

Zaire greets his friend with a handshake and one of those guy hugs. He then smiles, turning to us, and says, "Everyone, this is my best friend since childhood, Cody."

Peter's jaw drops. "Wait… Cody? As in Brent's right-hand man?"

Cody smiles. "Peter, nice to see you again. I was a spy within the FBI ranks. I'm a rebel. I've been running this base for a long time. You can ask Zaire."

Carissa steps forward. "My father spoke highly of you."

"Thank you, Ms. Williams. I'm sorry for your loss.

Andre was a great man."

Carissa nods once, but doesn't say anything. I don't think she has it in her to reply to the condolences yet. The wound to her heart is still fresh.

Cody gives us a tour of the base. It's not large, but it's big enough that we have space to plan.

When he finishes, he turns to us and says, "Why don't you all get some rest? We can finalize the plan later. We won't get any work done if you're too sleepy."

Carissa agrees and sends us on our way. I start off towards one of the guest rooms Cody has indicated we'll be staying in. Peter winds his arms around me from behind and whispers, "Wanna cuddle?"

The idea of sleeping alone in this strange place terrifies me, so I say, "Yes. I don't trust it here, yet."

"I know. I don't, either. Zaire seems to trust Cody. And if Andre said good things about him, then I know we're probably safe. But I'm on edge."

"Yeah," I agree.

We find an empty room with a nicely made bed. Peter shuts the door, locking it. He then turns to me and says, "You know, there's no interruptions here."

I smirk, but my cheeks begin to burn. I quickly raise my hands up to my face. Peter takes my hands away and says, "Don't hide."

"I blush way too easily."

"I love being the reason your face goes pink."

"That statement did not help my problem here."

He laughs, cupping my face in his hands as he leans in. "I wasn't trying to help," he murmurs before bringing my lips to his.

Soft, gentle longing turns to the unspoken words we haven't said. His hands find my waist. My hands tangle in his hair. Every one of my heartbeats falls into sync with his. My back presses against the wall, his hands run through my hair, down my back, back to my waist. My fingers run through his soft, blond hair. Hair I'm glad he refused to buzz.

His lips press to my jaw, down my neck as I catch my breath. "Peter," I say softly.

"I don't want to lose you," he whispers against my neck, bringing his lips back to mine.

My hands fall to his chest. His heart races against my palm. Everything is soft. Hushed words. Fear. A few tears escape my eyes and I feel a few of his fall against my cheeks. I wrap my arms around his neck.

He lifts me up, breaking the kiss, and carries me to the bed. He lies at my side, catching his breath. "We should rest. We have a lot ahead of us."

"Yeah," I say, my face still hot to the touch.

His lips are pink; I reach my fingers up to touch them. He takes my hand and presses soft kisses to my palm and each finger in turn. Everything inside of me melts.

I roll to my side, and Peter rolls to hold me in his arms. Our heartbeats grow steady, our breathing evens out. Sleep is coming, finally.

"I love you," he says, before he slips off to sleep.

So much for a calm pulse.

My eyes drift shut. My dreams are full of war and battles and the hope of winning.

THE MEETING ROOM IS a small, round and cramped. But it works for what we need. Carissa stands at the head of the table. "Our spies have agreed to help us attack at midnight. They will get us inside the White House where we can find Evan and capture him. I don't want anyone to kill him unless it comes to self-defense. I don't know if he'll be armed or not."

There's pain in Carissa's eyes when she talks about her brother. Despite all Evan has done to cause us pain, I know she still cares for him. He's still her brother.

"We're not here to take down the emperor," she continues. "Not yet. We're here to capture Evan and get answers. When he's captured, he needs to be blindfolded and gagged, as well as restrained. Once we have him safely here, we can make him talk to us."

The plan seems simple. Only a few of us will be going on this mission. There's no strength in numbers this time around.

As we wait for nightfall, Cody and some of his team bring us food. We eat. We discuss the plan. Then eleven-thirty rolls around and it's time to go.

Everything feels real now.

More real than this war has ever felt. This is our attack. We'll take Evan. We'll have answers. Maybe we'll even take down the emperor and restore peace in the country. I don't know how, but the hope resides in my mind and my heart, giving me strength.

When we pull up at the back of the the White House, Carissa gets out of the van first and leads the way. There's no time to admire the architecture or sheer awe of such a historical sight. The spies, who are stationed as guards at the back gates, nod at her as they let her in. They guide us through the halls and point out Evan's study. We enter, but it's dark. No one seems to occupy the room.

Carissa turns to Ainsley, one of Andre's spies. She worked under Brett until it was discovered he was double-crossing Andre and the rebellion. After that, she chose to become a spy for the resistance She knows this place better than we do. "Any other ideas of where he might be?"

Ainsley seems surprised. "The spy we had tailing him informed me he just entered his room, like we were hoping he would. No one saw him leave."

Peter frowns. "There must be a hidden passage somewhere in this room. I remember rumors of those existing. Just like a prison exists under the White House."

Carissa's fists clench at her side as she paces. "We need to figure out where he is. This mission can't fail."

Jackson glances around. "Should we wait and see if he comes back soon? Then we can hold him hostage in here. Not ideal," he turns to Ainsley. "How long can you keep the hallway clear?"

She glances at her wristwatch. "Not long. This was supposed to be in and out. If he's not back in five minutes, you're all screwed. Maybe we can retreat and regroup? I know for a fact he hasn't left the premises. My agents would've told me if he had."

Carissa runs her hands over her face as she talks with Ainsley further. I glance around, looking for anything suspicious. But nothing is out of place in the room. Almost like it was cleaned out.

Almost like he made an escape.

"Guys… I don't think he's coming back."

CHAPTER FORTY-THREE

Evan
THURSDAY, AUGUST 28TH, 2025

THE HALLWAY IS COLD, FAMILIAR.

I'm going to see Sam one more time. Confess my sins. Reveal my plot. I don't quite know why I have the need to do this. She's never going to want me the way I want her. And after our last discussion, there's no way she'll be expecting me.

But instead, I'm met with the unexpected.

Sam's cell is empty. The door open.

I hear voices further up the hallway.

"Take her to the emperor's audience hall. He's waiting," one of the guards says, voice rough as gravel.

I clutch the strap of my duffel bag. Sam is the only prisoner in this place.

I start up the hallway, hoping to catch more information. But the guards have left, presumably with Sam in tow. All is quiet.

Adrenaline surges through my veins as I rush back through the tunnel. I can't let them reach their destination.

Whatever the emperor has planned can't be good. And on tonight of all nights.

I arrive at the secret door to my room, but then I stop in my tracks: on the other side, there are muffled voices. I push the door open only slightly. The stone makes a scratching sound, and I'm certain whoever is on the other side will hear me. But somehow, they don't.

I can't see into the room, but I press my ear to the gap.

"He was last seen entering his room. This doesn't make sense."

I don't recognize the woman's voice, but she must be one of the agents who work within the White House.

"Where could he have gone? Are there hidden tunnels?"

That voice… that's my sister.

"No," the other female says. "At least… none that I know of. Not in this room. I suppose that's the only logical explanation."

"He must've known we were coming."

This comes from Peter. I should've known he'd be here. Contrary to what he believes, I did *not* know any of them were coming. If I had known, I would've been prepared for a battle.

"I don't think he'll be coming back," Carissa says,

defeated. "We'll have to figure out where he might be before it's too late."

I can hear the main door open as everyone files out of the room. It's clear I can't go back in there, though. They might be waiting for me outside. I make my way quietly back through the tunnel, back through the jail, and fly up the stairs that lead outside into one of the hallways. There are no guards here now; there's no more need for them now that the only prisoner is on her way to the audience room.

Of course, I've lost so much time evading my sister and her group that I'm probably too late now to stop Sam from being hauled in front of the emperor.

I drop my duffel bag at the entrance of the prison.

No more waiting around for the right time.

No more excuses.

I bend down and take the pistol from the bag, tucking it into the back of my jeans, and then head towards the east wing. I find my way through the halls and arrive outside the audience room without being spotted.

Carlos sees me and strides over. "Master Evan, His Majesty was just requesting to see you, but I could not locate you."

"I had a few errands to run," I say, hoping I don't sound as out of breath as I am.

I don't know who is helping my sister and the other rebels look for me, but I know they won't find me in time. I'll be done with this matter by the time they figure out where I am.

"Are you ready to enter, Master Evan?"

I nod once to Carlos as he pushes the doors open for me to enter.

Sam is seated in a chair, gagged, her hands cuffed behind her back.

My mind flashes to two years ago, when I did the same to Raegan.

Never in my life have I ever seen Sam truly terrified. But tears flow freely down her face now. The emperor is standing on his platform, his back to me.

"Your Majesty," I say, going to one knee. "Carlos said you were looking for me."

Emperor Morgan doesn't turn to look at me. Two of his trusted guards close in. I don't reach for my pistol. Not yet.

"Guards, you may leave us," the emperor intones.

The two guards share a look before retreating out of the room. The lock clicks from the outside.

"Evan, I think we have a problem."

I rise up from my kneeling position. I don't know what he's planning but I don't like it.

Sam looks at me, shaking her head as if I'm the reason she's here. I would never betray her like she did me. But I can't say that now. Not in front of the emperor. My heart can't take any more breaking.

"Whatever problem there is, Your Majesty, I will

do whatever it takes to resolve it."

He chuckles darkly, something that is never a good sign. My blood turns to ice in my veins. As he turns to look at me, I notice the pistol in his hand.

"I've tolerated your deceptions for a very long time. But you've gone too far this time."

"What are you talking about?" I don't bother with titles or pleasantries.

"You think you can do *anything* without me knowing about it? I know about the rebel camp. I know you blew up the base before we could make arrests. And I know you've come to visit Samantha Winters often enough."

Everything.

He knows everything.

He takes a step down the stairs, slowly. Deliberately.

"Your Majesty… I did everything for you. I was only trying to interrogate Samantha. And blowing up the base was an overstep. But I just wanted to prove my worth."

The lies fall off my tongue easily now.

But they don't hit the intended mark.

Emperor Morgan chuckles again. "You know, you're a horrible liar. You've gotten better. But it takes a liar to spot another one. I don't trust a word you've said to me in this room, Evan Williams. You will always have rebellion in your blood. However, I've come too far to kill you now. Your image is splashed across every newspaper, TV news special, and magazine. The people of this country look up to you. If I admit you committed treason, others will begin to get ideas about doing the same. There will be more rebellion. More anarchy. And we can't have that."

Emperor Morgan fully descends the platform now, making his way over to Samantha, pistol in hand. "So instead," he says, "I've decided to punish you. Giving you power and fame clearly isn't enough to ensure your loyalty."

A sick feeling sinks into my gut.

"Sir, please. Whatever you want from me, leave Samantha out of this. I swear to you, I—"

"SILENCE!" the emperor yells, his face full of disgust. "Your lies are getting out of hand. I've been gracious so far in letting this rotten, traitorous girl live. She deserved death the moment she aimed a gun at my head."

Emperor Morgan places the muzzle of his gun against Sam's head. Her eyes widen, full of fear. She chokes on the gag as sobs overtake her. Her body shakes in the chair. I reach into my belt for my own pistol, not fully brandishing it yet. He has to be bluffing. The emperor has never once done his own dirty work.

Never once raised a finger to commit his own crimes.

Other people commit his crimes for him.

"Your Majesty, please. Don't do this."

He chuckles again. There is no fear in his eyes. No hesitation.

Two gunshots fire, nearly simultaneously.

But I've never been fast enough.

The president crumples to the ground, bleeding heavily from a wound in his chest. I've never been fast, but I've never missed a target I've wanted to hit.

Sam's head hangs forward at an unnatural angle.

"NO!"

I rush to her, kneeling in front of her. But she's already gone.

I'm too late.

Tears blind me as I jump to my feet.

This isn't what was supposed to happen. We were supposed to get away. Live free. Away from all of this. Even if she didn't want me.

"I'm sorry," I sob, turning away. I'm so sorry.

The lock on the doors clicks again. Someone's coming in. I'm a dead man when the guards get inside this room.

I can't find it in myself to care.

The emperor is dead.

Just like I wanted.

But so is the woman I loved. There is nothing left for me to live for.

But when the doors burst open, I'm not met with an army of guards.

I'm met with rebels.

CHAPTER FORTY-FOUR

THE CLOCK IN EVAN'S ROOM SHOWS 12:30 A.M. We've waited. But he's clearly gone. Ainsley, one of the rebels that helped my father learn of Brett's true intentions all those years ago, works to clear the hallway again so we can make a safe escape back to the van.

A swift search has told us that Evan has taken things from his room. Some documents, maybe some clothes. I don't know if his aim was to escape or if these were intended for a trip of some sort.

But it's obvious he's not planning on coming back here anytime soon.

Suddenly Ainsley bursts into the room and says, "Evan's been spotted heading towards the emperor's audience room. Some of my contacts say that two pistols are missing from the armory. There's some rumor that he may be planning to kill the emperor."

My eyes widen and I jump to my feet. The others

follow me out.

"Kill the emperor? But he's the heir," I say, before realizing that that's actually a pretty good motivation.

Ainsley leads the way, rushing ahead of us. "We don't know what's going on. But I don't think you want Evan in prison for killing the emperor. The only thing that will happen is someone else will take over the country and continue Emperor Morgan's legacy. If you think Evan is the only heir, you'd be mistaken. The emperor has backup plans. His advisor, his chief judge—there are countless people in line to make sure everything operates smoothly even if he dies."

"Where do we need to go to head him off?"

She pauses, pushing a button on a wall. To my astonishment, a secret passage opens. "Follow me. This is our only chance."

Jackson keeps close behind me. Raegan, Peter, and Shaw hurry along behind him. The passage has many turns, but Ainsley seems to know where she's going. After a few minutes, she says, "Wait here. I need to check the hallway."

She opens another secret door and slips through it, leaving us alone for a moment.

No one speaks.

We hardly dare to breathe.

She returns and nods towards the door. "You can keep going. The audience room is at the end of the hall. I can't go further with you at this point. No one can know I've helped you."

I rest a hand on her shoulder. "Thank you. You've done so much already."

Ainsley smiles before retreating. I inhale, taking a step. Jackson takes my hand and says, "Whatever lies beyond that door, we're with you."

I look back to Raegan, Peter, Shaw, and of course Jackson. I grip his hand tighter. "Thank you."

We file quietly the door. The hallway is deserted— for now. The work of Ainsley, I'm sure. We make our way to the audience room. The doors are closed, but, strangely, the key dangles from the lock. Jackson reaches over and turns it. It clicks loudly, echoing through the hall. Whoever's waiting on the other side now knows we're here.

I take a deep breath. Jackson glances at me, waiting for me to give the okay.

"Let's go," I say to everyone. Or maybe to myself.

The doors grind open as we push them inward. My heart drops to my stomach as my brother rises from a kneeling position in front of a lifeless Sam, his hands coated with blood. At first, I don't know if it's his own. Then I see her terrible wounds.

A bullet to the head.

Her skin is already gray; it was a kill shot.

Nearby, the emperor lies crumpled on the floor in

an awkward position, blood pooling under his body.

Raegan is behind me, her breathing harsh and heavy. I glance back to see Peter take her hand in his. But nothing will calm anyone now, not after seeing this.

I return my focus to my brother, who still holds a pistol in his hand.

"Leave," he says, his voice coming out strangled. "While you have the chance."

"We're not leaving here without you," I say calmly, despite the flood of emotions rushing through me.

"Oh, I'm leaving, too. But not with you. Now go, and get out of my way." Tears pour from his eyes; manic energy radiates off of him.

"Evan," I begin, but he shakes his head.

"Look," he tells me, "I'm offering you an escape. Any minute, this place will be crawling with agents. If you don't leave, you'll all be apprehended. I have done everything in my power to make sure that doesn't happen. So, I'll tell you again, Carissa: get out of here before it's too late."

His words ignite a flame in me, snapping me out of my stupor. "You think you've *protected* us? Do you call bombing our headquarters 'protection'? And what about setting fire to the camp? Was killing Mom and Dad protecting them?"

I'm shaking, tears pouring out of my own eyes now. I hate myself for it. I never cry in front of anyone, except for Jackson. And yet, I've cried so much in recent days.

Evan falters. "What… what did you say?"

Jackson steps forward. "Andre and Maya—your parents, Evan—were killed in the blast. Many others were injured."

"No…"

Peter steps forward now, Raegan following him. "You need to come with us," he says to Evan. "We just want to talk."

Evan laughs bitterly. "Oh, you just want to talk? About my crimes? I will not come with you. But since you clearly don't want to leave while you have the chance, I have some things *I* would like to say. Let's start with this: Peter, I've hated you for a very long time."

Peter doesn't flinch. He reaches into his waistband for his pistol and aims it at Evan. His grip is steady, unwavering.

Evan aims his own gun at Raegan. "Drop your gun or I'll shoot her. And this time… I won't hesitate."

Peter grips the handle of his gun tighter. Evan's finger twitches on his trigger. Peter hesitates for a moment, considering, and then throws his gun down at his feet, holding his hands up in surrender.

Evan smiles wildly. "Kick it away from you."

Peter's gaze doesn't leave Evan's as the gun slides away from us, across the floor. "What did I even do to you? We were friends. You were like a brother to me before all of this."

Evan shakes his head. "What happened was my father started paying more attention to you, singing your praises. I worked my ass off to help him with everything he ever asked. And then you came along and got everything I wanted. My father never praised me, not even once."

I glance at the gun on the floor. It's not far. I can reach it if I'm careful.

Peter keeps his hands up. "Is that why you changed sides?"

"I was in the wrong place at the wrong time. All I ever wanted was to keep my family safe, despite what my father did to me. And now I've killed them. I've killed my parents. And then the emperor killed Sam, so I killed the emperor. And now," he narrows his eyes at Peter and tightens his grip on the gun, "here you stand in my way of the exit. Let me go."

Peter shakes his head. "I can't do that. We don't want to hurt you."

Evan chuckles. The sound sends a shock of fear directly into my heart. I inch closer to the gun. Evan doesn't seem to notice as he keeps his gun aimed at Peter.

"It would be so easy," he says. "One bullet through your chest. Everyone would be distracted, and then I could slip out, away from you. You'd take the fall for my actions. And I could disappear for good."

"So do it, then," Peter says, his mouth in a grim line.

"If you hate me so much. Obviously, you've proven you can kill others now. I'm sure you're itching to eliminate another person from your hit list. Does the blood feel good on your hands, Evan? Does it make you feel strong? Powerful?"

"Shut up! You don't know anything, do you?" His face is a deep, angry red now.

"I know a lot," Peter says. "I know you never wanted this. But I also know you've lost your mind."

I grab the pistol. Evan is too focused on Peter to notice. He cocks the hammer of his pistol and sights down the barrel at Peter.

The world seems to slow down around me.

This is it.

This is the only chance I have.

I fire the gun.

I've never been a great shot. I can defend myself, sure. But I'm no expert when it comes to fighting with weapons.

Evan lurches backwards and falls, his gun flying away to one side.

Blood pools from his chest as life drains from his body. He doesn't make a sound. Doesn't move. Everyone looks at me, horrified and shocked.

I drop my arm to my side and Peter's pistol clatters to the floor at my feet.

"No, no, no…" I rush to my brother's side. Jackson

is with me in an instant. He feels Evan's wrist, then his neck. I wait, holding my breath, bile rising in my throat.

Praying this wasn't a kill shot.

Hoping life still clings to him.

Jackson looks at me, shaking his head softly. In a whisper, he says, "He's gone."

The world spins around me. I stand numbly, staring at my brother's body. In a distant hallway, I can hear the sound of people running toward the audience room. Agents.

"We have to get out of here," Peter says, his voice shaking. "We don't have much time."

My mind blurs as we rush away from everything, scrambling out the door and back into the secret tunnel.

All I can think…

All I can remember…

…is that I killed my brother.

I killed him.

His blood isn't on my hands, yet it's all I can see.

Blood.

So much of it.

Outside, I collapse to my knees. My body heaves as I throw up the meager contents of my stomach. Jackson is with me, despite how much I wish he wasn't seeing this.

"It's okay," he says, running a hand gently down my back. "It's okay."

I spit to clear my mouth, wiping my face with my shirt

sleeve. "I killed him," I say out loud, sobbing into his arms.

"I know. It's okay. You were protecting Peter."

He helps me to my feet and we hurry back to the van. Ainsley meets us there. "You have to get out of here," she says urgently. "I'll make sure you're wiped from the security cameras."

"Thank you," Jackson says for me. I'm unable to speak.

Or breathe.

Once I'm safely in the van, I lean my head against Jackson's shoulder. The world goes black. And everything grows still.

MY EYES FLUTTER OPEN. White, blinding light is all around me. I wonder, for a moment, if this is heaven. But given my lack of faith in such a place, such a power, this is hardly likely. The soft whirring of machines and the beeping of monitors around me also don't sound like what I imagine heaven would.

I blink rapidly, trying to see clearly.

I'm in a cold, white hospital room.

I glance over to the chair by the window. Jackson

sits slumped in it, asleep.

I want to smile. But memories flood back in all at once. The monitor begins to beep rapidly as the panic rushes through me. Jackson wakes at this and jumps to his feet. He sees me awake and calms. But only slightly.

"Rissa? You're awake?" he says, coming to the bedside.

"How long have I been out?"

"Almost two days. The doctors said you were dehydrated and exhausted."

They have no idea.

"And the mental strain of witnessing your brother's death was too much. I'm sorry you had to go through all of that."

I shake my head slightly. "I caused it, Jackson. He… he deserved a chance."

"I don't know about that. But I do know this isn't how any of us wanted things to go. Still… you did what you had to." He strokes my forehead. "Now you need to heal."

Healing sounds so far away.

"How?" I say. My voice is raspy. "Most of my family is dead. I have nothing left."

Jackson leans over and holds me gently in his arms — as best he can, anyway. "You have me," he murmurs into my hair. "You have Spencer. And you know the rest of the resistance has your back. You won't have to go through this alone."

I turn my face into his shoulder and begin to sob, unable to bear it anymore. He holds me tighter, despite the awkwardness of the machines I'm hooked up to, and whispers calming words in my ear. I know I have him.

He's right… I won't be alone.

CHAPTER FORTY-FIVE

Raegan
MONDAY, SEPTEMBER 1ST, 2025

SUNLIGHT STREAMS THROUGH THE WINDOW. AT first, I'm confused. Then I remember this isn't the rebel camp anymore. This is Peter's bedroom. And Peter lies next to me, holding me in his arms. Nightmares have kept me up at night. Seeing Evan's body collapse to the ground. All the blood…

I squeeze my eyes shut, my body tensing. Peter holds me closer, placing a gentle kiss on my shoulder. "Shh," he murmurs. "It's okay."

Even half asleep, he's learned how to recognize when I'm beginning to think about everything.

Gunner trots into the room, his nails clicking against the honey-colored floor. Peter sighs. "I guess it's time to get up."

"We have a lot to do," I say.

Most of Bent Ridge is empty. But now that the war is over, no one has to believe I'm dead. The few who remained in town were shocked when they saw me return home yesterday. But my parents stepped in and took care of explaining everything to them.

Peter was excited to be back to his house. And since being next to him at night had been helping me sleep, I agreed to stay over at his house. Our parents weren't too keen on the idea, but we promised on our lives that all we wanted to do was sleep.

And it's true. Sleep was the *only* thing on our minds as we collapsed onto his bed last night.

Peter's up first, always the morning person. He pulls a t-shirt from a pile of clothes on the floor and goes down the hall towards his bathroom. I pull the blankets higher over my head. I am most definitely not a morning person.

Gunner walks over to my side of the bed and nudges me. I stick my head out from under the blanket to see him looking up at me with begging eyes, willing me to get up and let him outside.

"Needy dog," I grumble under my breath, unable to prevent the smile coming to my face.

I climb reluctantly out of bed and walk down the hall, past the bathroom where Peter is brushing his teeth.

I open the back door, and Gunner charges outside without hesitation. Peter comes up behind me a moment later and says, "I'm jealous he can make you get up in the morning, but when I try, you throw things at me."

"I throw a pillow. And don't be jealous. It doesn't suit you."

He smirks, resting his chin on my head. "How are you?"

"Struggling. But I'm more worried about Carissa. I want to go see her today."

"Then we should. But first, there's something I really want to do."

"What's that?"

"It's a surprise."

PETER HOLDS THE BUSHES back so I can walk through. The path has become a bit overgrown without someone walking it every day. But I know the way by heart.

It's something I could never forget.

When we get to the clearing, tears fill my eyes. Our wonderful oak tree still stands tall, despite everything that's happened in the world around it. It's too early for any of the leaves to begin falling. But there's a faint yellow hue to some of them.

Autumn will be coming soon enough.

I lean back against the rough bark, inhaling the earthy scent of the forest.

Peter smiles, pulling his knife out of his pocket. He climbs up a few branches and begins carving something into the trunk.

"What are you doing?" I ask curiously.

"Come up here and see."

I climb up after him; the leaves cloak us from sight.

He's carved a simple heart with two letters.

R+P.

I smile, running my fingers over the marking.

"No matter what happens, no matter who else finds this place… it will always be ours."

"I love it," I say, kissing his cheek.

We climb carefully back down and make our way back to my truck. Peter gets behind the wheel, since I don't feel well enough to drive yet. I look out the window as he drives us towards the hospital in Cyrus, where Carissa will be until tomorrow. After that, it's unclear what will happen. Williams Ranch is gone. It will take time to rebuild anything on the property, assuming Carissa even wants that.

Nothing is quite certain, even though the war is over.

EPILOGUE

Raegan
FRIDAY, OCTOBER 17TH, 2025

THE AUTUMN AIR SWIRLS AROUND ME. I TAKE A deep breath. Everyone's dressed in black as we stand in the open field where the rebel camp used to be. The ground is still covered in ash.

Carissa didn't want anyone to touch it.

A table has been set up with three pictures in frames.

Andre.

Maya.

Evan.

Carissa doesn't bother to hold it together as Jackson stands with his arms around her. Spencer stands by the table and begins to address the group.

"My aunt and uncle were some of the best people I've ever known. Even though my uncle was often misguided, his heart was always in the right place. They took me in when I was sixteen and I've always been grateful for that. My cousin had his issues. But I believe he loved us all. Even though y'all probably hate his guts—" He smiles sadly— "it was important to Carissa and to me that we honor his life anyway. He made poor choices. But he's still family."

Spencer steps away from the table to stand by Nicole, who takes his hand and leans her head on his shoulder.

I step forward now, Peter right by my side, and turn to face my companions.

"Andre didn't always get it right. But he knew what needed to be done. He wanted the best for all of us. Maya always welcomed us into her home. She'd feed us even if we weren't hungry. She'd take care of us. And Evan… maybe he never intended for this to happen. We will never know. But I hope Carissa finds peace. I hope Spencer finds peace. That is all we can hope and pray for."

A few more people speak. Callahan talks of Andre's friendship. Jackson tells stories about Evan that make him seem almost human, even to me.

As the memorial comes to an end and people begin to pack up, I approach Carissa. She pulls me into a hug immediately.

"Thank you," she sobs into my shoulder. "For not saying bad things about Evan. I know it's probably blasphemous to include him in the memorial, but he is—was—my brother."

"I know," I say.

After helping with the cleanup, we all leave. Peter drives my truck again, holding my hand. I glance out my window as we enter Bent Ridge. Everything is starting to look better. Some of the stores have reopened in Main Street Market. More people walk through the streets, less fearful of what might happen. It's a slow process, but it's happening.

After Carissa was released from the hospital, just days after killing Evan, she and the rest of the resistance had to go into hiding until the heat was off us a bit. Predictably, many of the emperor's numerous advisors fought to take over. But none of it mattered. The seed of revolution had been planted. People demanded a real election. And with no real leader in place, one of the agents Andre had planted in the government rose to the top as interim leader, and he has begun discussions on organizing a real election.

The overturning of Emperor Morgan's government seems to have lifted the spirits of so many across the country. Shortly after the deaths of the emperor and Evan, the agent who took over as interim leader wanted us to join for a speech. It was then people saw me again.

It was then I was allowed to be alive.

The people still living in Bent Ridge had so many questions. Many people did. My story made national headlines. The attention was frustrating. But after it was clear I wasn't going to answer many questions, the media left me alone.

And life was allowed to be… normal. To a point, anyway.

After everything we've been through, nothing will ever be normal.

Cities and towns have started to rebuild. Businesses have begun to reopen once more. And an election will be held in about a month. There're a few people in the race to be president. Shaw is one of them. We've all agreed to vote for him. While not always the kindest, he is one of the best candidates. He knows what needs to be done.

So much has fallen apart, but it's slowly coming back.

There's a long road ahead. Healing takes a lot of time. It doesn't happen in a straight line.

But it's healing nonetheless.

I glance at Peter, who smiles at me as he parks in front of my house.

What will we do now that the war is over? The possibilities are endless. There's no one stopping us from anything. It's a question we've asked each other many times. But neither of us ever has the answer.

We haven't considered the after.

A life after war.

A life after resistance.

"My mom is asking when I'm going to man up

and take you on a real date," Peter says softly.

I laugh, feeling the heat flood my cheeks.

He cups my face with his free hand. "So, Raegan MacArthur, would you delight me with your company and join me for dinner tonight?"

The concept of dinner is amazing.

"I don't know," I say after a moment, smirking. "I'm a busy woman."

"Too busy for me?" He's pleading now, his face taking on that pouting look that I can never resist.

"I suppose I can be free for dinner," I say, giving him a wink.

He leans in, kissing me softly, slowly. Then we climb out of the truck and he walks me to my front door, like the gentleman he is.

Rebuilding isn't going to be easy.

Healing isn't going to be fast.

But I know, looking into his eyes, that I'll take whatever adventures life has for us, as long as he's by my side.

ACKNOWLEDGEMENTS

I can't believe this book is finally real. It's so mind boggling to think you, dear reader, are holding this in your hands, taking in every word.

This series was built on something special in my heart, and I'm so happy with how it's ended.

There's a lot of people I need to thank for making this book possible.

First and foremost, God. Thank You for giving me this passion for writing and for always being there through the highs and lows of my life.

Thank you to my parents for supporting me and loving me. To my dad, who's words inspired this series to begin with. To my mom, who always provided encouragement. To both of you, for always being there for me every step of the way.

Thank you to my brother, who usually doesn't like reading, but always loved to read my writing.

Thanks to my sister, for being a little cheerleader and always wanting to know how it was going and when this book would be out.

Thank you to Faith, for being my critique partner, always making time to read the roughest parts of this book and making it shine. And for all the time you spent proofreading in between everything else you had to do. You're a rock star! For believing in this book when I couldn't. For not letting me give up when I wanted to. For reminding me to trust myself and the inner writing voice inside me. I hope this book is everything you dreamed it would be.

I also want to thank Abbie Emmons and Kate Emmons for providing insight into the self-publishing world. Abbie, for always taking the time to answer questions and help me figure out that pain that is formatting. Kate, for encouraging me in my self-publishing journey. You're both lights in the independent author world!

To my grandma… this book is dedicated to you. You didn't get the chance to read the final part of this series, but I hope this is the ending you wanted. Thank you for enjoying my books and reminding me that I'd always have at least one fan.

And I can't not thank the writing community on Instagram and Twitter for all their love and support. Being an independent author is hard, but someone always reminds me why it's worth it. I wish I could list every name and every person who has made a difference, but that is another book in itself. But you know who you are and you know you've all made a difference in my life. Thank you!

Thank you to Jen, my editor, for always letting my author voice shine through and for always giving me helpful feedback. I also dearly appreciate the birdwatching pictures and the encouraging comments.

Thank you, Megan for once again creating a stunning cover design. I'm always so blown away when I see your designs!

To have them for my books is an honor. I don't think I

could've found anyone else who would've been able to breathe life into the vision I've had for each cover. Thank you!

And finally, dear reader, thank you. This book was the hardest one I've ever written. It didn't always come easy or naturally. So, the fact that you're holding it in your hands means a lot to me. I hope the heart of the story shines through. I hope you've laughed and cried and celebrated with my characters just as much as I did.

ABOUT THE AUTHOR

Brooke Riley started her writing journey at fifteen when she had an idea about a world falling to ruin. Though the books have come a long way from their original conception, she has found a refuge in writing books. A lover of books and an avid bookworm, words have always been somewhere ingrained in her soul.

When she's not writing, she's dreaming up new worlds, making playlists, or hanging out with her family.

Follow her social media to keep up with all her new writing endeavors!

Instagram: @thebrookeriley
Twitter: @thebrookeriley